JOHNNY UNDER GROUND

JOHNNY UNDER GROUND

Patricia Moyes

FELONY & MAYHEM PRESS • NEW YORK

All the characters and events portrayed in this work are fictitious.

JOHNNY UNDER GROUND

A Felony & Mayhem mystery

PRINTING HISTORY
First UK edition (Collins): 1965
First US edition (Holt, Rinehart and Winston): 1965
Felony & Mayhem edition: 2018

ISBN: 978-1-63194-143-6

Manufactured in the United States of America

Library of Congress Cataloging-in-Publication Data

Names: Moyes, Patricia, author.
Title: Johnny under ground / Patricia Moyes.
Description: New York : Felony & Mayhem Press, 2018. | Series: A Felony &
 Mayhem mystery | Reprint. Originally published: "First UK edition
 (Collins): 1965; First US edition (Holt, Rinehart and Winston): 1965 " --
 Verso title page.
Identifiers: LCCN 2018006848| ISBN 9781631941436 (pbk.) |
 ISBN 9781631941597 (ebook)
Subjects: LCSH: Tibbett, Henry (Fictitious character)--Fiction. | Tibbett,
 Emmy (Fictitious character)--Fiction. | Married people--Fiction. | Police
 spouses--Fiction. | Police--Great Britain--Fiction. | England--Fiction. |
 Domestic fiction. | GSAFD: Mystery fiction.
Classification: LCC PR6063.O9 J6 2018 | DDC 823/.914--dc23
LC record available at https://lccn.loc.gov/2018006848

Born in Dublin in 1923, Patricia ("Penny") Packenham-Walsh was just 16 when WWII came calling, but she lied about her age and joined the WAAF (the Women's Auxiliary Air Force), eventually becoming a flight officer and an expert in radar. Based on that expertise, she was named technical advisor to a film that Sir Peter Ustinov was making about the discovery of radar, and went on to act as his personal assistant for eight years, followed by five years in the editorial department of *British Vogue.*

When she was in her late 30s, while recuperating from a skiing accident, she scribbled out her first novel, *Dead Men Don't Ski*, and a new career was born. *Dead Men* featured Inspector Henry Tibbett of Scotland Yard, equipped with both a bloodhound's nose for crime and an easy-going wife; the two of them are both a formidable sleuthing team and an image of happy, productive marriage, and it's that double picture that makes the Tibbett series so deeply satisfying. While the Tibbett books were written in the second half of the 20th century, there is something both timeless and classic about them; they feel of a piece with the Golden Age of British Detective Fiction.

Patricia Moyes died in 2000. The *New York Times* once famously noted that, as a writer, she "made drug dealing look like bad manners rather than bad morals." That comment may once have been rather snarky, but as we are increasingly forced to acknowledge the foulness that can arise from unchecked bad manners, Inspector Henry Tibbett—a man of unflinching good manners, among other estimable traits—becomes a hero we can all get behind.

The icon above says you're holding a copy of a book in the Felony & Mayhem "Vintage" category. These books were originally published prior to about 1965, and feature the kind of twisty, ingenious puzzles beloved by fans of Agatha Christie and John Dickson Carr. If you enjoy this book, you may well like other "Vintage" titles from Felony & Mayhem Press.

———◆•◆•◆———

For more about these books, and other Felony & Mayhem titles, or to place an order, please visit our website at:

www.FelonyAndMayhem.com

Other "Vintage" titles from

FELONY&MAYHEM

For Johnny

Do not despair
For Johnny-Head-in-Air.
He sleeps as sound
As Johnny-Under-Ground.

Fetch out no shroud
For Johnny-in-the-Cloud.
And keep your tears
For him in after years.

Better by far
For Johnny the bright star
To keep your head
And see his children fed.

—John Pudney

JOHNNY UNDER GROUND

CHAPTER ONE

"**O**F COURSE YOU MUST GO, darling," said Chief Inspector Henry Tibbett. He helped himself to a piece of toast. "When is it?"

Emmy Tibbett looked again at the Personal Column of the *Times*. "September 15th," she said, "Battle of Britain Day. Very appropriate."

"Dymfield was a fighter station, wasn't it? Spitfires and Hurricanes, I suppose."

"In the early days," said Emmy. "By the time I got there in 1943, it was all Typhoons and..."

"I hate to cut short the story of your service career, my love," said Henry, "but I have to go. I'm late already."

"Sorry. Are you in for a busy day?"

"Not that I know of. But then, murderers are apt to be forgetful about telling us in advance when they intend to operate."

Henry went out into the hall and took his mackintosh off the peg. Emmy called from the living room. "Don't forget your newspaper."

"You'd better keep it, so that you can write in about this reunion."

Emmy came out into the hall. "I'm not sure that I want to go, after all," she said.

"Of course you do. I know what's worrying you. You think I'm incapable of cooking my own supper for once. Well, I'm not. So just you write off for a ticket."

"Well…"

"No argument," said Henry. He grinned, kissed his wife, warmly, and went out into the thin sunshine of Chelsea in search of a bus to take him to his office at Scotland Yard.

It would do Emmy good, he reflected, as he stood at the bus stop, to meet up with some of her old friends. Henry's job in the C.I.D. meant long and irregular hours and frequent trips away from home. Emmy never complained, but she had been a bit restless lately, saying that she hadn't enough to do and talking of taking a part-time job. If only we'd been able to have children, Henry thought. Poor Emmy… The bus arrived. Henry climbed aboard, and began to think about work.

When the front door had closed behind her husband, Emmy Tibbett picked up the newspaper and read the announcement again.

> R.A.F. DYMFIELD. A reunion of officers, R.A.F. and W.A.A.F., who served on this station during 1943 will be held at the Suffolk Hotel, Blunt Street, W.C.2. at 6 P.M. on Saturday, September 15th. Write for tickets (5s. each including buffet but not drinks) to Mr. A. Price, 27 Oakwood Avenue, Edgware.

Dear old Arthur Price, the Equipment Officer, affectionately known as Pricey—Emmy remembered a jolly, rotund little man, who even in 1943 had been too old for active duty. Pricey *would* be the person to organize a thing like this. Who else might be there, Emmy wondered. Annie Day perhaps; it would be marvelous to see old Annie again. She and Emmy had been particular friends in the Air Force, and still exchanged

Christmas cards, although they had not met for twenty years. Annie had married a farmer, and now lived in Scotland. Her children must be grown up by now... Then there was Sammy Smith, the ex-pilot who was the station's humorist; wonder what he's doing now? Lofty Parker, the tall, fair boy who always had his nose in a book and for whom everyone had predicted a great future as a writer. Little Jimmy Baggot, the Radio Officer, with his pockets continually sprouting screwdrivers and bits of wire. One by one, the almost-forgotten faces came back to Emmy's mind. And with them, another face. A face which she had not forgotten; but someone who would not be at the reunion.

As if in a dream, Emmy walked slowly over to her desk and opened the lowest drawer. Then she hesitated. She had sworn to herself that she would never look at it. She should have thrown it away years ago.

"Hell, woman," she said aloud, "surely you're old enough by now to look at a photograph without going all to pieces?"

She rummaged at the back of the drawer and brought out a dusty, discolored envelope. She carried it carefully over to the table, opened it, and pulled out the photograph.

There was nothing very remarkable about the picture. It showed a group of two men and two girls, all in Air Force uniform, posed rather self-consciously, the girls sitting on straight-backed chairs, the men standing behind them. Both men were tall, one dark and the other fair. The dark one was looking straight at the camera with a lopsided grin, lopsided, because, even in the small photograph, it was painfully clear that his once-handsome face was heavily disfigured by scar tissue. His Air Force cap was very battered and was pushed back on his head. He wore pilot's wings above an impressive row of medal ribbons and the three stripes of a Squadron Leader on his sleeves. In front of him sat a slim girl in the uniform of a W.A.A.F. Section Officer. Her hair was short, dark and curly; her face smooth and unlined; and her waist could not have measured more than twenty-one inches.

"More than twenty years ago," thought Emmy. "I was just nineteen. Beau must have been about twenty-five. I thought he was terribly old then. Now he looks like a child."

She turned the photograph over and recognized her own youthful copperplate handwriting: "R.A.F. Dymfield. Tennis Team, 1943." Below this were three signatures: Annie Day, Lofty Parker, and at the bottom, a bold scrawl—"With my love, Beau."

A lump rose in Emmy's throat. "I won't!" she said, aloud. But in spite of herself, the tears came; and as she dabbed her eyes angrily with her handkerchief, she remembered that at the time she had not cried at all.

"I'm getting old," she thought, "old and maudlin, so help me. Suppose I go to that reunion, will I start weeping into my gin? How awful. I won't go."

"Coward," said a voice at the back of her mind. "You little coward, Blandish."

Emmy sat up straight and blew her nose. Then she found a pen and paper and wrote:

Dear Mr. Price,
I wonder if you will remember me? I used to be Emmy Blandish. I saw your announcement in *The Times*, and since I was at Dymfield for the whole of 1943, I hope you'll consider me eligible for the reunion. I'm enclosing a postal order for five shillings, and look forward very much to seeing you again.

Sincerely,
Emmy Tibbett

Three days later, a reply arrived:

My dear Emmy,
How delightful to hear from you! I enclose your ticket with great pleasure. I'm most gratified at the good response that my little advertisement has

drawn. Annie Day (that was) is coming all the way from Scotland—combining the reunion with a week's shopping expedition, so she tells me. Lofty Parker will be there, and Jimmy Baggot—did you know that he's a big bug in television these days?

A splendid surprise was a letter from Vere Prendergast, asking for a ticket. Naturally, I've told him we shall all be delighted to see him. I suppose you know that he married Barbara Guest, Beau's widow. I'm hoping she may come, too. I'm not inviting other husbands or wives, but I do feel that Barbara was a part of R.A.F. Dymfield, don't you? Funnily enough, the Prendergasts live in East Anglia not far from Dymfield.

    À bientôt, dear Emmy,
    Pricey

P.S. I'm afraid Sammy Smith won't be with us. He tells me he has to go abroad on business. I'm not sure what his line is now. Motors of some sort, I believe. At all events, he seems very prosperous, and was, I think, really pleased to meet me again.

Emmy read the letter at the breakfast table. She said nothing. Henry glanced up from his newspaper to ask, "Interesting letter?"

"Just my ticket for the Dymfield reunion."

"Oh, good."

After a little pause, Emmy said, "I'm still not sure that I'll go."

"What, and waste five bob? Don't be an idiot, darling. It'll be fun for you."

Emmy stood up and began stacking plates onto a tray. "I'll have to think about it," she said.

"Coward," said the voice in her mind.

"Yes, I'll think about it," said Emmy, and carried the tray into the kitchen.

The Suffolk Hotel was situated in a small street off the Strand. It was not too large, comfortable without being chic, and highly respected without being smart. It also had a reputation for providing excellent food and drink at reasonable prices, and Emmy mentally congratulated Pricey for choosing it.

The taxi came to a halt, firmly jammed in the rush-hour traffic of Trafalgar Square, and Emmy took advantage of the pause to pull out her compact and inspect her face. "Goodness, I look old—I hadn't noticed all those lines. And there's another gray hair." She pulled it out and immediately spotted two more. "And fat, horribly fat; they won't call me little Blandish anymore." And then she laughed, because it was so long since anybody had called her by the surname which she had happily relinquished fifteen years ago when she'd married Henry. "I must watch it," she thought, "or I'll start talking about wizard pieces of cake." The taxi moved on again with a jerk.

Walking up the steps of the Suffolk Hotel, Emmy nearly panicked. Her heart was beating unpleasantly fast as she asked the receptionist for the Dymfield reunion. She was directed along a corridor. As she approached the reception room, a wave of chattering voices greeted her, and she had a sweeping impulse to turn and run away; but the next moment, she had pushed open the door, and a warm well-remembered voice was saying, "Emmy Blandish! Come in, my dear. Come in and have a drink!" She found herself looking into the plump face and twinkling eyes of her old friend, the Equipment Officer. A little stouter, perhaps, a little more wrinkled, one extra chin; but the smile and the mop of gray hair were just as she remembered them. Pricey at sixty-five was really very much like Pricey at forty-five.

"You haven't changed a bit, my dear Blandish!"

"Nor have you, Pricey," said Emmy, gratefully. She accepted a drink, and looked around her.

The first thing that struck her, bringing a sense of relief, was that nobody looked very old. Of course, it was easy to forget how terribly young they had all been in the forties. Looking around the room, Emmy reflected that they had all worn pretty well. Then she saw Annie.

Annie in 1943 had been tall and gangling. Now, she was Junoesque. She wore unfashionable but well-cut tweeds—the countrywoman's concession to the city—and she looked magnificent. Her face, with its peaches-and-cream complexion, was practically unlined. Her corn-colored hair gleamed as brightly as ever. Certainly she had put on weight, but she had not become fat. In the old nursery expression, she had "filled out."

She saw Emmy, and called out, "Blandish! My God, how many years is it? In another minute I shall burst into tears!"

But there was laughter rather than tears in her deep voice, and Emmy hurried over to her friend, spilling her drink in her haste.

Annie, inevitably, was the center of a group of people. Among them, Emmy had some difficulty in recognizing Jimmy Baggot. The scruffy little Radio Officer now wore an impeccably-cut suit with a carnation in the buttonhole, and exuded an unmistakable aura of success, even celebrity. He talked easily, emphasizing his remarks by gesturing with a gold cigarette holder. In spite of his distinction, however, there was a reminder of the old Jimmy in the rebellious lock of black hair, now tinged with gray, which still leapt independently from his forehead defying the ministrations of expensive barbers.

"Yes, we're up to our necks in color T.V. now, of course," he was saying. "And that's only one of the new developments. In fact, it's pretty old hat. But I can't tell you about the latest research. All top secret, you understand."

"And we're such bad security risks," said a light, ironic voice. The speaker was a tall, fair man in a shabby suit. If

Baggot personified success, Lofty Parker did the opposite. He looked threadbare, even hungry, and his hand shook as he lit a cigarette from a battered pack. "Funny, isn't it, that we were trusted to work with the most secret aircraft during the war, and now Baggot tells us we can't be told about his miserable television developments."

"It's not a question of national security, Lofty," said Baggot. He had gone rather red.

"Oh, isn't it? Then what is it a question of?"

"Well—commercial security, if you like. We don't want our rivals to know exactly what we..."

"Just as we didn't want the Germans to know..."

"Oh, for heaven's sake, old man," said Jimmy Baggot. "Take it easy."

"You've been taking it easy for years, haven't you, Baggot?" said Parker. There was an awkward pause, and then Annie said, "Lofty, you remember Emmy Blandish, don't you?"

Lofty's strained features broke into a smile. "Little Blandish! Our first W.A.A.F. controller, if I remember rightly. What are you up to now?"

"She's controlling Scotland Yard instead of fighters," said Annie.

"Scotland Yard?" Arthur Price had joined the group and there was a distinct note of alarm in his voice.

"Not really," said Emmy, laughing. "I'm married to a bit of it, that's all."

"Henry Tibbett," Annie went on, proudly, "the famous Chief Inspector Tibbett, who's always solving murders."

There was a ripple of interest, and Emmy found herself quite a center of attraction. She was just insisting that she really had very little to do with Henry's work, and was even thinking of looking for a job herself to pass the time, when the door opened again. Arthur Price glanced quickly toward it, excused himself, and bustled off to meet the new arrivals. And then it seemed to Emmy that the whole room fell silent, as everybody turned to look toward the door.

Two people had come in, and were shaking hands with Price. The man was tall and lanky, and his brown hair was heavily streaked with gray. He looked, in spite of his dark suit, like a caricature of a country squire. His graying mustache—its wingspan undiminished by the passing years—bristled from a red-veined face, hiding his ineffectual upper lip, but powerless to conceal his receding chin. One glance at him told you that he inevitably had a loud laugh, a small vocabulary, a hatred of all forms of socialism, and a lot of money. The woman was of medium height, and had the figure of an emaciated fashion model. As a consequence, her neck was deeply wrinkled, and the skeletal hand that she held out for Arthur Price to shake was like a bird's claw. She was heavily and expertly made-up, and only a close observer would have remarked that her golden hair was dyed. She wore a white silk suit of breathtaking elegance, and her haggard face was still very lovely in a slightly macabre way. She looked a good ten years older than either Emmy or Annie; she also looked ten thousand pounds a year more expensive.

"So that's what happened to Barbara." Emmy heard Annie's voice, little more than a whisper, in her ear.

She tried to say something and failed. Then she felt her hand grasped by Annie's strong fingers.

"Get a grip, Blandish," said Annie. "You're a big girl now."

Emmy nodded, and smiled gratefully. The instinctive gesture of support, the old catchphrase, were marvelously heartening.

"Go on," said Annie. "Go and say hello. Get it over. I'll be right behind you."

"Yes, Annie," said Emmy. She took a deep breath, and walked across the room. Hoping that her voice sounded light and matter-of-fact, she said, "Barbara! How lovely to see you again!"

Barbara turned, with an attractive, vague smile on her face. "I'm sorry," she said, "so many people—I don't quite…"

"I'm Emmy Blandish," said Emmy, too loudly.

"Blandish—Emmy Blandish. Oh, yes, one of Beau's little girls. I remember now." She turned to her husband. "Vere, darling, this is Emmy Blandish."

"So it is, by Jove," said the man heartily. He shook Emmy's hand vigorously. "Good to see you, Blandish. How are you? Bearing up?"

"Yes, thank you, Vere," said Emmy.

"Feel a bit of a gate-crasher here, y'know," Vere went on. "There seem to be more Operations Room types than aircrew. Thanks, Price, old man, I'll have a whisky. Yes, as I was saying, we all know how clannish you plotters and controllers were..."

"Oh, don't be silly, Vere," said Emmy. She was beginning to feel better. "You were the chaps who flew the planes, and I've always maintained that we weren't fit to black your boots." She stopped, surprised at the warmth of remembered emotion. "I suppose I had too much to do with penguins," she added. "You know, they flap but don't fly. It was only when I was posted to Dymfield and started working directly with the fighters that I—well..."

Vere was not listening. "Actually, it was Barbara who insisted on coming along today," he said. He glanced toward his wife, who had moved away to talk to Jimmy Baggot. "Because of Beau, you know. I thought it was a mistake. Still do. Bloody dull party—present company excepted, of course—and she'll only get worked up and sentimental about—you know what..."

"I can understand her wanting to come," said Emmy steadily. "It's always better to face things."

"It's not as though he'd been killed in action." Hildegard St. Vere Prendergast was embarrassed. "*De mortuis*, of course, and all that, but suicide isn't a very nice thing, and when the type ditches an expensive kite into the bargain..." Vere's voice trailed off into uneasy silence.

Emmy could not for the life of her think of a suitable remark, and she was delighted when Annie came up, embraced Vere warmly, and started talking about dogs and cows.

Barbara had by now pinioned little Arthur Price in a corner, and was haranguing him with what looked like a mixture of charm and menace. Jimmy Baggot was holding court, the center of an impressed circle. Emmy spotted Lofty Parker drinking by himself, and went over to him.

"What are you doing now, Lofty?" she asked.

"Drinking," said Lofty, shortly.

"I mean, for a living?" Emmy cursed herself for having started such a tactless conversation. Whatever Lofty was doing for a living, it was patently not a success.

Lofty knocked back a neat whisky. "I am what you might call a failed odd-job man," he said. "I have been a small-part actor, a male model, a publisher's part-time reader and an encyclopedia salesman. About the only thing I haven't been is a cheerleader in a holiday camp. I have published a small volume of verse which sold fifty copies, and two short stories. If I didn't have a small income from my father's estate, I'd have starved several times over. So much for Dymfield's resident genius. At the moment I am eking out what is laughingly called a living by knocking on people's front doors to collect sales statistics. 'Excuse me, madam, would you mind telling me what detergent you normally favor? What furniture polish you use on the elephant's-foot table? And, if you'll pardon my frank speaking, what brand of toilet paper currently graces your bijou convenience?'" He stopped speaking and lit a cigarette.

Emmy said nothing.

Lofty went on, "I expect you wonder why the hell I came here this evening. Well, I'll tell you. Call me silly, but I haven't quite given up all hope of being a writer, and I knew that television's great James Baggot was going to be here. Would you believe it, as soon as I set eyes on him, I thought, 'You silly little bastard, you're just Jimmy Baggot after all,' and so I had to go and be rude to him. Now he'll never give me a job in a million years." Unexpectedly, he grinned.

Emmy grinned back. "I don't blame you," she said. "He's become pretty insufferable. It's rather sad."

Lofty looked sharply at her. "The sad person here," he said, "is Barbara Guest—sorry, Mrs. Hildegard St. Vere Prendergast. Did you ever see the like?"

Emmy hesitated. "She's still very beautiful," she said. "And she's kept her figure marvelously. Not like me."

"My dear Blandish, she looks a hundred and two. And as for poor old Vere—well—he never was very bright, but I never thought to see such a case of arrested development. I believe his life stopped at the moment when he climbed out of the cockpit of a Typhoon for the last time—which must be twenty years ago." He took another drink. "This whole bloody evening was a grave mistake. Old Price'll never realize it though. I bet you ten pounds to a button that he suggests making it an annual event. He just doesn't realize that he's asking for trouble, making people go back…"

"Lofty," said Emmy, "You're drunk."

Lofty beamed down at her. "Now *that* takes me back," he said. "Prim little Blandish. 'Beau, you're drunk.' I remember coming into the anteroom one evening and hearing you say that in the young, clear, innocent voice you had then. 'Drunk.' I don't suppose you knew what the word meant—probably still don't. And I thought at the time, 'That's a rum old way for a junior officer to speak to the Chief Controller.' Of course, I didn't realize then…"

"Lofty, please…"

"That can't have been very long before he did himself in, poor sod. And yet, you know, when I look around here, I wonder whether he wasn't right. 'They shall not grow old, as we that are left…'"

"Lofty," said Emmy quietly, "if you don't shut up, I shall throw my drink at you, glass and all."

"You always were hopelessly sentimental…"

"I wasn't, and I'm not…"

"If you weren't, you wouldn't bother to deny it."

A voice behind Emmy brayed shrilly. "Lofty! Lofty is the person! The ideal person!"

Barbara had arrived with Arthur Price in tow. "Explain the idea to him, Pricey."

Price was glowing with enthusiasm. "Barbara has come forward with a most intriguing idea," he said, "most intriguing. She thinks that a history of Dymfield should be written, a portrait of a wartime fighter station, as it were, told from the point of view of the Operations Room."

"We've had endless epics about ships and regiments and squadrons," Barbara put in, "but the backroom organization has been a complete Cinderella..."

"Possibly because it was less interesting than ships and regiments and squadrons," said Lofty.

"Nonsense." Barbara went on. "It would be fascinating and I'm convinced that *now* is the time, and *you* are just the person, Lofty darling..."

"My dear Barbara," said Lofty, "if you think I can afford the time for the writing, let alone the research, on a project that no publisher in his senses would..."

Barbara looked a little embarrassed. "I—I'd like to finance the project. As a sort of memorial, you see. To Beau."

"Left it a bit late, haven't you?" said Lofty, but there was a note of interest in his voice.

"I *knew* you'd agree," said Barbara, with a ravishing smile.

"Here, wait a minute. I haven't agreed to anything yet."

"You're so brilliant," cooed Barbara. "You could do it in no time. It shouldn't be very long, you see."

"It's not a question of the writing taking time," said Lofty. "It's the research. I have a job to do, be it ever so humble..."

"But all your expenses would be..."

"That's not the point, Barbara. If I give up my job, there's no guarantee that I'll get it back again. So unless you are prepared to support me for the rest of my life, if necessary..."

Barbara bit her lip. "There must be some way," she said.

"There is," said Lofty, and Emmy saw with surprise that he was looking straight at her. "Blandish can do the research and I'll write up the results."

Before Emmy could say a word, Barbara was yapping enthusiasm. "Brilliant! Perfect! You are clever, Lofty!"

"But," Emmy began.

"You were saying," said Lofty to Emmy, "that you had no children and a busy husband and were thinking of taking a job. This could be it."

"But…"

"Unless, of course," Lofty added, "little Blandish is too sentimental and squeamish to start digging up the dead past…"

The obvious thing, of course, would have been to treat the whole idea as a joke—no need to go to the trouble of turning down a suggestion which was clearly never meant to be taken seriously. But Emmy hesitated just too long, and the moment of escape evaded her.

It was then that she became horribly aware that everybody was looking at her. Lofty with a sardonic smile worthy of goat-footed Pan; Barbara with quick, hard-edged suspicion; and Arthur Price with the benign anticipation of an uncle about to distribute gifts. Beyond Price, Vere Prendergast and James Baggot had interrupted their conversation to turn and stare. Baggot seemed amused, and Vere faintly contemptuous.

It seemed to Emmy that her tiny hesitation had been as explicit as a public confession, a confession not merely of her feeling for Beau in 1943 but of the fact that those feelings still persisted, that in twenty years little Blandish had apparently not succeeded in growing up. To run away now would be an intolerable betrayal. This was the last chance of preserving dignity and keeping faith. Or so it seemed to Emmy.

"I don't see anything to be sentimental about," she said. "I think it would be very interesting work." She met Barbara's eyes steadily. "I can start any time you like."

So it was that Emmy Tibbett walked into a trap which was largely of her own making, and slammed the door of it behind her.

CHAPTER TWO

"I SUPPOSE," SAID HENRY later that evening, "that it *could* turn out to be a popular success, but…"

"It hasn't a hope," said Emmy.

"What makes you so sure of that?"

"Well, it's pretty obvious that Barbara isn't really interested in the story of Dymfield. She simply wants to create a—well—a memorial, as she said herself. To her first husband. A guilty conscience working itself out after all these years, I suppose."

"Guilty conscience? Whatever for? Presumably she couldn't help it if her husband was killed in action…"

"He wasn't," said Emmy shortly. She kicked off her shoes and stretched out her legs.

Henry looked up, inquiringly.

Emmy said, "He killed himself. You surely must have heard about it."

"If I have, I'm afraid I've forgotten."

"Well, Beau was one of the great heroes of the Battle of Britain. He piloted Spitfires, and because his name was Guest, he was nicknamed Beau. Come to think of it, I've no idea what his real Christian name was. He was very young then, of course, in 1940. Twenty-two."

Henry glanced sharply across the room at his wife. She seemed curiously withdrawn, and was talking to herself rather than to him.

She went on. "Heaven knows how many German planes he shot down. He won the D.F.C. and a couple of bars, and the miracle was that he survived. He became a sort of legend; he seemed to be indestructible. That was why it was so awful when it happened."

"When what happened?"

"When he crashed. The Battle of Britain was over, and Beau's squadron had been sent down to a quiet West Country airfield for a rest. He was on a routine patrol when his Spitfire got out of control and crashed into the sea. Beau was lucky to be picked up alive by Air-Sea Rescue—if you call it lucky. The plastic surgeons had to build his face up from a photograph."

"Poor devil," said Henry.

"He used to laugh about it. Apparently it wasn't a very good photograph, and by the time he emerged from East Grinstead, he looked more like the picture than—what he was before. Or so he said. Actually, it was difficult to tell what he must have looked like before; his face was badly scarred, you see, although the doctors did all they could. By great good fortune his eyes and teeth and bone structure were all undamaged, so that he wasn't an invalid in any obvious way. Oddly enough, I think that made it even harder for him to take the news that he could never fly again."

"But why couldn't he?" Henry asked. "If the doctors had made such a good job of him…"

"Because," Emmy said, "the accident had somehow upset his sense of balance; I didn't know the exact medical details, but every so often he used to get dizzy spells. He never talked about it and I wouldn't have known, only once I accused him of being drunk. And then he told me. You can imagine what a worm I felt. Anyhow, he was grounded and sent off to end his Air Force career as Chief Controller of a fighter station. Not a very heroic role for one of the fabulous few.

"Dymfield had what was known as a Sector Operations Room. That was where I worked. We controlled the fighters..."

"When you say 'control...'"

"Oh, literally control. We were in radio-telephone communication with the pilots—plain speech, not Morse—and we tracked the hostile bombers and our own fighters and directed the pilots until they were close enough to see the enemy. Our information came from radar stations, of course, and the aircraft tracks were plotted on our Operations Room Table." Emmy paused. "What made it even worse for Beau was that when he got to Dymfield, he found that one of our pilots was an old—well—a friendly rival, I suppose you'd call him—from the Battle of Britain days. A caricature of an R.A.F. type, handlebar mustache and all. He was called—if you'll believe it—Hildegard St. Vere Prendergast. Vere had survived unhurt, and he couldn't help being a continual reminder to Beau of—well—you can imagine."

Emmy paused, and lit a cigarette. Then she went on.

"There was another thing, too. In 1940, Vere and Beau were not only rivals as far as their score of enemy planes was concerned. They were also both crazy about the same girl, a bit-part actress called Barbara Brent. She was very pretty, in a—well—an actressy sort of way. She still is."

"I gather," said Henry, "that this is the same Barbara who is commissioning the book."

"Yes," said Emmy. "Well, in 1940 she turned Vere down and married Beau. Heaven knows whether she did it because she really loved him or simply because he was such a glamorous figure. I dare say she wasn't very clear about it herself. I don't know why it's always assumed that people know their own motives for..." She stopped, and took a pull at her cigarette. "Anyhow, Barbara and Beau were married and apparently were very happy. She gave up the theater and followed him around the country. Then he had this crash.

"They came to Dymfield, and Barbara took lodgings in the village. Beau had to live at the Mess, of course, but he spent as much time as he could with her and she was always in and out of the station."

Henry raised his eyebrows. "A civilian—on an airfield?"

"Oh, only the Mess, the living quarters. Quite separate from the airfield or the Operations Room. Several miles away. Anyhow, one of the first people Barbara met up with was her old flame, Vere Prendergast."

Emmy frowned. "It's terribly hard to tell you this with any sort of accuracy," she said. "I don't like gossip, as you know. But gossip is an integral part of the story. Beau hadn't been at Dymfield more than a few weeks before the place was buzzing with rumors about Barbara. Her name was linked with practically every man in sight—Vere, Lofty, Sammy Smith, even little Baggot. The story was that she'd never cared a rap for Beau, and that now he was badly burnt and grounded and doing a routine job, she was fed up with him. I've no idea whether any of the rumors were true or not. I can only tell you that Beau heard them and they upset him terribly. You see, he loved Barbara. People thought he didn't, but he did. I know.

"That was the situation in 1943, when Dymfield got its first Typhoons; in those days they were top secret fighters. Naturally, the pilots had to be especially trained in flying them. Vere, as a pioneer on this exciting new aircraft, became even more one-up than ever.

"The next thing that happened was that hideous Mess party at Dymfield. Everyone was there: Beau and Barbara and Sammy Smith—he was one of our controllers who had been a pilot and had known Beau in the old days. Then there was Annie and Lofty and Arthur Price, Jimmy Baggot, too, and Vere, of course—oh, everybody.

"Anyhow, it was a pretty lively party. I don't know how the argument started, but the first I heard, Vere was telling Beau, quite quietly and sensibly, that nobody could fly a Typhoon without a certain amount of training; and Beau was claiming that he could fly any bloody aircraft ever built. Barbara was egging Beau on, and the next thing we knew, he'd flung down his challenge. He would fly a Typhoon and single-handed at that.

"Vere told him not to be a fool, but Beau had suddenly become very lucid and seemed to have the whole thing worked out. He said he would take Vere's place on his next routine patrol. He'd pilot the aircraft himself—take-off, landing, acrobatics, and all—and he bet Vere a hundred pounds to a sixpence that he'd give a faultless performance. He knew that he'd be tracked on Dymfield's Operations Room Table all the time, as well as being in radio-telephone touch, so we'd be able to watch his performance.

"Vere told him he was crazy, but Barbara kissed him and told him he was marvelous and brave and clever, and, of course, after that nothing on heaven or earth would have stopped him. Vere remonstrated as hard as he could, but Barbara told him he was being a spoil-sport and that all he had to do was turn a blind eye for a few minutes. Vere went off muttering defiance, but they must have talked him around in the end.

"The fatal day was to be the following Friday. Vere was due to go up on a dusk patrol. All of us in the Operations Room were considerably worked up about it. I was on duty that evening. We all knew that Snowdrop Three-two—that was the call sign of Vere's aircraft—would in fact be piloted by Beau, and we were all keeping our fingers crossed for him. I certainly was.

"He took off all right, and I made radio-telephone contact with him. I called him and said, 'Snowdrop Three-two, Redwing calling'—Redwing was Dymfield—'are you receiving me? Over.' Back came that crackling voice over the loud-speaker, 'Hello, Redwing. Snowdrop Three-two. Receiving you loud and clear. Out.' Now, that was odd, because "out" is what a pilot said when he was switching off, and apparently that's what Beau did. After that, I called and called him, but there was no answer. The aircraft crossed the coast, made a big circle over the sea, and then swept the coastline again, flying at a level height. Then, suddenly, a voice came over the loud-speaker. It just said, 'Tally-ho.' Sorry..." There was a suspicious break in Emmy's voice and she blew her nose. Then she went on. "I expect you know, that was the code word meaning that the enemy was in sight, but there was no hostile aircraft that evening. Then Snowdrop Three-two headed straight out to sea and just—disappeared. Lost height rapidly and vanished. It must have nose-dived into the North Sea. Nothing was ever seen or heard of it again. Nor of Beau."

"Vere's commanding officer must have thought that he'd been killed."

"Yes. Poor Vere. It was awful. He'd carried out Plan A, which was that if he'd had no word from Beau by five o'clock, he'd lie low in his quarters and leave the field clear for Beau, which is what happened. Beau and Vere were much the same size and height, and one man in flying outfit and helmet looks very like another. The ground staff accepted Beau as Vere. You can imagine the shambles when Vere walked into Dymfield next morning—and found he was supposed to be dead.

"I must say, the powers-that-be were marvelous. Of course, the whole story had to be confessed, and Vere was in a lot of trouble, although he managed to convince the commanding officer that Beau had given him the slip and taken the aircraft up without his knowledge. Anyhow, there was nothing anybody could do."

"Poor fellow," said Henry. "I suppose he must have had one of his fits of dizziness and..."

Emmy shook her head. "That was the official explanation," she said, "but it didn't make sense, not to any of us. Why was he heading straight out to sea? Why had he switched off his radiotelephone? Why didn't he call for help?" She paused, and then said, "We all knew what actually happened."

"And what was that?"

"Beau obviously and deliberately killed himself."

After a long moment of silence Henry said, "Why?"

"You mean, why was it obvious?"

"No, why did he kill himself?"

Emmy hesitated. "Who knows? The story went that, earlier in the day Barbara had told him she was going to leave him for Vere. Heaven knows if that's true. The fact that Barbara did eventually marry Vere doesn't prove anything. Personally, I think Beau killed himself for quite a different reason."

"What was that?" Henry asked with interest.

"I was on duty that evening," said Emmy. "I watched the track of that aircraft. He didn't even attempt any sort of acrobatics, as he'd promised. Just made that rather clumsy circuit, and then flew out to sea. I think he just couldn't cope. Maybe he was plain scared to try to bring her back and land her—remember he'd crashed in flames once before. Even if he'd gotten down safely, he'd lost an enormous amount of prestige. Sammy Smith was in the Operations Room, for instance, and he was fairly gloating over the bad show Beau was putting up. He'd been a pilot himself and he's never liked Beau." Emmy paused and then said, "I think Beau killed himself sooner than have to face Barbara and Vere and the others as a failure."

"And what about you?"

"Me? What do you mean?"

Henry smiled. "You don't include yourself among the people he wouldn't want to face."

"Well, of course not. He knew that I—I mean, I simply didn't count. I hardly knew him."

Henry considered telling his wife that she was a very bad liar, but then decided to keep his mouth shut.

"Anyhow," Emmy went on, "it was all hushed up. The heroic image of Beau Guest was maintained. He was posted as 'Missing, presumed killed' on a training flight. Of course, the rumor of a gallant suicide leaked out and burnished the image, if anything. And unless I'm very much mistaken, Barbara has had a bad conscience over it for twenty years. She knows that he'd never have gone up unless she'd practically dared him to do it, and she knows equally well that he killed himself rather than face her when he failed. She'd have given him no sympathy."

"You don't like the lady very much, do you?" Henry asked.

Emmy raised her hands and let them fall again. "I do try not to be unfair," she said, "but one can't help... And now there's this business of the book. My guess is that Lofty and I will be handsomely paid for creating an elaborate whited sepulcher for Beau. And for Barbara. It's a revolting idea."

"Then why do it?"

"I was dared," said Emmy. She smiled, ruefully. "I'm a bit like Beau, I suppose. I hope I manage to live through it."

"So do I," said Henry.

The following day Barbara Prendergast telephoned Emmy Tibbett. She thought, she said, that they should get together as soon as possible to discuss plans. Of course, it was a little difficult for her, since she lived in the country, but she had been able to persuade Lofty to come and spend next weekend at Whitchurch Manor, and she did so hope that Emmy and her husband would be able to manage it, too.

"I don't know whether Henry's keen on rough shooting," she added. "If he is, Vere will be delighted. The two of them can amuse themselves shooting or fishing while we're in conference."

Emmy replied that she was afraid that Henry wasn't very keen on blood sports. "He has too much to do with violent death during business hours," she explained.

"I see," said Barbara. She did not sound pleased. "Oh, well, he can go bird-watching or plant-collecting or something. Anyhow, do say you'll come." And so it was arranged.

Vere met their train at Colchester. He looked more at home in the countryside than he had in London. He installed Henry and Emmy, with their suitcases, into his dark blue Bentley, and they purred off through the smiling countryside. After several days of heavy rain the weather had cleared. The September sunshine was bright and the air crisp, and cottage gardens had late roses blooming beside early chrysanthemums. The cloudless, deep blue sky reminded Emmy of another lovely September, twenty-five years earlier, when the only clouds in the sky had been the funeral pyres of brave men, when Beau Guest had been twenty-two, and Barbara Brent, nineteen, and Emmy Blandish still a schoolgirl, looking up from her lessons at the sound of gunfire in the sky and resolving fiercely to join the Air Force on her eighteenth birthday.

"Barbara tells me you're some sort of a detective type," Vere was saying to Henry, as the car whispered up a leafy lane.

"That's right." Emmy detected the amused note that always crept into Henry's voice when he met a character who appealed to him.

"I wouldn't mind your job." Vere sounded wistful behind his outsize mustache. "Chap against chap. Single combat. Like the old Battle of Britain in a way."

Henry laughed. "It sounds very romantic, put like that," he said. "In fact, I'm afraid, it's not true. The criminal may be a lone wolf, but *we're* a big and reasonably efficient organization."

"H'm," said Vere. He became owlishly thoughtful. "Interesting, that. You think the fighter type is apt to be on the side of the criminal, do you?"

"Good heavens," said Henry, "I certainly didn't intend to imply…"

"Many a true word, old sleuth," said Vere. "Keen on shooting?"

"I'm afraid not," said Henry.

"Fishing?"

"Not really, no."

"Well, what *are* you keen on?" asked Vere with a touch of irritation.

"Sailing," said Henry. "Sailing and skiing." He had the sense to realize that Vere's question had been concerned exclusively with sporting activities.

"H'm. I see." Vere sounded a little dubious. It was clear that in his view both these sports, while patronized by certain acceptable people, had a darker side to them. They were becoming popular. "Don't think we can help you much there."

"I also enjoy walking," said Henry.

"Walking?" echoed Vere, as if he had never heard the word before.

"It used to be known as hiking," said Henry, and winked at Emmy.

"Good God," said Vere, and lapsed into a gloomy silence. After a few minutes the Bentley turned into a driveway which led to Whitchurch Manor.

Barbara and Lofty were waiting to greet them on the flagged terrace. The house was long, low, beamy, and chintzy, and outside every window stretched a vista of park and farmland. Civilities were exchanged and drinks provided, and the party settled down to a relaxed preprandial conversation.

Barbara, haggard but elegant in dark linen trousers and a silk shirt, made much of Henry. *"Darling,"* she said to Vere, with exaggerated reproach, "you mean you actually didn't realize that this is *the* Henry Tibbett? The great detective, wizard of the Yard..."

"Oh, please," said Henry. "There's no need to exaggerate."

"But I'm *not,*" protested Barbara, opening her black-ringed eyes very wide. "Am I, Emmy? I'm continually hearing about Henry Tibbett, the detective. But nobody ever told me how fascinating he would be to meet."

Henry, well aware of his undistinguished appearance and of the fact that, far from shining in conversation, he had barely had the chance to open his mouth, decided that it would be more foolish to protest than to say nothing. He did, however, wonder what Barbara Prendergast was up to. Listening to Emmy, he had formed an impression of Barbara as a thoroughly silly woman. Now, he was not so sure.

Vere, meanwhile, had started to reminisce with Emmy about the war. As a momentary silence fell on the conversation, he was saying, rather too loudly, "—and there was this Hun in his Heinkel, y'see, straight and level at angels fifteen..."

"And there was I," said Lofty loudly, to nobody in particular, "upside down, nothing on the clock and still climbing."

There was a moment of dead silence. Vere looked at Lofty as though he could cheerfully kill him. Barbara turned away, embarrassed.

Emmy said quickly, laughing, "What a memory you have, Lofty! I'd completely forgotten that phrase. I haven't heard it for donkey's years."

"And I," put in Henry, "haven't heard anyone talk about 'donkey's years' since I was a schoolboy, which is longer ago than anyone here can remember."

This started a general conversation on the subject of slang. The awkward moment was forgotten. It was only later, in the privacy of their room, that Henry asked Emmy why Vere had been so angry.

"Well, you know," said Emmy, "'Lloyd George knew my father...'"

"Did he really?"

"Idiot. You know what I mean. Just as people used to start singing, 'Lloyd George knew my father' to take the starch out of name-droppers, so in the R.A.F., if anybody started to shoot a line about his heroic achievements, the others would begin chanting, in unison, 'There was I, upside down, nothing on the clock...'"

"And still climbing," Henry finished for her. "An interesting situation. So one is to gather that your friend Lofty was taking the starch out of your friend Vere."

"Obviously," said Emmy.

There was a pause, and then Henry said, "Well, Emmy love, it's up to you, but I'm beginning to wonder if you wouldn't be wise to keep right out of this business of raking up the past. Your band of old comrades doesn't seem to be a very united body."

"I said I'd do it," said Emmy.

"You were dared."

"That's right. So you see, I must."

"Oh, dear," said Henry, "it's all a bit childish, isn't it? If you want to back out all you have to do is say so."

"It's a bit more complicated than that," said Emmy. She kissed the top of Henry's head as he sat on the bed. "I feel I have to go through with it."

"Because of Beau Guest," said Henry.

"Yes," said Emmy, seriously. Then, looking hard at her husband, she added, "Oh, Henry. You can't really be *jealous*, not of a man who died twenty years ago and who never—who never..." She stopped.

Henry smiled at her. "I think it's only natural," he said, "that I should be jealous of the first man you ever loved."

"You're an idiot," said Emmy, and turned away.

Henry noticed that she had made no denial.

CHAPTER THREE

After LUNCH BARBARA became very business-like. First of all Vere and Henry were sent off firmly for a walk around the home farm, which comprised some eighty acres.

"I hope," Vere said to Henry, with overdone politeness, "that it won't upset you if I take a gun, old man. Always the chance of a rabbit or a few pigeons. For the pot, of course," he added.

"It won't upset me at all," said Henry. He borrowed a pair of enormous black rubber boots, and the two of them set out.

Barbara waved good-bye to them from the terrace, and then came back into the big drawing room, where Emmy and Lofty were chatting over a third cup of coffee.

"Right," she said, "now we can begin."

Lofty pulled a small blue exercise book and a ballpoint pen out of his pocket. "Have you got something to write on?" he asked Emmy.

"You won't need to write anything for the moment," said Barbara. She spoke briskly. "First of all I want to propose a slight change of plan."

"Good God, Barbara!" Lofty, never a respecter of persons, spoke rudely and explosively. "You mean you've dragged us all the way down here to tell us the whole thing's off? Of all the..."

"Of course it's not off," said Barbara, sharply. "Although I should have thought that a free weekend's board and lodging might have appealed to you, anyway."

Surprisingly, Barbara's counterattack seemed to please Lofty. He laughed. "That's my girl. God, you haven't changed, have you? All this lady-of-the-manor stuff is a pretty thin veneer."

Surprisingly again, Barbara took this in good part. "You haven't changed either, Lofty. As bloody rude as ever." She laughed, and lit a cigarette. "No, the project is not off. But—I've been thinking. The history of a fighter station is pretty dry sort of material, isn't it? Most readers want characters and personalities, people they can get to know, human interest, in fact."

"So what do you want me to do? Fill Dymfield with a lot of fictitious characters and weave a story of blood, lust, and glamour around them in the approved style?"

"I hadn't thought of *fictitious* characters," said Barbara quietly. She studied her carmine fingernails.

"Here, wait a minute," said Lofty. He sounded really taken aback. "There's such a thing as the law of libel, you know. I can't sit down and write a scandalous history about a whole lot of people who are very much alive and kicking…"

"I didn't exactly mean that either," said Barbara. She paused.

Emmy said, "I know what Barbara is getting at. She doesn't want a history of Dymfield. She wants a biography of Beau." She turned and looked full at Barbara. "That's what you intended from the beginning, isn't it?"

Barbara threw up her head nervously. "No," she said. "No, that's not true. I first had the idea of a book on Dymfield, and then, the more I thought about it…" She leaned forward. "This is how I see it. Lots of Battle of Britain aces had their biographies written; but my idea would be to put the emphasis on Beau's work at Dymfield—coming out of the hospital and starting a second service career, pointing out that he was doing even more vital work after his accident than before…"

"Not true," said Lofty shortly.

"Well, just as vital then. Don't you see? That way we could produce a history of Dymfield—at least, of its most interesting epoch—and still have our human interest. Isn't that a good idea?"

There was a moment of silence. Then Lofty said, "Bloody clever, Barbara. I believe Emmy's right; you've been after this all along. And it so happens that your reasoning is impeccable. If the book's going to have any general interest at all, that's the way to do it." Barbara looked pleased, and glanced down modestly. "You realize, of course," Lofty went on, "that we shall also have to include a full account of Beau's death."

Barbara's head came up with a jerk. "I don't see why."

"If you ask any member of the public," said Lofty, slowly and without emotion, "if he has heard of Beau Guest, he'll probably either say No, or he'll think you mean the fictitious hero of the Foreign Legion. But if by a remote chance he does remember Beau, he'll say, 'That was the fighter pilot who killed himself, wasn't it?'"

There was a silence which seemed to Emmy to be endless.

Then Barbara said, "How vile people are."

"Human is the fashionable synonym," said Lofty. "Look here, Barbara. You've just been talking about appealing to the popular market. Well, you can take it from me that the popular market isn't interested in airfields or Operations Rooms, except in the most incidental way. But it might well be interested in the reconstruction of a twenty-year-old human drama played out against the backdrop of Britain's finest hour, if I may coin a phrase." Almost in spite of himself, Lofty was growing enthusiastic. He got up and began pacing the room. "For the first time," he said, "I begin to see commercial possibilities. It could even be a best seller."

"But Lofty," Barbara began.

Lofty took no notice. He was talking to Emmy. "Your first job," he said, "is to get the details of Beau's early life—school, family, and so forth. Dates of joining the R.A.F., postings, marriage—everything that happened to him up to the time he ditched." He turned to Barbara. "Let's have a few dates and facts from you first, Barbara. We can fill in the details later."

"I'm not quite sure what you want," said Barbara a little uncertainly.

"Just tell us—what you want to tell us," said Lofty. For a moment Emmy had a strange feeling of a shared knowledge between these two; almost of a conspiracy. Then it vanished, as Lofty said, "Let's start with the date of birth, if you can remember it."

"Beau's or mine?"

"Beau's, of course."

Emmy had taken up her notebook and, at a nod from Lofty, she began to write as Barbara spoke. "Beau was born on January 19th," she said. "Let me see, it must have been in 1919. His father was a country clergyman, the Reverend Sidney Guest. A dear, gentle man. Beau was an only child. I believe his mother was very beautiful. Alas, I never met her. She became very ill when Beau was only a baby and had to go abroad for her health. So Beau was brought up by his father, who was perhaps the teeniest bit old-fashioned. He wanted Beau to train as an accountant or a lawyer or something conventional like that. He wasn't keen on Beau joining the Air Force, but, of course, once the Battle of Britain started, the old man was tremendously proud of his son.

"Beau joined the Air Force in 1938. You know all about his career with fighters. I met him in the spring of 1940, when I was playing a small part in *Summer Song*. We got married in August—at the height of the Battle."

"That's good," said Lofty. "We can work that up. I imagine you won't want Vere mentioned at this stage."

Barbara gave him an unfriendly look. "By all means, you can say that Vere was Beau's greatest friend in the squadron," she said.

"Make a note of that, Blandish," said Lofty. "Right, Barbara. Go on."

"You know the rest," said Barbara. "He shot down sixteen Huns, and won the D.F.C. three times, and then crashed on a routine patrol in 1942."

Lofty turned to Emmy. "Your first job," he said, "is to get at Air Ministry records for more details of Beau's operational career. Then talk to the people who served with him, Vere for a start. And I believe Sammy Smith knew him in the old days."

"Smith was at Falconfield," said Barbara, "where Beau was stationed when he crashed."

"Was he? I never knew that." Lofty sounded thoughtful. "He never mentioned it when we were all at Dymfield."

"Of course he didn't," said Barbara. "Smith was pretty uncouth, but at least he had the tact not to remind Beau of…"

"Incidentally, why was Sammy himself grounded? Anybody know?"

"*Anno Domini*, I suppose," said Emmy. "He was in his late thirties, after all. That's pretty old."

"You mean," said Lofty, "that it *was* pretty old. It sounds pretty young from where I'm sitting at the moment."

"Oh, God," said Barbara, and laughed. "Do you have to keep reminding us?"

"'Golden lads and girls must, as chimney sweepers, come to dust,'" said Lofty. "Except Beau Guest, of course."

Suddenly Barbara stubbed out her cigarette and stood up. "Lofty Parker," she said, "if you continue to take that attitude the whole thing is off."

"Attitude?" Lofty was full of unconvincing innocence. "What attitude?"

"You know very well what I mean."

"My dear Barbara, I haven't the faintest idea what you mean."

"You're a bloody liar," said Barbara. "You always were. Now listen to me. I'm paying you good money to do a job. You'll do it the way I want it done or the deal is off. Is that clear?"

"Perfectly, Barbara. Perfectly." Lofty grinned. "I thought you would have realized by now that your wildest whim is my command. If I was provocative just now, it was simply to establish where we all stood. It's all right, little Blandish," he added; and Emmy became uncomfortably aware that she must have been staring. "Don't bother your pretty little head about what the grown-ups are saying. You'll understand when you're older."

"Honestly, Lofty," Emmy began.

"I take that back," Lofty amended, not unkindly. "However old you may grow, your mental age will always be nineteen. That's your charm." Before Emmy could think of a suitable reply, he went on. "Right. We've got to the point where Beau ditches his Spitfire. We now come to a gripping and poignant chapter on his experiences in the hospital, which will have the lending libraries rolling in the aisles and not a dry eye in the house. Tell us about it, Barbara, dear."

Barbara sat down on the sofa. Twisting a fragile white handkerchief in her fingers, she said, "It happened on a Friday afternoon. I was out shopping, so they got no reply when they telephoned me. It was six o'clock before the call came through. They simply told me that Beau had had an accident and asked me to go to the hospital as quickly as I could..."

"Mrs. Guest? Do sit down. I'm Dr. Innes. Now, I don't want to distress you, but I'm afraid your husband has had rather a nasty accident. A very nasty accident indeed."

"He's not...?"

"No, no. He's alive, and he's going to be perfectly all right. Just get that into your head."

"Can I see him?"

"Not just at the moment, I'm afraid. What I really wanted to ask you was whether you have a good photograph of him?"

"Photograph?"

"Yes. Two, if possible. Full face and profile."

"But what on earth do you...?"

"Just to help us."

"My God—you mean—he's got no face left...?"

"Now, now, Mrs. Guest. Nurse, would you...? Thank you. Now, Mrs. Guest, you must be brave and sensible. I told you, your husband has been extremely lucky. His eyes are undamaged, and so are his teeth and bones. It's just a question of contours—always useful to have a photograph to work on..."

"When can I see him?"

"We'll let you know. Within a few days, you may be sure..."

"Falconfield 34? Mrs. Guest? Ah, how are you? This is Dr. Innes. You can come along to see your husband tomorrow, half-past two, if that's convenient for you. Yes, yes, we got the photographs. Thank you very much. Oh, yes, he's conscious and extremely cheerful, but you must be prepared for a little bit of a shock... The main thing is not to upset him, just be very gentle and sympathetic and calm. Above all, don't let him see that you're upset by his appearance in any way..."

"Oh, God, Vere. Give me another drink. It was hell. It was indescribable. Have you heard people say that eyes are expressive? Well, it's bloody well not true. D'you know what's expressive? It's the way the skin sort of wrinkles and straightens out around the eyes. Have you ever seen two eyes just gazing at you out of nothing, out of a lot of bandages, because there's no face left around them? Laughing eyes, sad eyes—bloody balls. Yes, that's exact. Two staring brown-and-white balls, like marbles. And what's going to happen when the bandages come off? Have you seen them, Vere? Have you seen those poor creatures in that hospital? Have you tried to keep the horror out of your face as you spoke to them? Don't try to cheer me up. Beau's going to be like that. I know he is. I had to take them a photograph. Oh, God, I wish he were dead. I wish he were dead…"

"…got to the hospital as fast as I could," said Barbara. "Poor Beau. He looked like an Egyptian mummy, all done up in bandages with only his eyes showing. I had to take along photographs so that they could rebuild his face. He was wonderfully brave. He was so cheerful that I was, too. Of course, I had perfect faith in the doctors, and you know what a superb job they did on him. Of course, it took time. It was eighteen months before the last operation was over and I was able to take him away to convalesce."

"That's all good strong stuff, Barbara," said Lofty. He was scribbling as he spoke. "On we go. Where did you take him?"

Barbara hesitated. "We couldn't go to Beau's father," she said. "He—it would have upset him too much. As a matter of fact, Vere was very kind and lent us one of the cottages on this very estate. It was winter. The weather was horrible, I remember, but nothing mattered except that Beau was back with me and was getting better every day. It was like a second honeymoon…"

"Must you have that phonograph blaring all the time, Barbara?"

"I don't *have* to. I just try to keep myself sane, that's all."

"You mean, my company drives you insane?"

"Oh, Beau, don't be idiotic."

"I only asked you a question."

"Well—if you want me to be honest—it's not much fun for me, is it? Stuck down here in this one-horse hole."

"Poor darling Barbara..."

"There's no need to be sarcastic."

"I wasn't. I swear I wasn't. I'm just so angry with myself for crashing, and giving you such a hell of a time. Never mind, darling. As soon as I'm fit we'll spend a week in town. We'll go dancing at Hatchetts."

"And be blown to bits in an air raid? Thank you very much."

"Now look, Barbara, you can't have it both ways. Either you live safely in Whitchurch or you live dangerously at Hatchetts."

"Or you just *live*; you *make* something of your life. Have you heard from Air Ministry about your new posting?"

"Yes."

"Oh, my God. That's ominous."

"What do you mean?"

"You didn't mention it until I asked. That means it's bad."

"I don't think it's particularly bad. I'm to be Chief Controller of the Operations Room at Dymfield—just a few miles from here."

"Chief Controller? You mean, commanding officer?"

"Of course not. I've done my nut with the doctors, but they won't let me fly. How could I be in command of an airfield?"

"Christ almighty! Controller of an Operations Room! How low can you sink?"

"It'll be a very interesting job, Barbara. And what's more, I'll be working with Vere..."

"Vere's flying Typhoons."

"That's right. And I'll be backing him up with..."

"Backing him up! That just about sums it up, doesn't it? Hanging around on the edge of things, never in the center. I tell you, Beau, you're finished! Finished! And I'll tell you another thing. I'm not! I'm bloody well not!"

"Barbara, darling, it's not as bad as all that. Come and sit down. No, don't have another drink."

"Why shouldn't I? Why damn well shouldn't I?"

"Very well. Please yourself. You're grown up, after all, despite appearances to the contrary."

"Are you trying to insult me, Beau Guest?"

"No. I'm trying to make you see that you're behaving in a rather childish way."

"Hark at grandfather! Twenty-five next birthday, and finished—finished…"

"…like a second honeymoon," said Barbara. "Then, when Beau was well enough, he took up his posting at Dymfield. We were both very thrilled about it. After all, it was a very important job. From there on, you know as much as I do." Barbara smiled engagingly and bent forward to throw a fresh log on the fire. "Of course, Beau wasn't very easy to live with in those days. He was absolutely heartbroken that the doctors wouldn't allow him to fly again, and it took quite a time for him to adjust to a ground job…"

"I'm sure," said Lofty, "that you were a great help to him."

"I did my best," replied Barbara, lowering her eyes modestly.

Henry and Vere came back about five o'clock. They had walked for some twelve miles across rough country. Henry was exhausted, filthy, and disgruntled. Vere was fresh and hearty and in the best of spirits, and he carried two pigeons and a rabbit in his gamebag.

They found Barbara, Emmy, and Lofty deep in discussion by the dying fire; Emmy and Lofty scribbling in their notebooks. The literary session broke up at once, however, with the return of the hunters. The guests dispersed to their bedrooms to wash and change, and Barbara exhorted everybody to assemble in the drawing room at six for a cocktail.

As Henry washed, Emmy gave him a short description of what had taken place during the afternoon. "It was—well— nasty, Henry."

"Nothing like as nasty as walking twelve miles through mud," he retorted through a mask of soapsuds.

"I mean, I can't explain. I wish I'd never started this…"

Henry spluttered, swallowing a quantity of soap in the process. "My dear girl," he said, finally, "didn't I tell you? Didn't I warn you?"

"Yes," said Emmy, "you did. Oh, maybe I'm imagining the whole thing, but I've got a feeling that there's a lot going on that I don't know anything about."

"Which makes you useful," said Henry, wiping his face.

"What do you mean?"

"Innocence is a rare quality and easily exploited."

"Oh, don't be a pompous idiot."

"Very well. But don't say you weren't warned."

On the way downstairs Henry was surprised to be waylaid by Vere, who grabbed his arm and urged him to come into the study for a quiet drink. Henry, who imagined that Vere would have had more than enough of his company during the after-noon, was considerably intrigued. He followed his host into the snug, book-lined room. After a lot of preliminary snorting and throat-clearing, Vere at last got to the point. "Been talking to Barbara, old man," he said.

"Oh, yes?"

"I dare say you've been talking to Blandish—your wife, that is. You'll have heard the latest."

"You mean, that the book is to be more of a biography of Beau Guest than a…?"

"Exactly." Vere handed Henry a whisky. "Soda? Say when. Yes, that's just what I mean. My dear old blood-hound, this has got to be stopped."

"It sounded a pretty good idea to me," said Henry, "a good commercial proposition. Better than the life story of an Operations Room."

Vere looked acutely unhappy, and breathed deeply, alternately sucking and blowing at his mustache. At length he said, "Poor old Beau's dead, isn't he? Committed suicide like so many others. Why can't Barbara leave it at that?"

"Emmy thinks," said Henry, "that your wife may feel she wants to create a sort of memorial to her first husband."

"Then she'd be better spending the money on a tombstone."

"But there's no tomb, is there?" said Henry, "no grave, no corpse, no coffin. Just missing, presumed dead."

Vere looked suspiciously at Henry. "What do you know about it?"

"Just what Emmy has told me."

"Look, my dear old investigator, it's difficult to explain, but take my word for it, *this must be stopped.*" Vere laid a hand on Henry's arm. "Your wife has some influence with Parker, I believe, and if Parker backed out, Barbara would drop the whole idea. Will you speak to Blandish about it?"

As a matter of fact, Henry had been fully intending to use his influence to get the project set aside; but as he followed Vere down to the drawing room, he was aware of a tingling sensation—half-physical and half-mental—which characterized the faculty which he called his "nose." Things he had heard, things he had been told were beginning to add up to something in Henry's mind. Nothing definite. Just an impression of things not being what they seemed. Suddenly he felt a great reluctance to let the matter drop until he had probed it thoroughly. He did not speak to Emmy after all.

CHAPTER FOUR

THE FOLLOWING DAY Lofty Parker started off by putting his foot into things, fair and square, with Vere. Hosts and house guests had all assembled in the morning room for a real English breakfast. Covered silver dishes stood on the hotplate, revealing in turn fried and scrambled eggs and bacon, mushrooms, kidney and sausages. Clusters of boiled eggs huddled under a huge tea cosy for warmth. The toast, butter and marmalade seemed purely incidental.

At first, conversation was general. It was another glorious day and Vere proposed a walk in the park, pointing out that the sun would have dried out the worst of the mud, so the going should be tolerable. Henry and Emmy agreed to the proposal with enthusiasm.

It was then that Lofty said, "My dear Vere, we aren't here to frivol about the woodlands enjoying ourselves, you know. We've got work to do."

"I wouldn't worry too much about that, old scout," said Vere, a shade uneasily. "You worked yesterday, after all."

"We roughed out a sort of ground plan yesterday. Today we start on the detail work."

"What do you mean by detail work?"

"I mean you, Vere," said Lofty.

Vere stopped dead in mid-mouthful. Then he spluttered as he swallowed a piece of bacon the wrong way and began to choke. Lofty, who was sitting next to him, began to slap his back in a bored manner, and Barbara giggled. When Vere recovered his breath, he glared around the table and said, "I've made no secret from the beginning that I disapprove of the whole enterprise."

"You didn't raise any objections at the reunion," Lofty pointed out.

Vere ignored this. "I shall certainly take no part in it."

"But, dear old soul," said Lofty, "you and Beau were practically inseparable at Dymfield."

"Rubbish."

"What's more," said Lofty, "you must have been one of the last people to see Beau alive."

"That's quite untrue." Vere sounded really upset. "I didn't see him at all the evening he—he died. You know that as well as I do. I waited in the Mess until five. I then went off to my billet and got into my flying outfit. When I came out to the hangar, Beau had already taken the kite up without my permission."

Lofty shook his head sadly. "It won't do, old man. You'll have to come clean. Everybody knows that you'd agreed to keep out of the way so that Beau could go up. After all, what does it matter if you tell the truth now? They can't court-martial you."

Vere had gone as red as a turkey cock. "I stand by the story which I told the court of inquiry," he said stubbornly. "I refuse to have my name blackened. Beau gave me the slip, turned up at the hangar, and took off in my place." Vere glared at Lofty. "I suppose I cannot stop you from advancing your own theories, but you will never get any endorsement from me. When I found Beau was already airborne, I naturally made myself scarce. Slipped out of the station on a bicycle, and put up at a pub some miles away." As if in explanation, he added to Henry, "Wouldn't have done, you see, to be sitting around in the Mess when I was supposed to be up on patrol."

"I wouldn't have thought it necessary to stay out all night," said Henry.

Vere turned on him, suddenly angry. "Just what are you driving at?"

"Nothing. Nothing at all. I just wondered…"

"You civilian types need everything explained in words of one syllable," said Vere. "Look. I should have been in that Typhoon and I wasn't. Beau was. Had all gone according to plan, he would have completed the patrol, landed, changed out of flying clothes in my billet, and gone quietly back to the Mess. Meanwhile, I had notified the Mess that after patrol I'd be leaving the station and sleeping out. I didn't dare turn up, of course."

"Why do you say of course?" Henry asked. "I should have thought…"

"It has apparently escaped your attention," said Vere, with growing impatience, "that we were a station with a Sector Operations Room."

"I know. But…"

"What Vere means," said Emmy, "is that all aircraft from Dymfield were tracked continually in the Operations Room, and it was very usual for off-duty pilots to drop in there in the evenings to watch what was going on. If Vere had gone back to the Mess, there would probably have been several chaps there who had followed his patrol—or rather, Beau's—on the Operations Room Table. It wouldn't have done for them to know more about the evening's air activity then Vere did."

"Thank you, Blandish," said Vere. "Very neatly put."

"You must have caused quite a sensation when you turned up the next day alive and well," said Henry.

Vere stood up. "I'm not prepared to talk about it," he said, and stalked out of the room.

Lofty made a face at Emmy. "What's eating him?" he asked.

Barbara said quickly, "Oh, don't mind old Vere. He—he's still very sensitive about the whole thing. Beau was his best friend, you see. I think he feels somehow responsible."

"Responsibility," said Lofty, "will have to be assigned, one way or the other. You are editor in chief, Barbara. I await your instructions."

"I don't understand you."

"What line are we to take about Beau's death? I presume that we plump fair and square for suicide?"

"Certainly not," said Barbara. "He lost his sense of balance, had a dizzy spell, and lost control of…"

"My dear Barbara," said Lofty, "don't be idiotic. Everyone knew that he deliberately killed himself, and if we simply stick to the official line, we may as well drop the whole idea, because Beau's suicide is the really interesting part of the story. The question is—what is to be the motive? I suggest something noble but not flashy."

"What do you mean by that?" Barbara looked up sharply, with unfriendly eyes.

Lofty tilted his chair back. "Possibility number one," he said. "Beau Guest, the dedicated pilot, realizes that he can never fly again. His life is therefore not worth living, and he chooses to die—as he had wished to live—at the controls of an aircraft. A bit too noble to be convincing, perhaps, but we could try it. Possibility number two. Beau Guest, golden boy of the Battle of Britain, has degenerated into a mutilated and unheroic ground staffer. Sooner than submit his beautiful wife to the humiliation of being tied to such a wreck, he decides to free her by…"

Without warning Barbara stood up and hit Lofty across the face. "You filthy swine!" she shouted.

Lofty rubbed his cheek and grinned imperturbably.

"I'm sorry," he said, "that I had to provoke you into that display, especially in front of Henry and Emmy. It was done quite deliberately."

"You're bloody right, it was." Barbara was so angry that Henry had the impression of smoke rising from the top of her head.

Lofty went on calmly. "Somebody had to rub your nose in a few facts. Don't you see, my dear idiot, that unless we produce a strong theory about Beau's death, people are going to draw their own conclusions. If they are charitable, they will probably pick one or the other of my two possibilities. If they are not…" He shrugged. "I think you'd better abandon the whole idea."

"I won't abandon it," said Barbara. She sat down again, her back to Lofty, like a child sulking.

"There is always," said Lofty, "possibility number three, which rather appeals to me. Without actually committing ourselves, we could hint that Beau was, in fact, on a special mission, so secret that it could never be acknowledged…"

"But he wasn't. Everyone knows that."

"How? How does everyone know?" Lofty was warming to his theme. "How do you know, come to that? Supposing that argument between Beau and Vere at the Dymfield party had been just a put-up job, a cover? I'll give you one or two other things to think about. First of all, if you recall, there was a German parachutist scare that evening…"

"I didn't know that."

"Well, of course, as a civilian, you wouldn't have. But I dare say Blandish may remember."

Emmy frowned. "Oh, yes. That's right. An Observer Corps Post started the scare. But Lofty, we had wild reports like that coming in all the time. It doesn't mean anything."

Lofty grinned. "It makes a nice, tantalizing red herring," he said. "Then there's another thing. Why did Beau arrive at the airfield at four o'clock, when he didn't take off till six? What was he doing all that time?"

Henry was surprised to see that Emmy looked upset, almost frightened.

"How do you know when he arrived?" she demanded.

"Because I saw him. I was wending my lonely way back to the Operations Room and duty. Beau was in the Guardroom as I came in—telephoning. I got a glimpse of him when the Duty Guard came out to open the gate for me. So there. Now more red herrings. Why did Beau sing out tally-ho when there wasn't another aircraft for miles? And why—this is very significant—why is old Vere carrying on like a prima donna now?"

"Because he doesn't want it published that he told fibs to the court of inquiry twenty years ago," suggested Emmy.

"Maybe," said Lofty. "But what about this as a more exciting theory. I have already demonstrated, my dear Watson, that Vere must have been in the know from the beginning. Supposing there are still secrets which can't be told, even after twenty years? Supposing that Vere is afraid we may stumble on the truth about Beau's mission?" Lofty looked at Barbara. "Well? How do you like it?"

"It stinks," said Barbara. She was very angry. "I absolutely forbid you even to hint at anything of the sort. In any case, it couldn't possibly be true."

"What couldn't be true?" said Vere's voice, loudly.

They all turned, almost guiltily, like conspirators. Vere had come back into the drawing room. He had put on a pair of rubber boots, and he carried a gun under his arm.

"Oh, nothing, darling," said Barbara quickly.

Lofty grinned. "Just a theory I was advancing about Beau's death," he said. It sounded impudent.

"What theory?"

"That it might not have been suicide after all."

"This has gone far enough," said Vere Prendergast. For a moment Henry found him almost impressive. "You may have found it amusing, Parker, but I have not, and neither has Barbara. I don't often put the old foot down, but I'm doing it now. This nonsense has got to stop."

"Dear old Vere," said Lofty. He sounded as though he were laughing. "You can't stop me. Nor can Barbara."

"I certainly could, if I wanted to," said Barbara.

"No you couldn't, imbecile. You could withdraw your financial support, but I'm interested now, and I intend to carry on until I find the truth. And so does Blandish, don't you?"

"I—I don't know, Lofty…"

Vere shrugged. He seemed to be making a great effort to control his anger. Then he said, "Well, Tibbett? Coming?"

"Yes, indeed," said Henry. He stood up.

"No use asking Barbara. You coming, Blandish?"

"Thank you, Vere. I'll go and change my shoes."

As the three of them walked out through the hall a few minutes later, Henry noticed that Barbara and Lofty were still sitting at the breakfast table. They did not appear to have moved a muscle between them.

The walk in the park was damp and uneventful. Vere shot a pigeon, which seemed to relieve his feelings. Conversation was desultory, punctuated by long silences, but this did not worry Henry. He was glad to have the chance of turning over in his mind the things that he had heard about R.A.F. Dymfield back in the nineteen-forties. He found himself much intrigued by those long-ago events. In fact, in his own mind Henry was beginning to think of the whole thing in terms of a case.

Whitchurch Manor was very peaceful when they got back from their walk. Barbara was arranging bowls of chrysanthemums in the drawing room, singing a number from a long-forgotten musical comedy to herself. Lofty had his feet up on a wicker-work chaise longue on the terrace, and was sipping his second Pimm's. Serenity reigned, and whatever conversation Barbara and Lofty might have had while alone, they were now clearly at some pains to present an innocent and united front. No more was heard of the projected book during luncheon.

The best train back to London left Colchester at four o'clock, so after lunch the house guests went to pack their suit-cases, and at a quarter past three Vere was waiting with the Bentley. Good-byes were said and thanks tendered with polite formality. Only the briefest of mutually understanding looks which passed between Barbara and Lofty betrayed—at least to Henry—that future plans had been securely laid.

The train had barely pulled out of the station when Lofty Parker began to laugh, aloud and apparently with genuine amusement.

"What's so funny?" asked Emmy.

"Better than I could have hoped," chortled Lofty. "What a performance, eh? And that's only act one. Wait until the real drama starts."

"Look, Lofty," said Emmy, "I've been thinking. I don't really want to go on with this. I'm sorry I ever got involved in it. Vere's dead against it, and I can't see any point in raking up old memories that would be better forgotten..."

"So you're backing out, are you, Blandish?"

"Not exactly backing out, but..."

"Good. Your next assignment—after you've gathered those dates and so on from Air Ministry—is a round of visits. I have not been idle this last week. I have collected all the addresses."

"Whose addresses?"

"They're all written down for you." Lofty produced a sheet of paper. "You'd better start with Annie, to make sure of catching her while she's still in London. Also in or around London are Sammy Smith, Jimmy Baggot, and Arthur Price. When you're through with that, you can have a day in the country as a reward. Beau's father, the Reverend Sidney, lives not far from Dymfield. That should be a particularly interesting visit. By the way, whatever you do, don't tell Barbara you're going to see the old man."

"But what am I to say to all these people, Lofty?"

"Just talk to them about Beau and Dymfield. Use your wits and keep your eyes and ears open, and make careful notes afterward. I've prepared a questionnaire, which I'm having duplicated in my office. Your ostensible purpose will be to give a copy of this to each person and persuade them to fill it in. I dare say most of them will simply tear it up. It doesn't matter much if they do, although the information on it would be useful. As far as Sammy is concerned, I'm chiefly interested in the time when he and Beau were both at Falconfield and

Beau had his crash. For the others—I don't mind telling you frankly, Blandish, that I'm more interested in Beau's death than in his life."

"That's surely not what Barbara wants…"

"What Barbara wants and what Barbara is going to get are two different things. This is my book, and it's not going to be a portrait of Dymfield, nor is it going to be a biography of Beau Guest."

"May one ask what it *is* going to be?" Henry said.

"Certainly," said Lofty. "A mystery story. The unraveling of a twenty-year-old enigma. Are you with me, Chief Inspector?"

"I follow what you mean, yes," said Henry carefully.

"If I'm not mistaken," said Lofty, "it will put several cats among a horde of pigeons." He smiled beatifically, delighted by the idea.

CHAPTER FIVE

THE FINCHLEY TELEPHONE number was answered by a young, languid, feminine voice. "Mrs. Smith speaking. Mr. Smith? Oh, no... Well, he's working, of course. What else would be doing? Who is it?"

"You don't know me, Mrs. Smith," said Emmy. "My name is Emmy Tibbett and I'm an old Air Force colleague of your husband's. I'm trying to get in touch with him about..."

"Oh, *lord*. Not again. That ghastly Mr. Price kept on and on at Sammy..."

"About the reunion, you mean?"

"It's all so *silly*," said Mrs. Smith.

Emmy, for some reason, had a clear mental picture of the woman at the other end of the telephone line. She was sure that Mrs. Smith was wearing tight black trousers with high-heeled shoes.

"Sammy didn't *want* to go, so why should he? The way Mr. Price went on..."

"I can assure you," said Emmy, "that I have nothing to do with reunions. As a matter of fact, I'm collecting material for a book."

"A book?" There was a quickening of interest in the voice. "You mean, you're going to put Sammy in a book?"

"In a way," said Emmy. "It's to be a biography of Beau Guest…"

"Come again. Of *who*?"

"One of the Battle of Britain heroes." Emmy was aware that she had spoken sharply. It irritated her unreasonably that this girl should never have heard of Beau. "Your husband was one of his colleagues."

"Battle of Britain? That's a long time ago…"

"We hoped that your husband would help us."

"Oh, yes. Well, I'm sure he will. If it's a book. I mean, it's all good publicity, isn't it? Will you be mentioning Sammy's name?"

"Almost certainly. That is," added Emmy, craftily, "if he can give us the information we need. If he's too busy, I can probably get it elsewhere."

"Oh, no. Don't do that. I mean, I know he'll want to help. Why don't you go around to his office? Are you in London?"

"Yes. I've just come from the Air Ministry. I'm in Whitehall."

"Well, Sammy's at Supercharged Motors in Euston Place. Do go and see him, Mrs.—sorry, I didn't get your name…"

"Tibbett," said Emmy. "Thanks very much, Mrs. Smith. I will."

Supercharged Motors was a large showroom fronted with plate glass, which looked exactly like many others in the same quarter of London. Gazing in from the pavement, Emmy was confronted by an array of burnished and lacquered motor cars, all well past their youth, most of which had been designed for the race track rather than the highway. Chromium pipes sprouted from their shiny hoods, and leather straps held many of their vital parts in position. Only one was effeminate enough to have a roof. The others disdained even the elementary comfort of a cloth top. Emmy pushed the door open and went in.

Almost at once a stout young man came out of an inner office. He wore a slightly passé carnation in the buttonhole of his blue suit and he was smoking a cigarette in a long black holder.

"Good afternoon, madam," he said, with all the warmth of a disc jockey. "Ah, I see you're admiring the Panther Special. Lovely job, isn't she? 1928, and in mint condition. Only one of her kind in London, I can promise you that. Twin overhead interconnecting camrods and triple..."

"Actually, I was looking for Mr. Smith," said Emmy, repressing a strong desire to giggle.

"Oh." The young man sounded damped. "You're sure I can't...?"

"It's personal," said Emmy.

"Oh, very well," replied the young man with a touch of petulance. "I'll see if he's in." He went back into the office and Emmy heard him calling, "Sammy! Someone to see you!" There was a pause. "Female... No, no, older than that—says it's personal... Oh, all right..."

He came out into the showroom again. "Mr. Smith is rather busy," he said. Emmy marveled that he could really imagine that she had not overheard every word. "If you'd just give me your name and..."

"Tell him it's Emmy Blandish from Dymfield."

He retired again, and once more Emmy heard the stage-whisper shout from the depths. "She says she's Sally Chandler. From Dim-something. No, she looks quite harmless."

There was a pause, and then the clatter of feet coming downstairs. A moment later Sammy Smith was in the showroom. He looked at Emmy for a moment in puzzlement, failing to place her; then, all at once, his face broke into a huge smile, and he cried, "Blandish! Emmy Blandish! Well, I'll be damned. What brings you to this neck of the woods, my dear?"

He had not changed at all in twenty years. Even in uniform he had given the impression of a smooth, plump, jolly fellow in a well-tailored suit, and this is what he now was in fact. His ruddy face was clean-shaven, his brown hair had receded a little at the temples but was still abundant. His hazel eyes twinkled as wickedly as ever, and his smart brown suit disguised any small increase in girth. It crossed Emmy's mind that he must be a very good second-hand car salesman.

"Well, well," he went on, "Dymfield seems to be in the air these days, if you'll pardon the pun. I had old Arthur Price pestering me a few weeks ago to go to some reunion. Couldn't make it, unfortunately. Did you go?"

"Yes, I did."

"What was it like? Who was there?"

"Almost everybody. Lofty and Jimmy Baggot and Annie..."

"Good old Annie! What's she up to these days?"

"She's terrific," said Emmy enthusiastically. "She's a farmer's wife, and she has four grown-up children, and she looks prettier than she did twenty years ago."

Sammy pretended to wince. "Ouch! That hurts! Can it be twenty years? Yes, by Jove, I suppose it is. Don't let any of my customers hear you. They say that life begins at forty—well—take it from me, Blandish, as far as I'm concerned, life stops there. I've been forty for more years than I can remember, and I have every intention of remaining forty until I drop dead. Well, what d'you think of the showroom? Had time for a look around?"

"It's most impressive," said Emmy.

"All my own work," said Sammy proudly. "It's a tough game, this, y'know, and I don't mind admitting that the going was rough for a bit. But now I've worked up a sweet little business here, *and* I'm my own boss. Yes, I think I can say that Sammy Smith has fallen on his tootsies."

"The cars are beautiful," said Emmy, putting out a tentative hand to touch a scarlet hood.

Sammy beamed. "My girls, I call them," he said. "Every one a beauty. Not a dud among them. Of course, these are specialist jobs. Not everybody's cup of tea. Can't expect a very brisk turnover. But the customers we do get are the right sort. Enthusiasts. Salt of the earth. Even so, it sometimes nearly breaks my heart to part with…"

The stout young man suddenly popped his head out from the office. "Mr. Trimble of Overtread Tires on the phone, Sammy," he said, unhappily. "It's about—that little matter. He says they can't wait any longer, and…"

"Tell him I'm out," said Sammy quickly. "You don't know when I'll be back. Probably next week. I've gone to Paris to see a client."

"But…"

"In fact, I *am* out," added Sammy. He took Emmy's arm. "This beautiful creature is an old flame of mine, and I intend to buy her a cup of coffee."

Ignoring the young man's whimper about the possibility of Mr. Trimble turning nasty, Sammy hustled Emmy out into the street. Safely outside, he looked at her, winked, and roared with laughter. "All right, all right, all right—I admit it. Things are still rough. Not out of the woods yet, but we survive, you know. We survive." He was as irrepressible as one of the weighted rubber dolls which always fall, if not on their feet, at least on an ample posterior and pop back in an upright position. Emmy had always enjoyed Sammy's company.

As they installed themselves at a corner table in a nearby coffee shop, Emmy said, "I must congratulate you."

Sammy looked startled. "Whatever for?"

"I rang your home and spoke to a charming girl who said she was Mrs. Smith. You were a bachelor last time I saw you."

"I was, wasn't I?" Sammy's voice had lost a little of its ebullience. "You married, Blandish?"

"Yes, Sammy."

"Happy?"

"Extremely, thank you."

"Got a brood of children, I dare say."

"No. None. We both wanted them, but they just didn't arrive. It's a pity, but there are compensations."

Sammy seemed to be brooding a little. "Bad luck, that," he said. "Still, I'm not sure I wouldn't rather that than—well, take us. We've been married five years. I've always wanted kids. But Marlene—well—she's twenty years younger than I am and a bit of a gay girl, you know. I suppose kids would be too much of a tie for her. Anyhow, that's the way she feels."

Emmy felt sorry for Sammy, and also embarrassed. It had been on the tip of her tongue to say, consolingly, "Well, there's plenty of time yet, Sammy," when she remembered that for all his bland charm he must be sixty. She hesitated and was lost. The only solution was to plunge into a new topic. "You haven't yet asked me why I came to see you, Sammy."

He seemed relieved to change the subject. "My dear girl, I haven't been allowed to get a word in edgeways."

"Liar. You've never stopped talking. Well, go on—ask me."

"Blandish," said Sammy solemnly, "why have you come to see me? Is it to make mock of an old comrade who's down on his luck or have you been searching for me all these years, driven on relentlessly by a passion which you dared not admit, even to yourself?"

"Idiot!" Emmy laughed. "If you'll stop talking for half a minute I'll tell you. I'm writing a book."

"You're—what? A book? Good lord, I didn't know you could read and write. Why didn't you tell us? We might have been able to get you transferred from the Sanitary Squad."

Emmy threw a lump of sugar, which hit him on the nose. She was enchanted to find how easy it was to pick up the threads of a free-and-easy friendship after two decades. "Shut up," she said, "and let me explain."

Briefly she told him about the reunion, about Vere and Barbara and Lofty and the projected biography. "And so you see, Sammy," she ended, "I've come to interview you—really to get your recollections of Beau and put them down in my little notebook for Lofty."

Sammy had grown thoughtful. He stirred his coffee several times and then said, "A bit ironic, isn't it, you being involved in this job?"

"I don't see why."

Sammy looked at her sideways and winked. "We weren't all quite blind you know, Blandish."

Defiantly, Emmy said, "Don't make nasty insinuations, Sammy. I was very fond of Beau. I admit it. But he was married, and—that was that. And now I'm married, and very happy, and..."

"...and, of course, you couldn't refuse this assignment because it would have looked like an admission, to say the least of it." He grinned at her. "What a bitch that woman is."

"Who? Barbara?"

"Of course. Who else? Never mind. We'll all rally around and do our best, but—seriously, Blandish—do you think this is a good idea?"

"No," said Emmy, "I don't. But I've said I'll do it, and I will. So please, kind sir, tell me your recollections of the late Squadron Leader Guest, missing believed killed on a training flight in October, 1943."

Sammy considered. "How far back do you want me to go?"

"As far as possible."

"Very well. R.A.F. Falconfield, Somerset. Day fighter station. Reserve squadron, piloted by old deadbeats in their thirties, like me. Beau was posted to us for a rest. He was the golden boy, fresh from the Battle of Britain. I didn't like him."

"Why not?"

"He—he seemed so arrogant. He had Barbara along with him, of course, and the pair of them burst into our quiet little station like a couple of golden eagles into a dovecote."

"You mean, he threw his weight around?"

"I'm trying to be fair," said Sammy. "No, he didn't throw his weight around, because he didn't need to. He was just naturally surrounded by a haze of glory—hell, Blandish, *you* know what I mean. Even if he just sat in a corner saying nothing, one was aware of him. This was Beau Guest. He'd done something glorious with his young life—and we'd done nothing. He could hardly expect to be liked."

"I don't think he did," said Emmy slowly. It was a point of view which had not occurred to her at the time.

"Well," said Sammy, "he might have succeeded in being liked in spite of everything, if it hadn't been for Barbara. Rude— God, I'd never met such a bloody rude woman in my life…"

"What's your name?"

"Smith, Mrs. Guest. Sammy Smith."

"What do you do around here?"

"I'm Messing Officer. I also fly an aircraft."

"You surprise me."

"Mostly routine patrols, I'm afraid. I'm considered too old for the rough stuff. Fair, fat, and forty—that's me."

"Oh, don't apologize. Don't you go out of your minds in this dump, with nothing to do, no action…"

"We were dive-bombed once last summer."

"How terrible for you. I suppose you all put on your tin hats and dived into the underground shelter and then claimed danger money."

"Something like that."

"God, Beau will *die* of boredom. After 11 Group…"

"We all admire your husband very much, Mrs. Guest."

"So you bloody well ought to. Well, don't just stand there. Get me a drink, can't you? God, when I think of the parties at Tangmere and Biggin—those *were* parties. Oh, there you are, Beau…"

"Enjoying yourself, darling?"

"I'll give you three guesses. I've just been having a scintillating conversation with a Flying Officer called Smith."

"Oh, yes. Sammy."

"He's getting me a drink, which I suppose is in his favor, but what an old *bore*. Honestly. Can't we go home?"

"Not really. Not just yet. It would look so rude. Stick it out a few minutes more, there's an angel."

"But Beau, all these *ghastly* people..."

"Ssh. Smith's coming back. He'll hear you."

"I don't care if they all hear me. As for Smith, he's a disaster. Tries to be funny, which makes it worse. Don't you agree, darling?"

"Yes, of course I do, but don't talk so loud. You'll get me lynched. Ah, Sammy, that's very kind of you, old man. I hear you've been entertaining my better half—well, cheers. Down the hatch."

"Beau, once and for all..."

"Yes—well, I'm afraid we really must go now. On duty first thing in the morning, you know—and Barbara's a bit tired. She's so enjoyed meeting you... Good night, old man..."

"...bloody rude. And he was patronizing, which was almost worse. Of course, I was sorry when he crashed. I wouldn't wish that on my worst enemy. All the same, I can't deny that I was glad to see them go, the pair of them. You can imagine that I was none too pleased when Beau turned up as my Chief Controller at Dymfield. Of course, he'd been taken down a few pegs by then. If I'm to be honest—and you know I'm honest, don't you, Blandish—well, I must admit that it did cross my mind that there was a sort of poetic justice about Beau Guest ending up as a penguin. My only regret was that I'd been grounded myself by that time. Couldn't take my revenge." Sammy stirred his coffee again, and then began to laugh. "So Barbara's set on a rehabilitation job, is she? She's pretty optimistic if she thinks anyone's going to be interested in her ridiculous goings-on."

"Aren't you being a bit hard on her, Sammy?"

"Hard on her? My dear little Blandish, if you took a hammer and chisel to that woman, you'd only break the chisel." He paused. "So she married Vere. Poor fellow."

"He seems to be bearing up all right," said Emmy. "The only thing he seems upset about is this book idea. It's funny, because he was quite keen on it at first."

Sammy looked up sharply, but said nothing. Emmy went on. "Lofty especially wanted me to ask you about Beau's crash at Falconfield."

"What about it?"

"Well—what caused it? Was it a fault in the aircraft, or…"

"I've no idea. Can't help you. Didn't Beau tell you himself?"

"No. I don't think he liked talking about it."

"I'm not surprised. Anyhow, tell Lofty that I'm sorry, but I can't help."

"Lofty has some odd ideas," Emmy went on. "He seems to think there was something strange about Beau's death."

"Well, of course there was."

"What do you mean?"

"The man was unbalanced, more than halfway around the bend, if you ask me. Most suicides are. One minute he's as happy as a lark, planning a leave in Scotland, and the next he's crashing deliberately. Mad as a hatter."

"He must have had some good reason, Sammy…"

"I don't know what makes you think that. Some imbecile reason, more like. I dare say Barbara refused to go on leave with him or something of that sort. It's all that's needed to push these nut cases over the top. The only mystery about the whole thing is why the trick cyclists didn't clamp old Beau in a strait-jacket before he went really barmy and did himself in."

"He didn't *appear* to be unbalanced that evening," said Emmy.

"You saw him, did you?"

Emmy, to her annoyance, blushed. "I—I met him. Just as I was going into Dymfield Operations Room for the two o'clock watch. He seemed a bit nervous, but otherwise all right." She paused. "Oh, well, I'm sure you're right and there's no mystery. But Lofty seems to fancy himself as a latter-day Sherlock Holmes."

"I see." Sammy took a box of small, cheap cigars from his pocket. "Do you object to these? Good. So Vere has taken violent exception to Lofty's detective fervor. Is that right?"

"Well—yes, I suppose you could put it like that."

"Interesting. Very interesting." Sammy lit his cigar and puffed at it. "I should follow up that lead if I were you. Where do your investigations take you next?"

"To Annie," said Emmy. "She's visiting London. I'm really looking forward to that. Then I'm to see Jimmy Baggot..."

"Ah, yes. Old Jimmy. I see quite a bit of him—from time to time."

"Then we're to visit Dymfield, Lofty and I."

"I don't suppose there's much left of it by now."

"Not a lot," Emmy admitted. "I've been talking to Air Ministry about it. A lot of Dymfield has been ploughed up, but apparently some of the runways and buildings are still there, including the Operations Block; it's on Care and Maintenance and used for training sometimes. The Mess has gone altogether. To tell you the truth, I'm rather dreading going back, but Lofty's absolutely adamant."

"You're still as sentimental as ever, aren't you, Blandish?" said Sammy with some affection. "Don't worry. It won't be moving or touching. It'll just be extremely cold and desolate, and I bet you a fiver that you'll be in and out within five minutes, after which you'll spend hours in the Duke's Head in Dymfield village, reminiscing and weeping happily into your beer."

Emmy laughed. "You are a comfort, Sammy," she said. "Anyway, one good thing about this job is that we've met again. I do hope you'll come and dine with Henry and me one day, you and your wife."

"Very civil of you, Blandish," said Sammy, but without much enthusiasm. "I'll be interested to hear how the book comes along. Keep in touch. And give my regards to Lofty, and tell him I think he's a sentimental ass."

"What do you mean by that?"

"Never you mind. Just tell him."

"All right. And if I meet anyone who's looking for a really special vintage sports car in mint condition…"

"My dear Blandish," said Sammy, lowering his voice, "if this hypothetical character is your worst enemy, send him to us. If he's not, steer him clear. These old heaps of junk in my showroom aren't worth five bob."

"But…"

"Ah, you're going to say, 'Then why make them your stock in trade?' I'll tell you why, little Blandish. It's because, glory be to God, there are still some mugs in the world who want to buy them. And who am I to tell the customer he's wrong?"

Emmy laughed. "You haven't changed one little bit, Sammy," she said. "I *am* glad I found you again."

"So am I," said Sammy, "but I don't seem to have been very helpful about the book."

"Oh, gosh, I almost forgot." Emmy rummaged in her bag and produced a typewritten form. "I have to give you this. It's a questionnaire that Lofty's drawn up for everyone to fill in. Will you be an angel and do it? It's mostly questions about dates and so on."

Sammy took the form and glanced at it. "Lofty's got consumer research on the brain," he said. Then he put on a pair of spectacles and studied the questions more closely. At last he said, "Lofty's certainly more interested in Beau's death than in his life."

Emmy shrugged. "I told you. The great mystery."

"Well." Sammy folded the paper and put it in his pocket. "I'll make this my homework for the next few days. What do I do with it after I've filled it in?"

"Send it to Lofty, please," said Emmy. "His address is on it. We're using his place as working headquarters. I'll be going along on Monday to correlate all the replies we get."

"Coo," said Sammy, "not giving us much time, are you?"

"Oh, don't worry if it's late. I go around there several evenings in the week. Lofty's out all day, you see, and I don't like to leave my husband on weekends."

"Sounds like a dog's life to me."

"It's rather fun, actually."

"You're welcome to it." Sammy stood up. "Well, back to the grindstone for young Sammy. Give Annie my regards. And if you should happen to run across a Mr. Trimble from Overtread Tires, tell him I'm dead. Really, the man has no sense of decency. Well, so long, Blandish. Keep your tail up."

Through the window of the coffee shop, Emmy watched the sprightly, bulky figure as it set off down the street, Homburg hat set at a jaunty angle, cigar in hand—and wondered whether to laugh or cry. "It's better than ending up like Vere, anyway," she told herself.

Then she became aware that the waitress was standing beside her with an inquiring look, and she realized that Sammy had left her to pay for the coffee.

CHAPTER SIX

ANNIE WAS STAYING at the Suffolk Hotel, where the Dymfield reunion had been held, and this time Emmy approached its swinging doors with no apprehension whatever.

"Oh, yes, Mrs. Tibbett," said the receptionist. "Mrs. Meadowes is expecting you. If you care to take a seat, madam, I'll just ring through. Mrs. Meadowes will be down in a moment."

Annie emerged from the elevator like Demeter come to greet Persephone at Eleusis. She towered over Emmy, throwing back her dark golden hair as she laughed with sheer pleasure—the essence of femininity, yet stronger than many men both in mind and body. In the old days Annie had always been a dominant character; even at twenty-two she had seemed almost like a mother to the slender, shy Emmy Blandish. Now, fulfilled in marriage and motherhood, she seemed like Mother Earth—universal, mellow, and mature. She embraced Emmy, and then said, "You don't want to stay indoors on a lovely afternoon like this, do you? I thought we'd walk in the park."

"Good idea," said Emmy. She was thankful that she genuinely did not want to stay indoors, for she might as well have argued with Niagara Falls.

"Come along then," said Annie. "And you shall tell me all about yourself and Lofty and this ridiculous book..."

Like a genial whirlwind Annie swept Emmy out into the street, where they found a taxi to take them as far as the Albert Memorial. Soon they were walking toward the Serpentine under the glowing September trees, and Emmy was telling Annie about her weekend at Whitchurch Manor and the scheme to produce a biography of Beau Guest. As they talked, the years dropped away, and Emmy was vividly reminded of other autumn afternoons when she and Annie had tramped for miles over the East Anglian marshes, and she had confided to her friend the misery of her first, hopeless love.

"So, you see, Annie, if you'll tell me all you can remember about..."

Abruptly Annie said, "I wish you hadn't started on this."

Emmy smiled, a little ruefully. "So do I, sometimes," she said honestly. "Still, there it is. Lofty is determined to go ahead, and I can't let him down."

"Why can't he do it all himself, if he's so keen on the idea?"

"He's too busy."

"Anyhow, I thought it was Barbara's scheme in the first place."

"So it was. But now that Lofty has latched on to Beau's death as the—the nub of the thing..."

"I don't imagine that pleased her much."

"No, it didn't. And Vere got quite worked up over it."

"Emmy," said Annie, "take my advice. Have nothing more to do with it."

"Even if I could give it up, I wouldn't," said Emmy doggedly.

"Supposing Lofty abandoned the whole idea..."

"Oh, that would be quite different. I certainly wouldn't go on alone."

"I see," said Annie. After a short silence she went on. "So Lofty thinks there was some sort of mystery about Beau's death."

"He pretends he does anyhow. To make a good story."

"Blandish," said Annie, "do you believe that Beau killed himself?"

"I—well, of course he did. I mean, he must have. Everybody said…"

"I'm not asking everybody. I'm asking you. Would he have killed himself?"

Emmy thought for a moment, and then said, "He wasn't handling that Typhoon at all well you know, Annie."

"You haven't answered my question."

For perhaps three minutes they walked on in silence. It suddenly occurred to Emmy how ludicrous it was—two middle-aged women tramping across Kensington Gardens, desperately concerned with the hypothetical state of mind of a man who had died more than twenty years before.

She said, "I was looking at his photograph the other day—you remember, the tennis team one that you all signed for me. Seeing him again brought it all back, how well I knew him, I mean. Even better than Barbara, I think, in many ways. It's almost impossible to believe that he would have killed himself."

"I quite agree with you," said Annie. "It's what I thought at the time. It worried me a lot, but then I was posted away and got married and forgot about it. But you see, if he didn't commit suicide, then his death was either an accident or deliberately caused…"

"Oh, that's not Lofty's idea at all," said Emmy. "He's trying to pretend Beau was on some secret mission—parachuting into Holland, or some such thing—and that only Vere was in on the secret."

Annie stopped dead in her tracks. "Emmy," she said, "supposing Beau is still alive?"

"Alive? After twenty years? Of course not. If there were any truth in Lofty's idea, and Beau had survived—well—he'd have come home long ago."

"He was posted missing, presumed killed," said Annie. "Shortly afterward, Barbara married Vere. You might just think about that."

"I won't," Emmy cried, appalled. "I won't! It's a terrible thought; it couldn't be true…"

"The only person who might know, and would have every reason for keeping it quiet, is Vere," Annie went on relentlessly. "And apparently he's putting up serious objections to this investigation..."

"I wish you wouldn't use that word."

Annie ignored the interruption. "Barbara obviously knows nothing. Vere knows something. And there may be somebody at Air Ministry who knows even more..."

"Annie!" Emmy heard her own voice shouting against the wind. "Stop it!"

Annie did stop. She put her arm around Emmy's shoulders, and said, "Poor Blandish. Let's go back to the hotel."

"Oh, I was going to ask you—would you fill this in and..." Emmy produced a copy of the questionnaire from her bag. She was delighted to change the subject.

"What in heaven's name is this?" Annie asked.

"You just write your answers to the questions and send them to Lofty..."

Annie glanced at the typed sheet. "Give a full account of your movements and those of your colleagues on the evening of October 11, 1943. When did you last see Beau Guest? My God!" Annie was really angry. "Lofty may be prepared to insult us with this sort of rubbish, but to think that you—*you* of all people—are prepared to support him..."

"I have to..."

"Then bloody good luck to you!"

"I only want to find out the truth..."

"The truth! My dear Blandish, that's obviously the last thing you want. What you want is to lay on enough whitewash to make sure that the definitive edition of Beau's life lives up to your romantic ideal of him. Well, perhaps if the truth does come out, you won't like it."

"But Annie..."

Annie did not even say good-bye. She strode over to the road, hailed a passing taxi, and climbed into it, slamming the door. Emmy was left alone under the September trees, dejected and not a little puzzled. It was quite unlike Annie to fly off the handle like that. As to the fantastic theory that Beau might be alive, Emmy put that resolutely out of her mind. There was enough trouble around without deliberately making more. She made her way to a telephone booth, dialed the number of Incorporated Television, Ltd., and asked to speak to Mr. Baggot.

"I'll put you through," said the operator sweetly. Emmy was surprised and gratified that it was all so easy. She had imagined that the celebrated James Baggot might be difficult for an outsider to contact. She was, of course, perfectly right.

The next fluting female voice introduced itself as the Production and Research Department, and asked Emmy her name and to whom she wished to speak.

"Mr. Baggot? Oh. I don't know. I'll see if... Hold on a moment, please."

A third, crisper voice announced that she was Mr. Baggot's office.

"May I speak to Mr. Baggot, please?" Emmy asked. She was beginning to get a little fed up.

"Who wants him?"

"Just tell him it's Emmy Blandish."

"Emmy Blandish. Can you tell me what it's about, Miss Blandish?"

"I'm afraid not. It's personal."

"Oh, I see. Just hold the line please."

After a long interval a fourth voice said, "Mr. Baggot's personal secretary speaking. No, I'm afraid Mr. Baggot is in conference... If you'd tell me what it's about? Oh, I see. Personal. Well, Miss Er—I really don't know what to suggest... No, I've no idea when the conference will be over, and he has another appointment immediately afterward... Yes, I'll certainly give him a message and ask him to call you, but he's extremely busy, you know... If you would just give me the details of your business with him, I might be able to arrange an interview..."

Emmy gave in. Business seemed to produce a better reaction than personal friendship. "Well, as a matter of fact," she said, "this is a business matter, although I'm an old friend of Mr. Baggot's. I'm collecting material for a book, you see, and I think Mr. Baggot can help me."

The voice became more cordial. "Well, now, Miss Blandish, I'll see what can be arranged. Just a moment—it looks as though Mr. Baggot could fit you in from ten to ten-fifteen A.M. next Tuesday... No, no possibility at all before then—you're very lucky that he has a moment free next week... No, he'll be in our Manchester studios on Friday, on to Glasgow on Monday, and flying back late Monday night, so you see, Miss Blandish, I really have done my best for you. Now, may I just take your telephone number? Flaxman 83694? Thank you. Will you be in this afternoon? Good. I'll telephone you to confirm the appointment... Not at all—good-bye..."

It was late that afternoon that Emmy's telephone rang.

"Emmy Blandish? This is Jimmy. Yes, Jimmy Baggot. My dear, I'm frightfully sorry that my cloth-headed secretary treated you so cavalierly... Of course, she didn't know who you were, and I've been frightfully tied up today—first I knew was when I saw your name on the list of appointments she produced for my approval... But of course you can see me before Tuesday... Certainly I can manage it—I can manage anything if I try... Anyway, I'm most intrigued that you're starting on a literary career—no, no, don't tell me about it yet; keep me in suspense; it's more fun. Now, what about tomorrow? Yes, Friday... I know I'm going to Manchester, but not until the afternoon. Now, does your business have to be done in an office or would you consider lunching with me? You would? Splendid. One o'clock at the Orangery? Good. I'm looking forward to it. 'Bye, Emmy."

James Baggot was waiting in the foyer of this very expensive restaurant when Emmy arrived the next day. He looked, if anything, even smoother and more prosperous than he had at the reunion.

"Ah, there you are, my dear," he cried warmly, and surprised her by a swift, brushing kiss on the cheek. He smelt of costly after-shave lotion. "Marvelous to see you."

"It's mutual," said Emmy. "And it's a great treat for me to come here. This is the first time I've actually crossed the threshold, but I've heard so much about it from Henry."

"Henry...?"

"My husband. He comes here sometimes on business lunches. Or at least, he did during the *Style* case."

"Oh, of course. The great detective. I must say I'd be most alarmed to be asked to a business lunch by him."

"He's not a bit frightening," Emmy assured him. "Rather mild and mousy, really."

"Deceptive," said Baggot cheerfully. "Iron hand in velvet glove. I've heard enough about Henry Tibbett to—ah, yes, Giulio. For two. My secretary phoned..."

They were ushered into the tangerine-and-golden inner sanctum, escorted to a corner table, and presented with menus at least a yard square. Emmy, thoroughly enjoying herself, ordered a lavish meal. She felt sure that it would all come out of Jimmy's expense account, and she only wished that Lofty could have been there to enjoy the scattering of crumbs from the rich man's table.

"What do you actually *do*, Jimmy?" she asked, when the gastronomic and oenological questions had been satisfactorily settled.

Jimmy laughed. "Nothing much," he said. "I'm just an executive."

"Don't hedge. Tell me."

"Well, after the war I went into the technical side of television. Most of us did, as you know. It was fascinating, of course, but after a few years I realized that there was more of a future in planning, if you see what I mean, than in messing around with actual wires and valves. And, of course, my technical knowledge came in useful."

"Jimmy," said Emmy, "I believe you've been Empire building."

Jimmy laughed. "Call it what you like," he said. "I notice you're not averse to tucking into some ill-gotten imperialist grub and booze."

"Of course I'm not," said Emmy. "I think you're tremendously clever. After all, anyone can be a mere technician."

"Don't mock me. Someone has to do this job, after all, and I think I do it remarkably well. So there."

"I'm sure you do," said Emmy.

"Now, put me out of my misery, what is this mysterious literary enterprise? Wait a minute. Don't tell me, let me guess. You have had a brilliant idea for a new TV series—'Tibbett of the Yard.' Mild and mousy, did you say? I see Peter Sellers in the part, with Sophia Loren as his fascinating Italian wife, Emmelina..."

"Don't make me laugh or I'll disgrace you by swallowing my martini the wrong way!"

"Well, it was an idea," said Jimmy. "All right. Go ahead and tell me what it really is."

They were interrupted by the arrival of the waiter bearing dishes. When the food and wine had been served, Emmy said, "I thought you'd heard."

"Thought I'd heard what? You talk in riddles, woman."

"At the Dymfield reunion. Barbara's idea for a book..."

"Good God. You don't mean she was serious?" Jimmy sounded taken aback. "It never even crossed my mind that it was more than party talk."

"She *was* serious," Emmy assured him, "although I think she may be realizing by now that she's taken on more than she bargained for; and Vere is dead against the whole thing. However, Lofty is determined to go ahead, and I'm sort of caught in the middle."

"But..." Jimmy sounded both amused and exasperated. "Surely even Lofty Parker had the sense to grasp that nobody in this day and age gives a rap for the history of R.A.F. Dymfield?"

"Oh, yes. He realizes that."

"Then..."

"It's no longer to be a history of Dymfield," said Emmy. "It's to be the life story of Beau Guest."

"The man's mad. The market for war heroes was finished in the middle fifties."

"I should say," amended Emmy, "not so much a life story as a death story."

Jimmy, who had just speared a morsel of tournedos Rossini, stopped with his fork in midair. "A death story? What on earth does that mean?"

Emmy explained. "Lofty's crazy about the idea," she ended, "the unraveling of a twenty-year-old mystery, with a glamorous central character. 'What really happened on that long-ago October evening?'—you know the sort of thing."

Jimmy was looking thoughtful. "You know," he said slowly, "Lofty may have something there. The public is absolutely insatiable when it comes to historical whodunits. Look at the Princes in the Tower. You only have to run a series on Famous Cases Rehashed or Unsolved Murders of the Fourteenth Century and the ratings hit the ceiling. If it's any good, we might even buy it."

"Honestly, Jimmy? Wait till I tell Lofty…"

"No, no. Better not say anything to him just yet. I know him too well; he'd make my life a misery. Besides, it's the merest of ideas. I've no guarantee what the thing is going to turn out like. There may be no mystery at all, when the truth is known. How are you setting about your investigations?"

"Well," said Emmy, "I'm going around talking to people who knew Beau—like you, for instance—and we're asking everyone to answer a questionnaire that Lofty's compiled. Then we're to visit Dymfield—though heaven knows what he expects to find there, except a depressing atmosphere and a sense of growing old. That's all I know. I'm just doing the research, you see."

"H'm." Jimmy leaned back in his chair and took a sip of wine. "Interesting. A mystery on two levels."

"Two levels?"

"Mystery number one: Why and how did Beau Guest die? Mystery number two—much more subtle. Why in heaven's name has Barbara stirred it all up? And, of course, there's a third mystery…" He was grinning at her.

To her disgust, Emmy felt the color rising to her cheeks. "I'm helping Lofty because I promised I would..."

"Keep your hair on," said Jimmy easily. "Actually, my third mystery was why Vere has suddenly taken against the idea. He seemed quite amenable at the reunion."

"I suppose, I don't know..." Emmy felt thoroughly rattled. Jimmy Baggot was altogether too—she couldn't think of the right word—too perceptive, too professional. Too dangerous. She wished that she could abandon the rich food and wine and escape to an atmosphere in which she felt at home.

Jimmy continued, unperturbed. "Well, now, what do you want from me, apart from this comic questionnaire? My recollections of Beau, I suppose. I disliked him cordially, but I admired him. I disliked him simply because he was a gold-plated hero and I was a despised technician. Funny, isn't it? These days, technicians are little tin gods, and purely executive types are regarded as manual laborers. There must be a moral there somewhere. I admired Beau because he accepted his grounding and his new job with philosophy. And that must have taken some doing, with the hellcat Barbara continually rubbing his nose in the fact that he'd fallen from his pedestal. It wasn't as though he'd been shot down in combat. Several times I heard Barbara imply that—by the way, what *was* the cause of his crash, do you know? The one that smashed his face up, I mean."

"I don't know," said Emmy. "I was hoping Sammy Smith would be able to tell me, but he doesn't know either."

"Sammy Smith. What a character. I see him occasionally. It's so *right*, isn't it? I always knew he'd end up that way—sad and seedy, saloon bars and..."

Emmy felt a surge of anger, a fierce desire to protect Sammy. "I thought he was doing very well," she said. "He has his own business, and a beautiful showroom, and a lot of very valuable cars..."

Jimmy looked at her cynically and lit a large cigar. Its rich aroma was markedly different from that of Sammy's cheap little weed. "Sorry I spoke, I'm sure," said Jimmy. "Well, as I was saying, I disliked Beau, but I respected him. I detested Barbara, and I despised Vere for hanging around her like a puppy dog. When I heard he'd married her, my worst suspicions were confirmed. The man is obviously feebleminded. As for Beau's death—let me think. I remember that Mess party, and Beau swearing he could fly any kite that could leave the ground, and I also remember Barbara encouraging him in a revolting manner, and you crying in the corner."

"I don't cry."

"You gave the impression of weeping," said Jimmy. "I agree that your eyes may have been dry. As far as the Friday evening is concerned, when Beau was killed—I can't help much. I saw Beau in the Mess early in the afternoon, about two, I suppose, before he went over to the airfield. He looked as white as a sheet and positively ill—not surprising, I suppose, if he'd already decided to kill himself."

"Can you remember how you actually spent the evening, Jimmy?" Emmy asked.

"I'm innocent, Inspector, I swear it!" cried Jimmy in mock alarm. "By God, you've picked up a tip or two from your old man, haven't you? I suppose you'll write it down as highly suspicious if I can't remember everything that I did on a certain night twenty years ago..."

"Not at all. It would be more suspicious if you *could* remember..."

"I knew it," said Jimmy. "Well, you'd better send for the handcuffs, because it just so happens that I *can* remember. I lunched in the Mess and then went to my billet, where I was working out a circuit diagram for a brilliant anti-jamming device which I only just failed to invent. I was about to go into the bar at six, when I got a call from the Operations Room— something about a radio transmitter going up the spout. So I trotted down there just in time to witness the dramatic disappearance of Snowdrop three-two."

"You were there? I never realized..."

"You weren't caring much who was there," said Jimmy. "Oh, don't get me wrong. You were cool as ice and completely self-controlled, which made it all the harder for the rest of us. You probably didn't realize that."

"No, I didn't," said Emmy. She was past denials or protestations.

"One never does," said Jimmy cheerfully. "At a moment like that, you were quite rightly thinking one hundred percent about yourself. However, the other people in the Operations Room were not quite without sensitivity, you know. I think it was the sight of you, and your calm efficiency and dry eyes, that made me go off and get drunk as soon as the transmitter was fixed. Sammy came with me. He was staying at the Duke's Head with his popsy, but he'd dropped into the Operations Room to see the fun. We went back to the Duke together and got as tight as ticks."

"I feel ashamed of myself," said Emmy.

"Why should you? My dear girl, everyone must be allowed his own reactions. Take Sammy, for instance. He always hated Beau, but he got quite maudlin that night." There was a pause while a waiter removed one set of plates and substituted another. "Do you remember that little poem by Pudney—the one Michael Redgrave quoted in *The Way to the Stars*?"

Emmy nodded. She hoped very much that Jimmy would refrain from quoting it himself, but in vain. "'Do not despair for Johnny Head-in-Air. He sleeps as sound as Johnny Under-Ground—remember?'"

"Of course I do."

"Old Sammy was reciting it all the evening, sobbing into his beer. He kept getting it wrong... 'Do not despair for Johnny Under-Ground,' he kept saying, as though Beau had been a subway station; and the drunker I got, the less I could remember what was wrong with it. It was a thoroughly nasty exhibition on both our parts," added Jimmy a little severely. "Sammy insisted he was a resident—which he was—and kept ordering more drinks after closing time. The popsy went to bed alone. She was livid. I got back to my billet about three A.M and was as sick as a cat. I felt hellish. And yet, in a way, I suppose we were mourning Beau in the only way we could." He paused and laughed a little awkwardly. "It all comes back with a rush, talking about it like this. Makes me feel old."

"You're not old, Jimmy," said Emmy. "Not like..." She stopped.

"Barbara *is* a mess, isn't she?"

"I didn't mean..."

"And don't talk to me about her bone structure and how well she's kept her figure. She looks like a revivified Egyptian mummy." Jimmy looked at his watch. "Heavens, it's nearly two. My plane goes in a trice. Sorry, darling, but I must be off."

He tucked the questionnaire into his breast pocket and promised to fill it in. He then escorted Emmy to a taxi, kissed her warmly, and said that they must meet again soon. She offered her address and telephone number, but Jimmy waved them aside, protesting that if he wrote them down he'd only lose them. He would look her up in the phone book. As the taxi drove away, he was standing on the pavement, a suave and distinguished figure, waving energetically. Then he turned on his heel and disappeared into the crowd of afternoon shoppers. Emmy felt reasonably certain that she would see neither Jimmy nor the questionnaire again unless she took determined steps to do so.

For the moment, however, she did not allow this thought to bother her. She went home and wrote up her notes carefully. At six o'clock she telephoned Lofty, made a full report on her progress, and arranged with him a working schedule for the following week. This included spending Thursday afternoon visiting Dymfield—it seemed that an old friend of Lofty's, now at the Air Ministry, had promised to arrange the necessary permission and passes.

It was while Emmy was cooking supper that the telephone rang. A gruff and grudging voice informed her that she was speaking to the Reverend Sidney Guest, that he had received her letter, and that she might, if she wished, visit him the following morning.

Henry was late getting home that evening. Routine jobs had kept him at his desk until nearly eight. By the time he put his key into the lock at half-past, he was feeling ready to be pampered. It was therefore disconcerting to find that Emmy was not only unsympathetic but angry.

"I have to leave for the country early in the morning," she said snappily, disappearing into the kitchen. "I suppose that never occurred to you."

"How could it, when I didn't know?"

"Dinner is ruined, of course. It was ready at half-past seven. I hope you'll forgive me."

"Now look, Emmy..."

"I'm sorry," said Emmy. She appeared at the kitchen door, wiping an arm across her damp forehead. "I know I'm being a bitch."

"You certainly are," said Henry crossly, and stamped off into the living room, where he opened his newspaper with an ostentatious crackling. For some ten minutes a silence of the kind sometimes described as pregnant permeated the small flat. Then Henry decided to swallow his pride and went into the kitchen.

"I really couldn't help being late, darling," he said.

Emmy was standing at the stove looking hot and bothered. "Dinner is ready," she said. "If you'll get out of my way, I'll serve it."

"But..."

Henry had no time to get more than one word out, when Emmy brushed dangerously past him carrying two steaming dishes. He followed her into the dining room. The table was laid for one.

"Which of us," he asked, "is having dinner?"

"You, of course. I don't want any."

"Now, Emmy..."

"I had a big lunch. Anyway, I'm too..." She stopped.

"Too what?"

"Why should I tell you? It's obvious that you don't care."

"If you think that I'm going to sit here by myself and eat dinner..."

"It is a matter of complete indifference to me," said Emmy with a slight fissure in her voice, "whether or not you eat. I have provided food, which I think is all that is required of me under the terms of my contract. Now, for God's sake leave me alone."

Henry heard her run into the bedroom and slam the door. After that, there was silence. He sighed deeply and with anger. Then, to his surprise, he found that he was extremely hungry. From the hotplate, one of his favorite steak-and-kidney pies smiled up at him, steaming and succulent, flanked by fresh green beans tossed in butter and a fluffy mound of pommes mousseline. On the side table an iced gooseberry fool stood beside a bowl of whipped cream. Henry decided to postpone the domestic peace talk until after dinner. As he ate voraciously, his chief emotion was pity for Emmy. She was missing an excellent meal.

By the time he had reached the coffee (which was bubbling in a thoughtfully-provided percolator), he was wondering what could have come over Emmy. Certainly he had been late getting home, but that was not so unusual. Certainly dinner had had to wait, but it was none the worse for that. It wasn't a soufflé, after all. He could only suppose that it was something to do with this book of Lofty's that had upset her.

He was honest enough to admit to himself that he felt a sort of jealousy. He had done all he could to encourage Emmy to take up outside interests, but he certainly had never intended that those interests might become more important in her life than he was. *That* had not been his intention. Immediately he pulled himself up and felt ashamed. "Like a Victorian paterfamilias," he admonished himself; and went to face the inevitable reconciliation.

Emmy was lying on the bed reading *Winnie-the-Pooh*. One look told Henry that she had been crying. As he came in, she put the book down, smiled, and said, "I'm terribly sorry, darling. Please forgive me. It's," she hesitated. Then, raising the book again, "'It's a little Anxious,'" she quoted, "'to be a Very Small Animal Entirely Surrounded by Water.'"

Henry sat down on the bed. "What makes you think you are?"

"I have to go and see Beau's father tomorrow," said Emmy, "the Reverend Sidney."

"Well, he can't eat you."

"If it were only the Reverend Sidney... Oh, well. Never mind." She held out her arms to him. Sometime later, her voice blurred by the fact that her face was buried in his jacket, she added, "It's so much more friendly with two."

Henry did not even attempt to interpret this remark. He realized, however, that his wife's earlier fit of temperament had been caused not by anger but by fear.

CHAPTER SEVEN

THE REVEREND SIDNEY Guest was a robust, white-haired man who wore his seventy-five years not so much lightly as with impatience. In the course of a life ostensibly devoted to the service of others, he had, in fact, never given a serious thought to anybody but himself. Being therefore quite unaware of the strain which consideration for others puts upon the human constitution, he was a picture of hale heartiness and was continually irritated by the spinelessness of his nearest and dearest. Mrs. Hardwater, for example. Mrs. Hardwater was a gentle, widowed lady in straitened circumstances, who had come to housekeep for him after the lamentable episode of his wife's defection. For the bitter fact was that Mrs. Guest (her name had been June, of all things) had tired of her husband as long ago as the early nineteen-twenties, and had run away with a jazz saxophonist.

The Reverend Sidney had never, of course, considered Mrs. Hardwater as anything but a housekeeper. Even had he wanted to marry again, his cloth and convictions would have made it impossible. He had steadfastly refused to divorce June, even though she had had a child whom she wished to legitimize. That, reflected the Reverend Sidney with satisfaction, should teach her a lesson.

Meanwhile, he became quite attached to Mrs. Hardwater. She could be relied upon, which was a great blessing. He seldom had to make an unpleasant scene more than once about the exact cooking of his eggs or the precise way he liked his bed made. It seemed, therefore, like a betrayal when one day, after more than thirty years in his service, Mrs. Hardwater had collapsed. Just before the Harvest Festival, too. The doctor had insisted on removing her to the hospital, and in three days she was dead at the ridiculously early age of sixty-nine. The doctor's opinion was that Mrs. Hardwater's heart attack had been brought on by mental and physical exhaustion.

"Tcha!" said the Reverend Sidney. "Lack of stamina, that's all." He did not add, "Most inconsiderate of her," because he knew that the doctor was foolishly sentimental when it came to physical disability, nevertheless he appended the phrase mentally. The Reverend Sidney Guest, as he himself frequently remarked, had never had a day's illness in his life. He was very proud of this fact.

At the time of Mrs. Hardwater's death, Sidney Guest was seventy. After several unhappy experiments, he came to the conclusion that in these days of too much pay for too little work, it was impossible for him to find a good, honest woman who would look after him as he wished for the salary which he offered. Consequently, he was prepared to listen sympathetically when his Bishop spoke of the desirability of a move to a smaller house. The Bishop, who was the soul of tact, never mentioned the word "retirement." He proposed that the Reverend Sidney should give up his rambling rectory and his straggling parish and move to a small modern bungalow, which was situated equidistantly from the East Anglian villages of Upper Charwood, Snettle, and Dymfield. The vicars of these three parishes, said the Bishop, were grossly overworked, and would welcome assistance in the form of occasional officiation at services.

When the Reverend Sidney looked dubious, the Bishop played a small but telling trump card. "The vicar of Snettle," he said, "is—this is between ourselves, Guest—is a very *elderly* man of sixty-two. He finds the early morning Communion service rather too much for him."

"How far did you say it was from Snettle Church to the cottage?" demanded Sidney. "Six miles? Tell him I'll ride over on my bicycle to take the seven o'clock service. Perhaps he'll be kind enough to give me breakfast afterward, if he has succeeded in leaving his bed by then."

So it was arranged. And so it was that Emmy—having taken a train from London to Colchester, and then a smaller one to Snettle, and finally an asthmatic bus—found herself at eleven o'clock on Saturday morning ringing the bell of a whitewashed modern bungalow a few miles from the village of Upper Charwood.

To tell the truth, the Reverend Sidney had been much disturbed when he received Emmy's letter. His son, twenty years dead, belonged to the same category, the same world as June. Certainly, Sidney had kept and reared the boy, but there had never been any real contact between father and son. The boy grew up looking far too much like his mother. And he had developed, as he grew older, the same slyness, combined with physical beauty and a warped sense of values, which had finally made the Reverend Sidney heartily glad to see what he hoped was the last of June.

There had been a monumental row when the boy had insisted on joining the Air Force in 1939 when he was barely twenty. The Battle of Britain had been an embarrassing period for the Reverend Sidney, for people were continually congratulating him on his heroic son—and it seemed hardly the moment to deny him openly. Nevertheless, at that epoch as at every other, Sidney's good sense told him that the boy was a scamp and a scallywag, exactly like his mother. At the time of the first crash, and through the long weeks of plastic surgery, Sidney was heartily thankful that his son expressed no desire to see him. After the way that Sidney had expressed his views on his son's marriage to a loose, painted Jezebel from the variety stage, any interview between father and son could only have been painful.

When it came to his son's death, the Reverend Sidney felt even greater resentment than in the case of Mrs. Hardwater.

She, poor woman, had behaved with singular feebleness, but at least she could not help dying. His son, on the other hand, had apparently committed suicide when in a state of health so nearly perfect as to make no odds and in a manner calculated to bring notoriety and opprobrium to his family. This disregard for a father's feelings seemed to Sidney the most self-indulgent kind of behavior.

For many years now he had succeeded in burying any thought of his son so deeply in his subconscious that he himself was unaware that it might persist. Marriage and fatherhood were linked together in his mind as a single, lamentable event. Emmy's letter jolted the Reverend Sidney's memory in a most unpleasant way, and caused him to be even snappier than usual with the Vicar of Snettle at their weekly meeting. His first instinct was to tear up the letter, unanswered. On reflection, however, he decided that this would be foolish. If these tiresome people were set in their purpose of writing a book about his late son, then it was only prudent for him to take a hand in order to insure that the final result was as innocuous as possible. So he telephoned Emmy and made the appointment.

Emmy was not easily intimidated, but her heart sank when the front door opened and she found herself looking up into the unfriendly brown eyes of the Reverend Sidney Guest. For a start, he was disquietingly like his son—Emmy could see now that the strength of Beau's face had come from his father. Sidney, with his shock of snow-white hair and his rugged chin, looked like an Old Testament prophet. Emmy noticed, too, the lines of intolerance around his mouth and his thin lips. He did not look at all like the kindly old clergyman of Barbara's description.

"Mrs. Tibbett?"

Emmy's heart turned over. It was a deeper version of a voice she remembered so well. "Yes. You must be Mr. Guest."

"Come in."

The old man turned on his heel and led the way into what might ordinarily have been the drawing room of the bungalow;

but drawing rooms, with their associations of social gatherings, soft chairs, and pretty furnishings, played no part in the Reverend Sidney's austere life. As the largest room in the house, it had automatically become his study. There was a large, plain desk covered with papers. Floor-to-ceiling bookcases were crammed with leather-covered volumes, whose contents promised to be even weightier than their bindings. A paperback book of crossword puzzles—the impossibly complicated and erudite kind—gave the only clue to the old man's recreation. There was a rigidly upright wooden armchair behind the desk. In front of it stood a dining chair, which Emmy rightly concluded had been brought into the room expressly for this interview. Normally, the Reverend Sidney neither expected nor received guests.

Silently, he indicated to Emmy that she should sit on the dining chair, while he established himself in his usual place behind the desk. Then he said, "I understand that you wish to speak to me of Alan."

"Alan?"

"My late son."

"Oh—yes. I didn't know his name was Alan."

"You didn't? How remarkable. I understood from your letter that you had known him well."

"Yes, but..."

"Ah, I understand. In the Services only surnames were used."

"No, no. But he had a nickname."

"Indeed? I was not aware of that."

"He was called Beau," said Emmy. "B-e-a-u—on account of his name being Guest, you see. Beau Geste."

The Reverend Sidney's thin lips clamped down further in disapproval. "I dare say," he said, "that the name also reflected his love of ostentatious living."

"Oh, no. It was only..."

"We seem to be straying from the point, Mrs. Tibbett. What do you wish to ask me about Alan?"

Emmy felt tongue-tied. Faced by this unexpected hostility, the questions she had prepared seemed inept and futile. She was still hesitating when he spoke again.

"I suppose you know," he said, "that by an ironic coincidence, this bungalow is only a few hundred yards from the airfield from which Alan took off on his—em—fatal flight. I try not to think about it, as it might distress me. But there it is. And another thing. Are you aware that my son's widow, now married to a man named Prendergast, lives but a few miles away? I dare say you will want to interview her."

"Oh, I've talked to her already. You know what she's like…"

"I have never had the pleasure," said the Reverend Sidney glacially, "of meeting Mrs. Prendergast. I made my views perfectly clear at the time of my son's marriage to a painted hussy from the lower reaches of a disreputable profession. I am glad to say that she has never set foot in my house."

There was an agonizing pause, and then Emmy pulled herself together and said, "I'm really interested in finding out about Beau's—that is, Alan's—boyhood. His schooling, his early enthusiasms—you know the sort of thing I mean."

"I am not sure that I do, Mrs. Tibbett. His academic record was singularly undistinguished. At considerable sacrifice I sent him to an excellent public school"—and he named an establishment much patronized by the sons of the clergy. "I regret to say that he barely scraped through his School Certificate. Even so, I encouraged him to try for a decent university, but believe it or not, he flatly refused. Defied me to my face. Apart from an excessive preoccupation with personal adornment, he had only three interests at that time—playing tennis, riding motor bicycles, and flying airplanes. Naturally, I forbade the last on the grounds that it was not only dangerous but expensive. The boy got his own way, as usual, by clandestinely joining the Auxiliary Air Force, as I believe it was called. He did his flying training on weekends. He deliberately deceived me by telling me that he was visiting his mother—a thing which, in Christian charity, I felt I must allow. Of course, she was a party to the conspiracy of deceit. The whole episode was typical of them both."

"I understood that his mother had gone abroad, for the sake of her health…"

"For a short time only."

After a pause Emmy said, "Well, his flying came in useful later on, didn't it?"

"Useful? You call it useful? It warped Alan's character by turning him into a tinpot hero at the age of twenty; it then mutilated him and left him horribly scarred; and finally it killed him. A very useful accomplishment, I am sure."

"Useful to England," said Emmy a little sharply.

"Tcha!" said the Reverend Sidney. "There were plenty of young men only too eager to profit from the public acclaim given to airmen at that time. I remember once hearing a modern expression which sums it up very neatly—to climb on the band wagon is the phrase I mean. Of early American origin, I presume. Any young man of modesty and sense would have kept well clear of the Air Force."

"And been alive today, growing fat and middle-aged and rich," Emmy burst out angrily. She had forgotten to be intimidated.

"My son Alan," said the Reverend Sidney, slowly and deliberately, "was not killed in action, you know. I find it inappropriate that he should be remembered in any heroic light."

"How can you hate him so much, after all these years?" cried Emmy.

"I do not hate him. My feelings toward him have never varied. Naturally, I had affection for my own son. That did not blind me to his shortcomings, nor did his selfish and unnecessary death." The Reverend Sidney leaned forward across the desk and addressed Emmy with some solemnity. "Mrs. Tibbett, you seem to me to be a not altogether unreasonable young woman. I beg you to remember that you were very young and doubtless impressionable when you knew Alan. I advise you most strongly to abandon this ill-judged meddling with the past. If you want to preserve your girlhood idol intact, do not start digging around his feet, lest they prove to be of clay."

Emmy looked at him steadily. "Thank you for your advice, Mr. Guest," she said. "I'll remember it. Now will you tell me one more thing. Is your—is Alan's mother still alive?"

The old man reacted to this remark not by a movement or change of expression but by a perceptible stiffening of his whole body. "She is," he said.

"May I have her address please?"

"I do not advise you to see her. You will gain nothing."

"Of course, you don't have to give me her address," said Emmy, "but if you don't, I can probably find it elsewhere."

Sidney Guest sighed. "Very well," he said. He scribbled something on a piece of paper and passed it to Emmy.

"Thank you," said Emmy. She stood up. "You've been very kind, Mr. Guest. I won't keep you any longer. You might like to glance at this…" She laid a copy of Lofty's questionnaire on the desk. "Most of it refers to Service information, but we'd be grateful for any more information that you can supply. Don't bother to post it; we're coming down next week to look at the old base at Dymfield, so we can pick it up."

"I see. Which day do you expect to call here?"

"Thursday, in the afternoon."

"I shall make a point of being at home."

The Reverend Sidney made quite a business of escorting Emmy to the door. The interview had been less unsavory than he had feared it might be. Sidney considered that Emmy was misguided in many of her opinions, but to her credit he set that she seemed to be a gentlewoman and not hysterical. She would probably listen to sense in the end.

As for Emmy, her feelings toward the Reverend Sidney had passed from fear through active dislike to something not far from pity. She considered him harsh, intolerant, narrow-minded, and selfish; but he was also just, according to his own patriarchal standards, and completely unsentimental. More than anything, his utter solitude entitled him to pity, a solitude which was mental as well as physical. He was as frightening and as pathetic as the last of the dinosaurs, a magnificent specimen, but doomed because of his inability to adapt to changing conditions.

All the same, Emmy was heartily glad to get away from the Calvinistic gloom of the bungalow and into a corner seat of the crowded, cheerful train as it roared and rumbled toward Liverpool Street. As she hurried down the steps of the subway, Emmy ran into a crowd of young people—the extravagantly dressed youths and girls whose more outré doings were currently causing unfavorable comment. They were noisy and they did not move out of the way to let Emmy pass. On the other hand, they had that vitality which is the essence of youth.

Emmy remembered the Reverend Sidney's words: "... an excessive preoccupation with personal adornment...riding motor bicycles and flying airplanes..." Emmy felt a surge of sympathy toward the long-haired young men in their black leather jackets. Twenty-five years ago they would have been fighter pilots; and had Beau been twenty years old now, he, too, would wear his hair long and ride a motorcycle at a hundred miles an hour.

"And as for the Reverend Blooming Sidney," thought Emmy, blowing a mental raspberry, "I don't believe he was ever young."

In the District Line train she opened her bag and took out the paper which Beau's father had given her. It bore the words, "Mrs. Guest, Sandfields Hospital, Kent."

When Henry got home, he was cheered to find Emmy in a gay, relaxed mood. After dinner she regaled him with a blow-by-blow account of her conversation with the Reverend Sidney. Then she said. "By the way, do you know where Sandfields is?"

"Sandfields?"

"Yes. Somewhere in Kent."

"Oh, yes. Where the loony-bin is."

"The what?"

"I beg your pardon. The celebrated hospital specializing in nervous diseases. I gather they are particularly hot on alcoholism."

"Are they?" said Emmy very quietly.

"Why do you ask?"

"Oh—nothing…"

CHAPTER EIGHT

LOFTY PARKER TELEPHONED Emmy on Saturday evening. "Things are moving," he said with some relish.

"What do you mean?"

"Rummy communications are arriving at my sordid abode," said Lofty. "They have obviously been stirred up by dropping a plump Blandish into deep waters."

"Don't be so beastly," said Emmy, laughing. "What sort of rummy communications?"

"Item one," Lofty replied. "A pithy and well-expressed abusive letter from a Mrs. Meadowes, whom I have identified as Annie Day. What on earth did you say to her?"

"It was what she said to me," answered Emmy. "I'll tell you later. Go on."

"Item two, a completed questionnaire from Sammy—very amusing and quite illuminating—ending up with a request of the loan of ten pounds till next Friday. Poor Sammy. If only he knew!" Lofty laughed in genuine amusement. "Item three, a letter from Vere's solicitors."

"*What!*"

"Oh, don't worry; he's not suing us. On the contrary. The firm of Pringle, Pringle, Pringle and Sprout have been instructed by Mr. Prendergast to put themselves at the service of Mrs. Prendergast, myself, and any other collaborators in our proposed work, in order to discuss fully the legal implications of the libel and other relevant laws before publication. Mr. Prendergast will be financially responsible for the consultations. He wants us to have the best legal advice, because our enterprise might, in Mr. Pringle's delightful phrase, 'be beset by legal pitfalls not readily obvious to the layman.'"

"How fascinating," said Emmy.

"You haven't heard the half," Lofty went on. "I've kept the best one till the end."

"Whatever is it?"

"A letter from Incorporated Television, Ltd., dictated by Mr. Baggot and signed in his absence by one Prunella Fotheringay. A splendid mixture of the old-pals act and careful business phraseology. The gist is that J. Baggot would like to see the manuscript, without prejudice, before anyone else gets a glimpse of it, so that if it turns out to be good television material he can buy it for much less than it's worth before any of his competitors have a chance."

"He said that?"

"Not in so many words, but it's there in block capitals between the lines. I'm beginning to think we may need a good agent, Blandish."

"Oh, Lofty, I'm so glad. He sort of hinted to me at lunch, but made me promise not to tell you..."

"A bit discourteous, I thought, not to sign the letter himself."

"Oh, no. He couldn't. You see, he was off to catch a plane to Manchester immediately after our lunch yesterday. He must have nipped back to his office and dictated that letter on his way to the airport. It just shows how keen he is."

"Or something," said Lofty.

"What do you mean?"

"There is such a thing," said Lofty, "as buying a property not for use but to keep it off the market."

"You mean, he might buy the rights and never use them, just to stop publication? Why on earth should he do that?"

"Don't ask me. The plot thickens, that's all. How did you get on with the Reverend gentleman?"

Emmy recounted her interview with Beau's father.

"A proper old bastard," said Lofty. "I always suspected it. So I've got to go with you to see the old Gawd-help-us on Thursday, have I?"

"I thought it would give you local color."

"Yes," said Lofty. And he added, with a sort of relish, "I'm almost looking forward to it. Meanwhile, Emmy, when you come on Monday—oh, blast."

"What's the matter?"

"Front doorbell. I'm alone in the house, so I'll have to answer it. There goes the blasted thing again. All right, all right, I'm *coming*. I'd better give you a ring on Monday morning. 'Bye, Blandish."

The telephone clicked and Lofty had gone.

"Who was it on the phone?" Henry called from the kitchen, where he was making coffee.

Emmy came and stood in the kitchen doorway. "Lofty," she said. "He's had exciting news. Jimmy Baggot may be interested in buying our book for T.V."

"Fame at last," remarked Henry, pouring out his coffee.

Emmy glanced at her watch. "It's only nine," she said, "and I haven't written up my notes. Lofty's so full of energy, he's given me a bad conscience. I'll go and work in the bedroom for a bit, darling. I know you want to watch that play on B.B.C. One."

"There's no need to wear yourself out, you know," said Henry. "Anyhow, have a cup of coffee to help you along."

When Henry came to bed a couple of hours later, Emmy was already asleep, although the bedroom light was still burning. Her notebook lay on the bed—she had apparently fallen asleep over her work. Henry picked up the open book and saw that it contained nothing new except the underlined words *Interview with Rev. S. Guest*. Emmy must be really exhausted, he reflected.

When it was mentioned on the southeast news broadcast next morning that the body of a man had been found that morning in the gas-filled kitchen of a house in Earl's Court, Emmy paid no particular attention to the item. It was not until she opened her newspaper on Monday that a small paragraph informed her that the dead man had been identified as Mr. Charles Parker, aged forty-two, unmarried, a consumer research worker who lived in the house. Foul play, the statement added, was not suspected.

Emmy's first reaction was misery and despair; but after a few moments of most sincere mourning, she pulled herself together and telephoned Henry at Scotland Yard.

Henry listened attentively. Then he said, "I hadn't heard. It's obviously being treated as suicide. I'll get hold of the details and ring you back. Exactly what time did you speak to him?"

"Well—you remember, we'd just finished the washing-up when he phoned, and I suppose we spoke for about five minutes. Then he went off to answer the doorbell and I came out to the kitchen—and that was just before the T.V. play started at nine-fifteen. So call it five past nine."

"Maybe he did kill himself," said Henry. "He seemed a fairly unstable sort of character."

"My dear Henry, he was as excited as a schoolboy last night. That letter from Jimmy Baggot meant the first chance of a real break for him, and—oh, Henry!"

"What is it?"

"Oughtn't somebody to go around and see if everything's there, the letters he told me about, I mean. If any of them are missing…"

"Don't worry," said Henry. "We'll check on everything."

In the middle of the afternoon Henry rang Emmy. He sounded worried. "Can you come around here to my office, darling?" he said. "Things seem to be developing."

"Of course I'll come," said Emmy. "But what…?"

"I'll explain when you get here."

There was a little group of men in Henry's office. He introduced them to Emmy as Detective Inspector Buttery, Detective Sergeant Reynolds, Mr. Riggs from the laboratory, and Dr. Matthews. Then he sat down at his desk and said, "Well, Emmy, it looks as though your friend didn't commit suicide after all."

"That's what I told you," said Emmy.

"I know," said Henry. "And it was thanks to your hunch that we looked at things rather more closely than is usual in a straightforward suicide case. I'd better begin at the beginning. As you know, Lofty shared the ground and first floors of a converted house in Earl's Court with a couple of his colleagues in consumer research, both of whom were away for the weekend, as usual. The upper flat, consisting of the third and fourth floors, is empty at the moment. So when Lofty said to you that he was alone in the house, it was the truth. Not another soul on the premises. The alarm was raised by one of his flat-mates, who arrived unexpectedly at half-past eleven on Sunday morning. Otherwise, he probably wouldn't have been found until Monday.

"Lofty's friend smelled the gas as soon as he opened the front door. The kitchen door wasn't locked, so of course he burst straight in, and found the body—destroying some valuable evidence in the process, but that can't be helped now. Well, as I said, normally this would have been treated as a routine suicide. The windows of the kitchen had been sealed up with insulating tape, and the door, which was well-fitting, had evidently had a mat jammed up against it; but, of course, this was pushed out of the way when young Mr. Chalmers went in. The fact that the door was unlocked was not surprising, since Lofty was alone in the house and not likely to be disturbed. Sergeant Reynolds was called in and spoke to Chalmers."

Henry looked encouragingly at the sergeant, who took up the tale. "I didn't see nothing suspicious about it," he said. "Quite straightforward, it seemed to me. This Mr. Chalmers, what shared the place with Mr. Parker, told me as how the dead gentleman was highly excitable, how he drank too much and never had enough money, and how he was always behind with his rent. From what I could gather, Parker was always either on top of the world or down in the depths, just the sort of temperament for your typical suicide."

"Manic-depressive," remarked Dr. Matthews sagely.

"I shouldn't wonder. Just the type, too, that doesn't bother to leave a note. It seemed an open-and-shut case. But then the Chief Inspector took a hand, and…"

"I went along to Lofty's flat myself," said Henry.

"Were the letters and things there?" Emmy asked.

"The letters were there, all right, but something else was missing."

"What?"

"When we were at Whitchurch Manor," said Henry, "I seem to remember Lofty making notes in a sort of school exercise book with a blue cover."

"That's right," said Emmy.

"Well," said Henry, "there was no sign of it. Nor was there any trace of a manuscript. Had he started on it, do you know?"

"Of course he had. In another blue notebook. That is, he told me he'd sketched out the plan of the book, and started on the writing of some of the vital bits. He was going to let me see it this evening."

"Well," said Henry, "unless those notebooks turn up somewhere else, which I very much doubt, it means that they've been deliberately destroyed. Which in turn means that it was to prevent the book being written that Lofty was murdered."

"Murdered." Emmy repeated the word without surprise, but all the same it brought a sense of shock. "Can you be sure?"

It was Matthews, the doctor, who answered. "It certainly looks like it," he said. "Parker died of coal-gas poisoning, but my view is that he was unconscious before the gas was ever turned on. He'd received a severe blow on the side of the head before he died. Of course, he could have fallen and hit his head when he blacked out, but then you'd expect to find traces on the edges of the stove."

"And there weren't any," said Mr. Riggs. "Anyway, he hadn't fallen. He was lying comfortably on a pile of cushions. Most suicides like to be comfortable. But it's the fingerprints that clinch it."

"You found fingerprints?" Emmy asked.

"No. None at all. That's just the point. None on the gas tap, none on the door handle, none anywhere. Everything had been wiped clean. And no suicide's going to do *that*."

Henry looked at Emmy. "So you see," he said, "it seems pretty certain. And it's a fair assumption—though by no means a sure one—that whoever killed Lofty was the person who rang the doorbell while you were speaking to him on the telephone. So you see, you are a vital witness."

"Yes," said Emmy miserably. "I see. It's all my fault."

"Of course it's not," said Henry. "If it's anybody's fault, it's mine."

"Yours?"

"I should have talked you out of this crazy project right at the beginning. If you'd dropped it then, Lofty might well have done the same, and he'd be alive now."

"It was none of your business," said Emmy. "If you'd tried to dissuade me, it would just have made me more determined to go on. No, I should have..."

Dr. Matthews cleared his throat. "Well, Tibbett, if you don't need me anymore—bit busy today..."

"Of course, doctor," said Henry. "In fact, you can all get back to your jobs. Just leave the appropriate reports here with me, will you? And thank you very much." He grinned. "I think I can handle this witness myself."

When the door of the office had closed behind Sergeant Reynolds and Henry and Emmy were alone, Emmy said violently, "It's horrible!"

"I know it is," said Henry, "but at least, thanks to you, we've been able to..."

"I mean," said Emmy, "it's horrible the way that all your experts are so casual. To them, it's just another case. To me, it's Lofty, and he's dead."

"The best thing you can do now," said Henry, "is to be a bit more casual and expert yourself. Sentimentality won't help Lofty now."

"He said I was sentimental…"

"There you go again."

"Sorry, darling. By the way, what about—I mean, I knew so little about him. Have you been able to contact his family?"

Henry glanced down at a document on his desk. "He had no one, apparently. The complete lone wolf. The only lead we got was from the Air Ministry, who looked up his papers for us. Back in 1942, he gave his father as next-of-kin—a Mr. Jeremy Parker, with a Manchester address."

"Come to think of it, Lofty had a very slight Manchester accent, hadn't he? I'm trying to remember—he said something about his father at the reunion—oh, yes, that he had a small income from his father's estate. So Mr. Jeremy Parker must be dead."

"Perfectly correct. He died in America ten years ago. And that seems to be all there is to know. The money—and it was a pittance, a hundred pounds a year—was paid into Lofty's bank quarterly by a firm of Manchester solicitors. Lofty apparently never made a will, so there'll be some legal unraveling about the capital involved, I suppose, but that's nothing to do with us. What I'm interested in his Lofty's immediate past—and that's where you can help me."

"What do you want me to do?"

"To rack your memory," said Henry, "for every detail you can about the conversations you had with your various Dymfield colleagues."

"That shouldn't be too difficult," said Emmy. "I've got the facts jotted down in my notebook, and I've brought it with me, by luck."

"Good. Now, first of all, take a look at this and tell me if it's accurate."

"What is it?" Emmy asked, taking the sheet of paper which Henry handed her.

"It's a list of all the people who knew about the projected book—unless I've forgotten anybody."

The list, written in ink in Henry's neat hand, read:

Barbara Prendergast
Vere Prendergast
Annie Meadowes (née Day)
James Baggot
Sammy Smith
Sidney Guest
Emmy Tibbett

"You've put me on it!" exclaimed Emmy indignantly.

"Of course I have. If anybody knew about the book, it was you."

"But…"

"But since I know you were at home from the time you spoke to Lofty on the telephone until eight o'clock this morning, I think you can consider yourself in the clear. Not that it's a list of suspects anyhow."

"That's a relief," said Emmy. She considered. "There are two more names to add. Arthur Price, for a start. Barbara told him about the idea before anyone else. And Sammy Smith's wife."

"Was she at the reunion?"

"No, no. Neither of them were. But I mentioned it to her on the telephone."

"In detail?"

"No. I just said I was doing research for a biography of Beau. But Sammy may have told her more about it."

"Okay," said Henry. He took back the paper and added the names. "Anybody else?"

"I don't think so. Of course, there were other people at the reunion, but it was only our little group that was discussing it, and the party broke up almost immediately afterward."

"I'm not interested, in any case," said Henry, "in people who knew about the proposal to write a history of Dymfield. I'm interested in the people who knew that it had changed from the story of an R.A.F. station to the story of one man. And those are the people on this list."

"Of course, any of them may have told…"

"I know, I know." Henry sounded tired and a little irritable. "I have to start somewhere. Now, bring out your notebook and tell me about your conversations with these characters."

It was nearly two hours later that Emmy finished her account and Henry closed his own notebook. "I expect I've forgotten a few things," she said, "but I've told you all I can remember."

"Good. It gives me plenty to talk about when I interview the people myself."

"Oh, dear," said Emmy, "I suppose I'll see nothing of you for days."

"It won't be as bad as that," said Henry. "Most of them are in London, except Guest and the Prendergasts…"

"That's what I mean. You'll be away for days."

"*We* may have to go away for a few days, certainly," said Henry.

"We? What do you mean?"

"I mean," said Henry, "that I didn't include your name on that list for fun."

"But you said…"

"I said that it wasn't primarily a list of suspects. And it isn't. It's a list of people who may know too much. In fact, a list of potential victims."

"Oh, no! Henry, I…"

"And I'm not going to say that I don't want to frighten you, because I do. You are in danger, and I want you to realize it and be sensible. We'll take all the precautions we can. You are to write to all the people on that list and tell them that the projected book has been abandoned because of Lofty's death. That you couldn't possibly carry on because Lofty left no notes or draft for you to work on. You'll also imply that you weren't altogether surprised that he killed himself, in view of his unstable character and rickety financial position. Scotland Yard will take the official line that Lofty committed suicide and that they aren't interested. Meanwhile, my love, I do not intend to let you out of my sight until this business is cleared up. You will come with me to Whitchurch and anywhere else that I may have to go. And, darling, I know you'll think I'm fussing, but for God's sake take care of yourself. All the time, I mean."

Emmy smiled. "Don't talk to strange men…"

"It's not strange men I'm afraid of," said Henry. "On the contrary. It's old friends."

Emmy got her letters off by the last mail that night. While she wrote them, Henry sat by the fire and studied his notes of the case. He read carefully through the details of Lofty's R.A.F. career. He had joined up in 1942, giving his age as twenty and his profession as Assistant Stage Manager. He had applied for air crew duties, but had been turned down on medical grounds, owing to a very slightly unreliable heart— the result of a childhood bout of rheumatic fever. He had been accepted for ground duties, however, and had trained as a controller. He had served at two stations on the South Coast before being posted to Dymfield in August, 1943, with the rank of Flight Lieutenant. He had apparently made numerous requests, especially after D-Day, to be transferred to a unit in the fighting lines, but each time was turned down on medical grounds. He had been transferred in 1944 from Dymfield to a station in Scotland, and finally demobilized—still as a Flight Lieutenant—in 1946.

Here, all documentation of Lofty's life ceased. Like so many other young men, he had been thrown out on the labor market, unqualified for any civilian occupation and accustomed to a standard of life far higher than he had any right to expect outside the protective circle of the R.A.F. His jack-of-all-trades career would eventually be traced in detail, of course, but would take time. For the moment Lofty disappeared from sight at the demobilization center in 1946, and turned up two decades later at the Suffolk Hotel, Blunt Street.

Henry sighed and decided to go to bed early. He was making a round of visits the following day, and he had a feeling that they might be pretty taxing.

CHAPTER NINE

NUMBER TWENTY-SEVEN Oakwood Avenue, Edgware, turned out to be altogether grander than Henry had expected. It was a large prewar house of mock-Georgian design, surrounded by a carefully tended garden. Mr. Arthur Price, of whom Emmy had spoken with slightly amused affection, was evidently a man of substance. Instinctively, Henry straightened his tie before he rang the front doorbell.

The door was opened by no less a personage than a butler, who informed Henry coldly that Mr. Price was at his office. At the sight of Henry's official card, the butler grew chillier than ever. Mr. Price, he remarked glacially, was expected home for luncheon soon after noon; but, of course, it was perfectly possible that Mr. Price's secretary might telephone to say that the master had decided to lunch in the City after all.

Grudgingly, the butler went on to divulge the information that Mr. Price was a bachelor who lived alone in this house, attended by himself, Albert Bates, and Mrs. Bates, who acted as cook–housekeeper. A Mrs. Manfield came in daily to attend to the rough work, and Mr. Summers was responsible for the garden. Henry felt faintly repelled at the thought of four adult human beings spending their lives ministering to the wants of one lonely, elderly man. He said he would call back at half-past twelve.

After the austere splendor of Oakwood Avenue, Supercharged Motors came as a great relief. The seedy and rakish atmosphere of the place restored Henry's good humor at once, and he was frankly fascinated by the cars. As far as work was concerned, however, he drew a blank.

The stout young man, after an agonized moment when he mistook Henry's name for that of Trimble, confided that Mr. Smith was in Paris. On business. Oh, yes, he went over frequently; they had many clients on the Continent. He had left England on Saturday afternoon, and would not be back until the day after tomorrow, Thursday. If Henry would like to leave his name...

Henry, rather unkindly, produced his official card, which caused the young man's face to change color from red to yellow to green, like a traffic light.

"I'd just like to have a word with Mr. Smith sometime," said Henry.

The young man gulped and made a great effort to sound nonchalant. "Oh, yes, Inspector? What is it? Stolen cars, I suppose. Far too much of that sort of thing going on these days. Happily, all *our* young ladies"—and he patted the flank of an evil-looking monster—"have impeccable pedigrees, I'm glad to say. However, if we can help you at all..."

"Thank you," said Henry gravely. "We're always delighted to come across wholehearted cooperation."

The young man gave him a suspicious look. Clearly he was not sure whether or not he was being mocked. "Anything we can do," he said again.

"You might tell me," said Henry, "what time Mr. Smith left this country."

"I told you, Saturday afternoon."

"By air?"

"No. The old train and boat. Cheaper, you see."

"And do your clients in Paris do business on Saturday night and Sunday?" Henry asked.

"Do our...?" For a moment, the young man seemed at a loss. Then he slapped his thigh and said, "Ah, I see what you're driving at, Inspector. Well, now—you don't know Sammy, do you? No, I thought not. If you did, you'd realize that he's not the chap to pass up the chance of a weekend in Paris, all chalked up against expenses." An unpleasant thought suddenly seemed to strike him. "I say, you're nothing to do with the Inland Revenue, are you?"

"No, I'm not," said Henry.

"Oh, that's good. Well—I'll tell Sammy you called, and any time after Thursday…"

Henry next made his way to the Finchley address which Emmy had told him was Sammy Smith's home. He found a small, ugly, semidetached house firmly locked up and with the curtains drawn. Before he had time even to ring the bell, he was hailed from across the fence by a thin, gray-haired woman in a flowered apron, who introduced herself as Mrs. Tidmarsh.

If Henry was looking for the Smiths, said Mrs. Tidmarsh, he was wasting his time. They were away. Left on Saturday morning, bound for Abroad, she wouldn't wonder—and not the first time either, added Mrs. Tidmarsh with a meaning sniff. She'd thought there was something up when Mr. Smith had taken a suitcase with him to the office on Saturday morning. And sure enough, about midday *she* had gone out with a suitcase, too, and the house was all locked up, as Henry could see. No doubt about it, the pair of them were in Paris, or worse. They were that type of person, if Henry followed.

Henry took his leave quietly, without revealing his identity. He took some comfort from the thought that even if the occasion arose, he would never need to put a plainclothes sleuth on this couple. Mrs. Tidmarsh would be every bit as efficient and far cheaper.

It was twenty-five minutes past twelve when Henry found himself once more ringing Arthur Price's doorbell. This time Bates agreed unwillingly that Mr. Price was at home, and invited Inspector Tibbett to step toward the drawing room.

"Inspector Tibbett! Emmy Blandish's husband! Well, well, well. What a very pleasant surprise. Come in, come in. Do sit down. What may I offer you? Sherry? Whisky? Vermouth?"

Arthur Price was exactly as Emmy had described him— gray-haired, rosy-cheeked, cherubic. Apparently he was a high-powered businessman. Yet he gave the impression of a kindly old fuddy-duddy, about as astute as a newly-hatched chick. He was also, at the moment, extremely nervous. Henry was intrigued.

Having poured Henry a sherry and begged him to be seated, Arthur Price ensconced himself in an armchair which fitted him closely around the hips, licked his lips nervously, and said, "And now, my dear sir, how can I help you? I don't flatter myself that this is a purely social call."

"No, it isn't," said Henry. "I wish it were. I suppose you haven't received Emmy's letter yet."

"Letter? No, no letter..."

"Then you may not know that Charles Parker is dead."

Price seemed to have relaxed a little, and now registered no more than simple bafflement. "Charles...? I don't think I..." A thought struck him. "You don't mean Lofty, do you?"

"Yes, I do."

"You must forgive me. I never knew his name was Charles. Fancy that. Dead, did you say? But he was so young, Inspector. Was it an accident?"

"That's what we don't know, yet," said Henry.

"Dear me. Please tell me more. How did the poor boy die?"

"He was found dead in a roomful of gas."

Price sighed deeply and clicked his tongue. "Oh, dear; oh, dear. I see what you're hinting at, Inspector. Suicide. And I blame myself. I blame myself."

"You—what?" Henry's surprise sounded in his voice.

Arthur Price did not seem to have noticed the interruption. He went on. "Our little reunion—I dare say Emmy told you about it—a splendid response and a most delightful gathering—hope to make it an annual event... However, that's beside the point. To get back to Lofty." He looked at Henry reproachfully, as though accusing him of straying from the point. "As I was saying, at our little reunion I couldn't help noticing that Parker was—that he looked—how shall I put it…?" He took a deep breath and started again. "It struck me, Inspector, that all the members of our little band had done very creditably for themselves. James Baggot is a household name these days; Barbara and Vere Prendergast hold a very honor-able position in society; dear Annie is a picture of good health and domestic bliss; and as for your good lady wife…"

"You mean," said Henry, who was getting bored by the catalogue, "that Lofty Parker was the only obvious failure in your group."

Price sighed. "Alas," he said. "I can't deny it. And—this is the ironic thing, Inspector—Lofty is the person for whom a brilliant future was prophesied in the old days. Brilliant. It only goes to show…" And he shook his head sadly.

"I still don't understand," said Henry, "why you should blame yourself for…"

"No, no, you wouldn't. You wouldn't understand." Price sighed again, while Henry waited patiently. "I am a lonely old man, Inspector, and I have a great deal of money. I will confess to you—so long as you promise me it will go no further—that one of my reasons for arranging that reunion was to see whether any of my younger friends were in need of assistance. I saw a chance of doing a little good for my fellow men."

Henry looked at him steadily and a little skeptically. "Did you have to go back twenty years to find objects for your philanthropy?"

"Oh, yes." Price was very serious. "Oh, indeed yes. Young people nowadays have everything made easy for them. The generation which deserves our pity is the one which is now in its forties. The generation whose young lives were wrecked by the war, and which is now conveniently forgotten. I myself belong to an earlier epoch, of course, but I had the unforgettable privi-lege of serving in His Majesty's Forces alongside those splendid young men. The fact that they are no longer so young should surely entitle them to more consideration rather than less."

Henry was aware of mixed emotions. On the face of it, Price's sentiments were unimpeachable and should have sounded attractive to someone like Henry, who was in his late forties and had served as a soldier during the Second World War. Nevertheless, there was something nauseating about the whole thing. Perhaps it was Price's calm use of the word "wrecked" that irritated him. The war had been an experience; like most real experiences, a mixture of the squalid, the beautiful, the boring, the amusing, and the horrific. Some people—a lot of people—had been killed. For them, the war had written a full stop, and Henry, personally, remembered his friends among them vividly and frequently and believed in a muddled sort of way that it was important to do this. As for the others, they had survived and resumed their lives in the postwar world. It angered him to hear those lives referred to as "wrecked."

Aloud, he said, "So you felt you wanted to help Parker."

"That's right." Price beamed benevolently. "I—em—I am the owner of a not unsuccessful business enterprise. You may have heard of Price's Peppo-lollies? And Krumbly Kandy? And Creemichocs? You have? All lines of mine. Then, of course, we have what we called the upper end of the trade. Spicer and Pratt is another of our firms."

"Spicer and Pratt?" Henry was amazed. "The fabulously expensive chocolate shop in Mayfair...?"

"That's right. We kept on the old name when we bought it, of course. It's a question of prestige. We have a factory in the Midlands and a head office here in London. I'm telling you all this," Price went on with a sort of proud modesty, "so that you will appreciate that when I say I was in a position to help Lofty Parker, I'm not shooting a line, as our gallant pilots used to say."

"I do appreciate it," said Henry.

"Well, Inspector, the fact is that I had made up my mind to offer him a job. I confess that his behavior at the reunion party did not inspire me with confidence as to his potential usefulness, but this was, for me, an act of pure charity. I had made up my mind to telephone him the next day and offer him a position in our sales department. And then Barbara Guest—Prendergast, I should say—came up with this suggestion about a book, and it seemed to me to be—well—a better solution for the boy. After all, he had always shown literary talent. And so I encouraged her to employ him and did no more in the matter myself." He shook his head. "You may have heard about the book?"

"Indeed I have. The project is off."

"Yes, of course. I see it all so clearly. I suppose Barbara changed her mind and let the poor lad down. He had probably thrown up his job and had no money, and in his despair—oh, dear, how I regret not having offered him that position..."

Henry did not correct Price's assessment of the facts. Instead, he said, "Just a formality, Mr. Price, but would you mind telling me how you spent last Saturday evening? Between seven and eleven, say?"

The nervousness came back with a rush. Price's spectacles quivered. "What an extraordinary question, Inspector. What deduction am I supposed to draw from it?"

"None," said Henry. "Just answer it, if you would."

"By all means. By all means. But I must say... Now let me see. Saturday. Saturday—ah, yes. I went into the office in the morning. I nearly always go in on Saturdays—chance to get some work done in peace and quiet..."

"Yes, but it's the evening that..."

"Lunched at my club—Batt's in Pall Mall... After lunch—let's see—I went into the card room and made up a four at bridge. Played until about half-past six, precisely half-past six come to think of it. Willie Carruthers had an appointment at seven and insisted on breaking up the game in the middle of a rubber. I had a drink at the club and then went out for a bite to eat."

"Where?"

"You'll laugh at me, Inspector. Lyons Corner House in Coventry Street."

"I certainly won't laugh at you. They serve some of the best food in London."

"You think so too? Then we are fellow connoisseurs, Inspector. I always maintain that, apart from a few of the City restaurants..."

Price was clearly settling down to a lengthy discussion on the merits of London's catering establishments. Henry brought him firmly back to the point.

"After I'd eaten? Well, now—let me think—what *did* I do?"

Henry was intrigued by this amnesia. After all, he was only asking the man to recall the events of three nights ago.

"Ah, yes, of course. I remember now. Stupid of me." Price had brightened suddenly. "I went to a film."

"Which one?"

"The Majestic in Leicester Square. That epic picture about the Ancient Britons, *Boadicea*, it's called. Have you seen it? Oh, you should. Most entertaining. There's a most effective scene where Boadicea invites Julius Caesar to a—well, I suppose you'd call it an *orgy*—at her palace. I question its historical accuracy, but as entertainment, it is most diverting—and then there's the famous chariot fight, of course..."

Once again Henry had to stop the flow. He asked Price if he could remember the times at which he had entered and left the theater.

"Well, now—I got in just before the showing of the news, and then there was an amusing Mickey Mouse—I think it was about a duck, as a matter of fact, but I always call them Mickey Mouses, or should it be Mickey Mice?—and after that came the big picture. The last showing. So we can check the times easily enough from a newspaper." He picked up his midday edition of the *Evening Standard*. "Let's see—theaters—Majestic—oh, dear, how provoking..."

"What's the matter?"

"The program has been changed. I must have seen the last performance. However, I am sure the theater could tell you if you telephoned them..."

"And after the film?"

"I took a taxi home. I remember I arrived back at a quarter past eleven because Bates had kindly waited up for me and I told him he shouldn't have bothered. 'It's quarter past eleven, Bates,' I said. 'You should be in bed.' I am really lucky with my servants, Inspector, and they are generally such a problem, don't you find?"

Henry remarked that it was not a problem which troubled him overmuch. He finished his drink, refused a second one and an offer of lunch, and took his leave. He then made his way to a modest-looking restaurant in the suburb's main street and ordered a meal.

He felt irritated with Arthur Price. He had told Henry a classic example of a story which cannot be checked. Saturday evening in the busiest part of London's West End. Dinner at one of the biggest and most popular restaurants in town, followed by the crowded darkness of a vast theater. Henry felt a strong suspicion that the story was not true, but he saw precious little hope of proving it. He ate his lunch quickly and then asked if he might use the telephone.

The girl in the box office of the Majestic was most helpful. They were no longer showing *Boadicea*, she said, but if Henry would wait for a moment she would check on last week's time-table. After a few moments she came back to announce that the news had come on at seven thirty-five, followed by trailers and a cartoon film. The big picture had started at five past eight and finished at a quarter to eleven. "It was long," she added, "being an epic spectacular, if you see what I mean."

Henry thanked her despondently. If Price's story were true, the times gave him a complete alibi. The girl was still talking. "I do hope you'll come and see our present attraction, sir," she was saying—evidently a well-trained saleswoman. "*Wet Sunday in Wigan*. Ever so good. You may have seen pictures of the gala premeer in the papers. It was..."

"Wait a minute," said Henry. His memory had flipped up a recollection of photographs of toothy celebrities in mink and diamonds, contrasting conspicuously with the theme of the film they had come to honor. "That was last Friday night, wasn't it, the première?"

"That's right, sir."

"So you weren't showing *Boadicea* on Saturday?"

"Oh, no. That finished Thursday evening."

"Thank you very much indeed," said Henry.

On his way back to the center of London in the subway train, Henry considered the matter of Arthur Price. It had been a stroke of luck, certainly, to be able to prove so quickly and conclusively that the man was lying; on the other hand, Henry was too experienced a policeman to build too much on the fact. He knew that people may have many and varied reasons for concealing the truth, and to prove a man a liar is not to brand him as a murderer. On the face of it, Price was the least likely of Henry's suspects. He had actively welcomed the idea of the book—or had he? He had welcomed a portrait of R.A.F. Dymfield. As far as Henry knew, Price had never heard of the change of plan. For the time being he decided to leave Price alone. If he were guilty, there was no point in alarming him before sufficient evidence for an arrest had come to light; if innocent, it might not be necessary to cause him distress by dragging out the personal reasons which had prompted him to lie. The train pulled up at Charing Cross. Henry got out and walked up the hill to the Strand. Soon he was in the imposing marble foyer of Cathode House asking a supercilious blonde receptionist if he might see Mr. James Baggot of Incorporated Television.

He had very much hoped that he would not have to flaunt his official identity, but in vain. Mr. Baggot was altogether too important a person to see a Mr. Henry Tibbett, and without an appointment at that. The receptionist gasped, and fled. She was back half a minute later with the news that Mr. Baggot could see Chief Inspector Tibbett immediately, and that if the Chief Inspector would take the elevator to the fourth floor, Mr. Baggot's secretary would escort him...

So Henry was passed from the care of the blonde into the capable hands of an attractive brunette, and eventually found himself in a vast, soft-carpeted, sunny office where James Baggot sat in a leather armchair on the far side of a dazzling expanse of polished desk.

Once again, Henry thought, Emmy's description had been exact. The aura of smooth success was almost tangible; yet, beneath the surface, lurked the brilliant, untidy technician, not quite submerged. For the moment, however, James Baggot was concentrating on charm, and doing it very well indeed. He advanced from behind the desk, both hands outstretched.

"My dear Inspector Tibbett," he said, "this is a very great pleasure. Am I right in thinking that I owe the honor of your visit to my acquaintance with the adorable Emmy?" When Henry did not answer at once, Baggot went on. "It's so seldom, believe me, that we can lure *really* distinguished people like yourself across our humble threshold. We spend our lives surrounded by spurious celebrities—film stars, popular novelists, publicity-minded university dons—all the superficial trash. I expect Emmy told you what a sincere admiration I have for you and your work. Now, do sit down and have a cigarette."

"Thank you," said Henry, and did so.

Baggot leaned across the desk to light Henry's cigarette from a gold-plated lighter, and went on. "Now, you must tell me what I can do for you. I know what a busy man you are, and I don't flatter myself that this is a purely social call—although, believe me, I wish it were."

"No," said Henry, "it isn't. Didn't you get Emmy's letter?"

"My dear chap," said Baggot, "to tell you the truth, I only got in from Glasgow an hour ago. The wretched aircraft was delayed by fog. It's almost incredible, isn't it, that after the advances made in radar during the war, fog can still paralyze our air services. However, that's beside the point. So Emmy wrote to me? What about?"

"About Lofty Parker," said Henry.

Baggot, who was lighting his own cigarette, stopped in mid-gesture. He did not look at Henry, but an extremely wary expression crossed his face. Then he said, "Oh, yes? About the script, of course." He leaned back, relaxed again, and puffed at his cigarette. "I don't know what your interest is, Tibbett, but I presume you're here to represent your wife. Now, I must make it quite clear that in the event of a contract being signed— and it's by no means certain that it will be, you know—such a contract would be between Incorporated Television and Lofty Parker. Any rights which Emmy may feel she has in the property are no concern of ours. She must negotiate that side of it privately with Lofty. I hope I don't sound harsh, but it's so much better to get these things straight right from the beginning…"

"I'm afraid," said Henry, "that you don't quite understand…"

"It's perfectly true that I wrote the man a letter," said Baggot, waving his right hand airily as if to demonstrate the ephemeral nature of letter-writing, "but you must remember that I have not yet set eyes on a single page of manuscript…"

"No," said Henry, "and you never will."

Baggot sat up straight. "What do you mean by that? Are you implying that Parker has already sold the rights to…?"

"I'm implying," said Henry, "that he's dead."

"Dead?" Jimmy Baggot had gone very pale. "Good God. But how…?"

"Found gassed in his kitchen on Sunday morning."

"And you think he was murdered."

"I never said any such thing, Mr. Baggot."

"Of course you didn't. But it's obvious, isn't it? For a start, he was doing better than he'd done for years. He was doing a job that interested him, and it might well have led to a lot of money. If Lofty had been going to kill himself, he'd have done it long ago, when the going was really rough. And to go on with—Chief Inspector Henry Tibbett doesn't concern himself with cases of suicide."

There was a little pause, and then Henry said, "It's being treated as suicide. I'm naturally interested, because of Emmy, and so I'm making a few inquiries. In his flat—by the way, do you know where he lived?"

"I haven't the faintest. Why should I?"

"Wasn't his address on the questionnaire that my wife left with you?"

"Oh, that thing? Yes, of course it was. I remember now. After I'd lunched with Emmy, I drove to the airport and telephoned my office from there. I dictated the letter to my secretary and read her Lofty's address off the questionnaire thing. Then, I must confess, I threw it into the wastepaper basket and caught my plane to Manchester."

"That was on Friday afternoon, wasn't it?" Henry asked.

"That's right."

"Can you go on from there? Your movements over the weekend?"

"Of course. I was in the Manchester studios by teatime, and I worked there until quite late—between nine and ten. Then I went back to the Midland Hotel, had a bite to eat, and went to bed. On Sunday I flew up to Glasgow. Had a conference there yesterday. I should have flown back last night, but, as I explained, the fog closed in and—here I am."

"You've left out Saturday," said Henry.

"Saturday? I had a day off, for once."

"How did you spend it? Did you come back to London?"

Baggot hesitated. Then with a wide-open smile he said, "I see I'll have to tell you the truth, Inspector, or you'll suspect something much worse. But keep it under your Homburg, there's a good fellow. Yes, in point of fact I flew back on Saturday morning, and by the afternoon I was ensconced in a quiet country pub with a rather special popsy. I left her regretfully on Sunday to catch my plane to Glasgow. You won't bruit it about, will you? You know how people gossip, and her husband..."

At length Henry elicited the information that the pub in question had been the Fisherman's Arms at Dingley-on-Thames, and that the couple had registered as Mr. and Mrs. Derbyshire-Bentinck.

"One of the oldest dodges in the business," remarked Jimmy complacently, "but it never fails. If you want to fool a hotelkeeper, use a fancy name. None of your Smith or Brown stuff. In the good old days I used my own name quite shamelessly, but nowadays—well—there's always the chance that someone will start saying, 'Not the *television* Baggot,' and I'd be in the consommé. So I've evolved this rather attractive alter ego, Mr. Reginald Derbyshire-Bentinck. Quite Bunburyish, in his own little way."

"So you and your friend were together in Dingley for the whole of Saturday afternoon and night."

"I'm afraid so, Inspector. That's my guilty secret."

"I suppose the lady could confirm this..."

Baggot raised his hand. "No," he said. "There I draw the line. It would take the entire majesty of the law to drag her name out of me. But you can check with the pub and"—he scribbled something on a piece of paper and pushed it to Henry—"there. You'll recognize the writing in the hotel register. Further than that I am not prepared to go."

Henry looked at the paper. Baggot had written, "Mr. and Mrs. Reginald Derbyshire-Bentinck." He tucked the paper into his wallet.

"Well," he said, "I'll have to be content with this for the time being. But you must understand that you may possibly be required to give us the lady's name later on. Still, I hope not. Thank you very much, Mr. Baggot."

"Oh, for heaven's sake, call me Jimmy." Baggot was quite at ease. "Now, tell me more about poor old Lofty. Did he leave—I mean, had he started on the manuscript, do you know?"

"We found nothing to indicate that he had."

"No notebooks, nothing of that sort?"

"Absolutely nothing."

"It did occur to me," said Baggot, "that Emmy must have all her notes. She's been doing the research, hasn't she? If I were to put one of my scriptwriters on to the job, cooperating with Emmy..."

Henry stood up. "That is where *I* draw the line, Mr. Baggot."

Jimmy looked surprised. "What on earth do you mean, old man?"

"Emmy," said Henry firmly, "is having no more to do with this business. The project has been cancelled, and I would advise you to drop any idea you may have of reviving it."

"But why on earth…?"

"That is, if you want to be absolutely sure of staying alive," said Henry. "Good-bye, Mr. Baggot, and thank you very much."

For several moments after Henry had left, James Baggot sat quite still at his desk, doodling on his blotting pad. Then, suddenly, he began to laugh. "Poor old Lofty," he said aloud. "Poor bugger." Then he picked up his house telephone and said, "Get me the script-writing department…"

CHAPTER TEN

THE SUFFOLK HOTEL was only a short walk from the offices of the television company. The receptionist informed Henry courteously that Mrs. Meadowes had left the hotel. She had paid her bill and checked out shortly before midday that very morning. Once again Henry produced his official card, but it caused hardly a ripple on the surface of the receptionist's serenity. The Suffolk Hotel was so unimpeachably respectable that it would have taken more than a visit from a Chief Inspector to ruffle it.

The receptionist did, however, agree to make some inquiries, and came back with the news that, as Henry had suspected, Mrs. Meadowes's luggage was still in the hotel. She had checked out before noon in order to avoid paying for an extra day, but had left her baggage in the care of the porter, telling him that she would return for it later, as she was catching the night train for Aberdeen. Henry suggested that it might be worth paging the lounge in case Mrs. Meadowes had returned to the hotel for tea; and, sure enough, it was only a matter of minutes before Annie appeared from the direction of the gilt chairs and tinkling tea cups. She was dressed for her journey in comfortably shapeless tweed, and Henry could almost smell the heather and honeysuckle of her native habitat.

Annie greeted Henry briefly. "Emmy's husband?"

"Yes."

"Good. I'm glad you came. D'you want a cup of tea?"

"I really want a quiet chat with you, Mrs. Meadowes."

"You couldn't have chosen a better spot," said Annie. "There are only three other people in the lounge, one of whom is stone deaf and the other two asleep."

Annie led the way back to her table, ordered more tea for Henry, and then said, "I suppose Emmy is furious with me. I did behave very badly, but I want to tell you straight away that I'm not sorry. I'd do it again. So if she wants an apology from me, she can whistle for it."

"I'm sure she doesn't want an apology," said Henry, intrigued. Emmy's account of her talk with Annie had been noncommittal, merely recording that the latter had been strenuously opposed to the idea of the book and had mentioned a fantastic theory that Beau Guest might still be alive. "I told her this was utter rubbish, which it is," Emmy had added. Nevertheless, Henry had not forgotten Emmy's strange frame of mind on the evening following that meeting.

Annie was smiling. "Well, that's good," she said, "because I'm very fond of Blandish and I hate parting this way with an old friend. Do explain to her that everything I said was for her own good." She gave Henry a direct look from her clear blue eyes. "You seem a sensible sort of man," she added—an unwarranted assumption, Henry thought, for he had barely had a chance to open his mouth. "Surely you must see how dangerous it is for her to go on with this crazy scheme?"

"Why do you call it dangerous?"

"I don't think I'm betraying any confidences," said Annie, "if I tell you that Emmy was madly in love with Beau."

"I had gathered as much," said Henry.

Annie sighed impatiently. "It's all so long ago now," she said, "and it was never more than a schoolgirl infatuation. Unfortunately, Beau didn't live long enough for Emmy to realize that. The whole episode had become crystallized in her mind as a great, tragic, doomed romance."

"I don't think Emmy is quite as foolish as that," said Henry.

"Don't you? I do. In any case, what frightens me is that if she carries on probing into the past, she may uncover things which—well—which would be better left covered up. People might get hurt."

"I'm afraid it's too late, Mrs. Meadowes. People have been hurt already."

"Not seriously, as yet," said Annie. Evidently she had not heard about Lofty—Emmy's letter had been sent to her Scottish address. "You see, Emmy, in her innocence, didn't realize some of the things that were going on."

Henry leant forward. "What things?"

"Even if I knew the details I certainly wouldn't tell you," Annie replied, calmly. "It can do Beau no possible good to try to whitewash him after all these years, just as it would be pointless to dig up dirt about him. As for Barbara—she's paid for her sins in many ways, poor woman. And Vere has got what he deserves, no more and no less."

"Emmy tells me," said Henry, "that you think Guest may still be alive."

There was a tiny pause. Then Annie laughed. "Surely she didn't take that seriously?"

"You mean, she shouldn't have?"

"She certainly didn't appear to," said Annie.

"But of course," said Henry, "things are different now. One has to make what are known as agonizing reappraisals."

"What on earth do you mean?"

"Lofty's death," said Henry, "has changed everything."

Annie put her cup gently on the table and said quietly, "Why didn't you tell me at once?"

"You were doing the talking," said Henry.

"So I was. And you hoped I'd give something away. Is that it?"

"I was interested to hear what you had to say."

"I sincerely hope," said Annie, "that you are none the wiser for it."

"That's not a very cooperative attitude." Henry grinned at her, but there was no answering smile. Annie seemed lost in brooding thoughts.

"Poor old Lofty. What happened?"

"He was found in his kitchen with the gas turned on full."

"Suicide?"

"So the police think."

"But you don't."

"What makes you think that?"

"My dear man," said Annie, "the fact that you are here at all. And anyhow, Lofty wasn't the type. He had the resilience of rubber; he'd bend, but never break. When did this happen?"

Henry said, "He was alive at nine on Saturday evening. He was found dead on Sunday morning. We think he had a caller about five-past nine on Saturday and I'm anxious to trace who it was, to get a line on Lofty's frame of mind."

"It wasn't me," said Annie promptly. "I don't even know where he lived. And on Saturday evening I went and dined with an old school friend and her husband in Kensington."

"Any idea of times?"

"Roughly. I took a cab from here at seven, so I suppose I got there about half-past. Poor Mary had a nasty cold coming on, so I made my excuses and left early, around ten-thirty."

"Getting back here before eleven."

"No. It was nearer midnight. I walked most of the way back, you see. It was a fine night and I couldn't find a cab. Anyhow, I like walking." After a pause Annie added, "What will happen now? About the book, I mean?"

"The whole thing is off."

"Definitely?"

"Yes."

"Well, thank God for that anyhow."

"Mrs. Meadowes," said Henry, "will you tell me some more about the mysterious things that were going on at Dymfield that Emmy didn't know about?"

"I really don't know what you mean."

"A few minutes ago, you hinted..."

"I hinted nothing. Don't put words into my mouth."

"Mrs. Meadowes," said Henry, "you quite definitely..."

Annie stood up. "Excuse me, Mr. Tibbett," she said, "I must go. I have a train to catch. Give my love to Emmy and tell her I hope to meet her again one of these days."

She left the lounge majestically, like a great ship leaving harbor, and Henry heard her commanding voice in the lobby ordering a taxi and checking her luggage. She was going to be a good two hours early for her train, and in view of this interesting fact, Henry decided that it might be worthwhile following her taxi at a distance.

It turned out to be a waste of time. Annie was driven straight to St. Pancras Station, where her cases were wheeled away to the Left Luggage Office. Annie herself, followed unobtrusively by Henry, made her way to the Ladies' Waiting Room. Unable to penetrate this sanctum, Henry hung about on the platform outside, among the rush-hour travelers. Twice, as the door opened to admit a Lady, he caught a glimpse of Annie. She was sitting at a table writing a letter. At half-past seven she came out, collected her luggage, and boarded the first-class sleeping car compartment of the Aberdeen express.

Henry made his way home, cross with frustration, and well aware that he was late for dinner again. He found Emmy in the kitchen stirring a sauce with a look of worried concentration. Her face lit up as he came in.

"Oh, darling, I'm so glad you're back. I was beginning to..."

"Sorry, love. I know I'm late. But you need never worry about me, you know. Safe as houses."

Emmy kissed him. "I wish I could be sure of that," she said. "Anyhow, I was longing to see you, because I want to know if I've done the right thing."

"What about?"

Emmy stirred the sauce again. "Barbara rang me half an hour ago," she said.

"What did she say?"

"She knew that Lofty was dead."

"She'd had your letter I suppose."

"Yes. But she knew already. She'd seen it in the paper. She must be one of the few people who knew his real Christian name. She was obviously livid about my letter, in a honeyed way—if you know what I mean. She said it was quite out of the question to abandon the project now and that I had already done *such* valuable work, and so on. She's as stubborn as a mule, that woman," added Emmy with an extra-vicious stir of her wooden spoon.

"So what did you say?"

"I'm afraid I was rather spineless. She—she *fillets* me," said Emmy resentfully. "The best I could do was to bleat something about you not wanting me to go on with the book. Passing the buck, I'm afraid. She replied sweetly that it was too unfortunate that you should be against the project just when she'd managed to get Vere really enthusiastic about it. I said, 'I suppose that's why he got his solicitors to write to Lofty, is it?' That really rattled her. She obviously didn't know about it. She seemed quite relieved when I told her what was in the letter; I suppose she thought Vere might have been threatening to sue or something. Anyhow, she calmed down and said that obviously the whole matter should be discussed quietly, and she invited both of us to go down there for lunch tomorrow. So I said we'd go. I do hope I did right. I feel a bit out of my depth."

Henry put his arm around her shoulders. "You did splendidly, darling," he said. "I was wondering how I could engineer an invitation to visit the Prendergasts, and here it is, tied up with blue ribbon. At their suggestion, what's more."

"At Barbara's suggestion. There's no guarantee that Vere will even be there."

"What do you mean?"

"It's just a hunch," said Emmy, "but I think that Vere imagines that Lofty's death has put an end to the project and that he has no notion that Barbara's planning to carry on with it. I've no real reason for thinking it, only instinct."

"Your nose, perhaps?" said Henry smiling. He was referring to his own instinct for detection known to his colleagues as "Tibbett's nose."

Emmy smiled back. "I dare say," she said. "Anyhow, supper's ready."

"Before we eat," said Henry, "I ought to make a phone call."

"Where to?"

"If we're going to Whitchurch tomorrow we ought to call in and see the Reverend Sidney Guest."

Emmy stopped in mid-gesture, the wooden spoon held up like a conductor's baton. "Do you have to?"

"I said 'we,'" Henry pointed out. "I'm sorry, darling, but I think you should be there. Anyhow, he's expecting you, isn't he?"

"Not tomorrow. Thursday."

"In that case I'll have to ring him."

Emmy was suddenly brisk. "Come along," she said. "If we don't eat now everything will be cold."

With which patent untruth, she swept the piping-hot dishes onto a tray and carried it into the living room. Henry, taking the hint, did not refer to Beau's father again until they had finished their meal. Then, glancing at his watch, he said, "Ten to nine. I don't suppose the reverend gentleman is in bed yet. Can you give me his number?"

"It's on the pad by the telephone. I'll go and do the washing up." Emmy's voice was so deliberately light as to be almost unrecognizable. She assembled a trayful of dirty plates and vanished into the kitchen.

Henry found the number scribbled in his wife's handwriting and dialed it. For some time the telephone buzzed, unanswered. Then a bad-tempered masculine voice said, "Well? What is it?"

"My name is Tibbett," began Henry.

"What? Speak up! What's the matter? Who are you?"

"Is that Mr. Sidney Guest?"

"Of course it is. Who do you think it would be? I asked who *you* were. Don't you understand plain English?"

Loudly and deliberately Henry said, "This is Chief Inspector Henry Tibbett of Scotland Yard."

"Tibbett? Tibbett? Where have I heard that name? Oh, yes. Some fool of a woman. Came around here asking questions about my son Alan. Well, I told her all she wanted. Isn't that enough, without bothering me with telephone calls at all hours of the night...?"

"Mr. Guest," said Henry very firmly. "I am an officer of the Criminal Investigation Department, and I shall be calling on you tomorrow in connection with..."

"Oh, dear me." The voice at the other end of the line seemed to collapse, to become suddenly old. "I suppose it's about—yes, yes—again. Can't the hospital manage to...? Oh, well—can you tell me...?" The voice became pathetically tentative. "What—what is it this time? Nothing—too serious, I hope...?"

"Don't worry, Mr. Guest," said Henry briskly. "I just want to ask you a few routine questions."

"Routine—I've heard *that* before..." The voice was recovering a little of its truculence.

"We'll be with you at half-past four tomorrow afternoon, if that's convenient," said Henry quickly. "Good. Until then, good-bye, Mr. Guest."

He rang off. With suspicious promptness, Emmy appeared at the door with two cups of coffee.

"He's an old beast, isn't he?" she said. "Was he very rude?"

Henry shook his head. "He was pathetic," he said.

Emmy put the coffee on the table. "Good heavens," she said, "he must have changed since I saw him."

"The other evening," said Henry, "you asked me about a hospital—Sandfields."

"That's right. You said it was a loony-bin."

"Why were you interested in it?"

Emmy looked embarrassed. "Oh—no special reason."

"Don't be silly, Emmy," said Henry sharply. "Somebody connected with Sidney Guest is a patient at Sandfields. Who is it?"

For a moment Emmy did not answer. Then she said, "I don't know why I didn't want to tell you. Some sort of protective mechanism coming into action, I suppose. You must have guessed. It's Beau's mother."

It was some time later that it occurred to Henry that Emmy had referred to the invalid as "Beau's mother" rather than as "Sidney's wife." In fact the thought struck him as he lay sleepless during the despairing hour between three and four o'clock in the morning. Beside him, Emmy turned, moaned, and settled herself to sleep again. Henry looked at her serene face, etched by white moonlight. "In her innocence...," Annie had said. Emmy was innocent still; but forces that were far from innocent were gathering in the shadows. Henry shivered.

With maddening predictability, sleep eluded him until the moment when dawn began to lighten the late September sky. His last waking impression was of a whispering murmur from outside the open windows, which he failed to identify as falling rain. When Emmy woke him a couple of hours later, at eight o'clock, he roused himself slowly and reluctantly and surveyed the world in a disgruntled mood. Emmy had closed the windows, but the rain streamed dismally down the panes. Outside, the plane trees on the pavement jostled and complained, as a vicious wind whipped their flat leaves together like clapping hands.

Henry took a gulp of tea. "A charming day for a visit to the country," he said.

"We were lucky last time," said Emmy philosophically. She added, "I wish I had some rubber boots."

"Don't worry. Whitchurch Manor is lousy with them. You needn't think you'll be able to avoid a tramp around the park by pleading the inadequacy of your shoes." Henry finished his tea and shook himself. "I feel awful. I didn't sleep a wink."

"Liar. You were snoring like a pig when I got up."

"Yes, I know. But I was awake from three until about half an hour ago."

"Oh, dear." Emmy paused in the doorway. "Was it something you ate?"

"I expect so," said Henry, rather too quickly.

Emmy looked at him accusingly. "Henry, you're worrying."

"No. Not really."

"You are. Is it about me?"

"Of course not. Don't flatter yourself, woman. My insomnia was due to an equal mixture of Camembert cheese and the Reverend Sidney Guest, both taken too late at night."

"I hope that's true," said Emmy, doubtfully.

"Of course it is," said Henry. After all, it nearly was.

CHAPTER ELEVEN

THE DRIVE TO THE COUNTRY was every bit as dismal as Henry had foreseen. The glowing countryside of the previous week had been reduced by the dead hand of the rain to a uniform drab dampness, and the chrysanthemums in the cottage gardens sagged limply, bedraggled by the wind.

"Today's weather is more in keeping, anyhow," said Emmy suddenly.

"More in keeping than what, with what?"

"Than the sunshine, with—with everything. Poor Barbara and poor Vere. I feel terribly depressed every time I think of them."

"I don't see why you should," said Henry. "They are an attractive couple in early middle age with a great deal of money and a beautiful house."

"It's strange, isn't it?" said Emmy. "All that is perfectly true, and yet—you agree with me, don't you? Why is it?"

"You tell me," said Henry. "I'm interested. Of all the people from Dymfield that you've met recently, why is it only the Prendergasts whom you find depressing?"

"Oh, I don't know." Emmy mused a little. "Well, take Jimmy Baggot. He's obviously not depressing. He's blossomed."

"He's made a successful career for himself quite away from the Air Force."

"Yes. Of course, it was the R.A.F. that gave him his start in television, but that was years ago. Then there's Sammy. He's not a success exactly, but he's back leading the outrageous sort of life he's always led. The war was just an interlude to him, just another chance for a bit of fun and a bit of a fiddle..." Emmy looked at Henry. "I see what you mean."

"You see what *you* mean," he corrected her.

"It's because Barbara and Vere have—stopped. Physically they're living now, but emotionally they're still back in the nineteen-forties. That's what you were leading up to, isn't it?"

"Yes," said Henry. "And it brings us to the second question. Why?"

"Well—they haven't done much since those days. Vere's just got his estate, and Barbara..."

"Vere is a farmer in quite a big way," said Henry. "Barbara is rich and social, and my spies tell me she does quite a bit of sitting on committees of charity balls and so on. Why should they be less able to adjust to living in the present than Annie Meadowes or Sammy?"

"They're married to each other, remember," said Emmy. "I mean, they have a mutual past, whereas Annie and Sammy have both..."

"We're getting closer now, I think," said Henry. "Has it occurred to you that they may have married each other precisely because they were both—haunted?"

"Haunted?"

"By Beau Guest." Henry paused. "I don't want to be unkind, Emmy darling. I know you were very fond of the man. But suicide can be used as a very cruel weapon, you know. It can be the ultimate revenge, leaving a scar that a living person may carry to the grave."

Henry knew by the quality of her silence that his words had hurt and upset Emmy. She seemed to retreat into herself, slamming the door behind her. It was five minutes before she spoke again, and then she said, "But Lofty didn't commit suicide, did he?"

Barbara Prendergast was alone on the steps to greet them. Emmy's hunch about Vere's absence had been correct. Barbara apologized for him—"Gone to Snettle—long-standing date for some rough shooting."

A big log fire was blazing in the drawing room, and for a moment it seemed to Henry that the conversation in the car had been ridiculous. This house could not be called depressing. Then he caught sight of something which had not been there on his last visit. It was a large, silver-framed photograph of a dark-haired young man in R.A.F. uniform. He wore the thin stripe of a Pilot Officer on his sleeve, and very new-looking pilot's wings. His face, with its almost too-perfect, regular features, was vaguely and disturbingly familiar. A ghost had moved into the cheerful, chintzy drawing room.

Barbara dispensed drinks and small talk. "Lunch will be ready soon," she said, "and we can't get down to serious talk until it's over. So not a word about poor Lofty or the book until afterward." She glanced quickly at the photograph, and it seemed to Henry as though she exchanged a conspiratorial wink with it.

"I presume that's your first husband," said Henry. The photograph was so placed as to demand rather than invite comment.

"Yes." Barbara smiled fondly. "Taken when he first got his wings. Before I even met him. I've always loved it. But would you believe it, when I offered it to the hospital, after the crash, they wouldn't have it. Said he looked too young. I had to give them a more recent one which wasn't nearly as good. This one was *exactly* like him."

An awkward silence followed, which was mercifully terminated by the entry of an elderly parlor maid announcing lunch. They went into the dining room.

Afterward, over coffee, Barbara started the ball rolling. She took a deep breath and said, "Now, what is all this I hear about Henry Tibbett refusing to allow his wife to carry on with her work?" She eyed Henry accusingly. "This is the twentieth century, you know. If Emmy wants to go on with the book, as I gather she does, I really don't think you've got any right to stop her."

Henry was interested that Barbara had decided to open the proceedings with a frontal attack upon himself. Clearly her idea—and a good one—was to drive a wedge between Henry and Emmy. The more she could manage to take it for granted that Emmy wished to continue the work, the harder it became for Emmy to deny it. Barbara was looking full at Henry now with all the power of her huge hazel eyes. "I warn you, Henry Tibbett, I shall fight you all the way." For all the banter in her tone, she sounded dangerous.

Henry said, "I think you've got it wrong, Mrs. Prendergast. I'm not playing the heavy husband. But I agree wholeheartedly with Emmy in her decision not to continue with the book."

Barbara now turned her accusing gaze on Emmy. "That's hardly what you told me on the telephone, Emmy darling."

"I—well—actually, Barbara..." Emmy was floundering. She was, in her own phrase, filleted.

"I can explain very simply," Henry began, coming to the rescue.

Barbara turned on him. "The least you can do is to let your wife speak for herself without putting words into her mouth," she said.

Emmy flashed Henry a despairing distress signal with her eyes.

He said, "Go on, then, darling. Speak for yourself. You must."

Emmy swallowed. Then she said in a rush, "I don't want to go on with it."

"What Emmy means..."

"Let her say what she means."

Fortunately, Emmy seemed to recover. She said, more calmly, "There are several reasons why I've decided to give up. First, Lofty left no notes of any sort, as I told you in my letter, Barbara. Second, I'm not a writer. I couldn't do it. Thirdly I—I don't think it's healthy." Involuntarily Emmy glanced at the photograph. It smiled blandly back at her. "For heaven's sake, Barbara, leave it alone! What are you frightened of?"

As soon as she had said the last words Emmy felt a cold shock, as if she had fallen through thin ice. She had no idea why she had said them. She hadn't thought of Barbara as being frightened. The words had come, of their own volition, and now they lingered in the air, spreading their poison.

Barbara had gone very pale. "It would have been simpler," she said, "if you had been more honest with me on the telephone."

"I know. I'm sorry. I..."

"In fact," Barbara went on relentlessly, "it is you that are frightened. We all knew, of course..."

Henry felt it was time to intervene. "Mrs. Prendergast," he said, "if anybody is frightened, it is me."

"You?"

Barbara was sufficiently surprised to allow herself to be diverted, momentarily, from her attack on Emmy.

"What Emmy has not told you," he went on, "because she would never betray my confidence, is that personally I am not convinced that Parker killed himself."

Barbara sat quite still, looking at Henry. "Go on," she said.

"I must ask you to keep this strictly to yourself, Mrs. Prendergast," Henry went on. "Officially, the case is being treated as suicide. I am acting quite on my own when I say that I have a strong feeling that Lofty was murdered. If he was, then it seems likely that the motive was to prevent further work being done on your book. Now do you understand why I am not anxious that my wife should step into his shoes?"

"You seriously believe that Emmy would be in danger if she took over the job?" Barbara's delicately outlined eyebrows rose mockingly. "How very melodramatic. And what about me?"

"You?"

"I think you will agree, Mr. Tibbett, that I am the driving force behind this project. If Emmy refuses, it doesn't necessarily mean that *I* shall give up. Am I then in danger of being murdered, too?"

"I have no idea." Henry spoke so simply that Barbara laughed again, with more sincerity. "You see," Henry went on, "I don't think that it was the actual undertaking of the book that sealed Parker's fate. It was something to do with the way he was tackling the job—and I have no idea what that something was. I'm not prepared to risk Emmy making the same mistake."

"I see," said Barbara. "So I'm wasting my breath, am I? And playing a dangerous game into the bargain?"

"Yes," said Henry. "That about sums it up."

"Too bad."

Henry leaned forward. "Mrs. Prendergast," he said, "just why are you so keen on this idea? It's over twenty years since the death of your first husband. If you'd wanted to do something of this sort, surely the time to have done it would have been years ago."

Barbara looked down at her knees where her bird-talon hands were twisting and tearing a fragile handkerchief. "I couldn't—it was all so terrible at the time. I didn't even think about it. Then I suddenly got this idea, and—I want to do it. For his sake." She looked up and her voice was harsh as she said, "I hope you're not implying that you think I was responsible for Lofty's death, even indirectly."

"Of course not," said Henry. "But I would like to ask you a few questions. When did you see him last, for instance?"

Barbara seemed eager to help. "Let me see—what's today—Wednesday… Yes, it must have been just a week ago today. I didn't actually see him, of course, but I spoke to him on the telephone."

"What about?"

"Oh, I just rang to ask how things were going. He seemed in very good spirits. He was reading me…" She stopped. "Wait a minute. I thought you said he left no notes."

"That's right."

"But he read them to me. 'Wait while I get my notebook,' he said, and then he read me what he'd started on. You must have found that book."

"We didn't," said Henry. "That's one of the interesting aspects of the case. Can you remember what he read to you?"

Barbara frowned. "Not word for word, of course," she said. "It was mostly about Beau in the Battle of Britain, his sixteen enemy planes and all that. Really heroic stuff, although being Lofty, he'd managed to keep his tongue pretty firmly in his cheek all the time. Oh, and there was an earlier bit about Beau's childhood. The country rectory, the stern but kindly father, the beautiful but ailing mother, the closely knit English family circle—you know the sort of thing."

Emmy opened her mouth, and then shut it again.

Henry said, "Do you know where Lofty got that information, Mrs. Prendergast?"

"Of course," said Barbara blandly. "From me."

Emmy became articulate at last. "But it's untrue—his family wasn't…"

"Isn't it appalling," said Barbara, with a gently pained smile, "how false rumors stick, even after years? Of course, people believe what they want to believe, which is always the worst. And that talk about Beau not getting on with his father was nonsense. And as for the really scurrilous things people said about his mother—just because she had to go abroad for her health. Well, the only thing to do with slander like that is to ignore it. Of course, I haven't seen either of his parents for some years, because when I remarried I thought it was better to make a clean break. But I can assure you that the Guests were a really happy family."

In the face of Barbara's sad but firm smile, Emmy said nothing. She was extremely glad that she had not mentioned to Barbara her visit to the Reverend Sidney. As it was, she was now in a position to gauge the thickness of the whitewash that was being prepared. She became aware that Henry was speaking again.

"I believe that your husband's solicitor wrote Parker a letter shortly before he died."

Barbara was well in control now. "So I understand," she said.

"Do you know what it was about?"

"Not really. Vere never told me about it, the forgetful creature, so the first I knew of it was when Emmy told me yesterday. I asked Vere about it last night, and he said it was something to do with libel laws. All rather above my head, I'm afraid."

"I see," said Henry. "And now, would you mind telling me what you were doing between seven and eleven last Saturday night?"

Barbara's eyebrows went up. "I don't think," she said, "that you can compel me to answer that."

"No, I can't. Not here and now. But it would save a great deal of trouble if you did, and I can't imagine that you have anything to hide."

"Certainly I haven't. I was here all the time. As a matter of fact, I was"—her eyes strayed briefly to the photograph—"I was sorting through some old things in the attic. It took me the whole evening."

"Well, that's straightforward enough," said Henry. "I suppose your husband will be able to confirm it."

"Oh, no. Vere was out. At one of these reunions he adores so much. An Old School affair—I think it was at the Dorchester. He left here before six and came home at half-past two in the morning. I remember that, because he woke me up."

Henry received this information with some depression. Of course, it would have been too much to expect all his suspects to have neat alibis, but he had seldom come across a less satisfactory bunch than this. He felt certain that nobody would have noticed if Vere Prendergast had slipped out early from the Old

Boys' Dinner; and, in any case, he would have had plenty of time to visit Earl's Court after the dinner and still be home by half-past two. After all, Henry reminded himself, there was no proof that Lofty's mysterious visitor had been his murderer. The doorbell might well have been rung by a political canvasser or a charity collector or some other anonymous but harmless caller.

Barbara seemed to sense what was going through Henry's mind. She smiled with rather more satisfaction than sympathy, and said, "Not very helpful, I'm afraid. I was alone here, and Vere was actually in London, and therefore highly suspect—along with the other six million people who might have chosen to while away Saturday evening by murdering Lofty."

Henry decided to change the subject. "I'm a little puzzled, Mrs. Prendergast," he said. "Last time we were here, I somehow got the impression that the project was rather running away from you, out of control, and that you'd have been quite glad to pull out..."

"Lofty was so impulsive." Barbara was demure again now. "He was full of this ridiculous idea of making a mystery out of Beau's death. As you know very well, that was not my intention at all. Now, I shall go ahead on my original lines—when and if I find somebody to help me," she added, with a nasty look at Emmy.

"So in fact," said Henry, "it's very convenient for you that he's out of the way."

Barbara looked amused. "You surely can't mean that you think it would be an adequate motive for murder."

Henry looked steadily at her. "No," he said with regret, "I can't imagine that it would. But in my job one is continually being surprised by people and their motives."

"Not only in your job," said Barbara. And Henry realized that she had transferred her gaze from him to the photograph. Then she turned back to Henry. "Inspector Tibbett," she said, "have you any idea why Lofty was so keen to visit Dymfield airfield?"

"No," said Henry.

Barbara smiled. "That's a straight answer anyway," she said. "Everyone else I've asked just shies away from the question, as though it were something indecent."

"Well," said Henry, "I hope I may be in a better position to tell you by next weekend. Emmy and I are visiting Dymfield ourselves on Friday, and I intend..."

He got no further, for at that moment the door opened and Vere Prendergast came in, followed by a pack of leaping, enthusiastic dogs.

"Good lord," he said, "the Tibbetts. What brings you here, eh? Nice to see you. Hope Barbara's been entertaining you adequately. What about poor old Lofty—shocking business, wasn't it? Can't think what made him do it. You never can tell, can you?" He rubbed his large hands together in front of the fire, and began to hold forth about his morning's bag of six pigeons and a hare. Then he said, "Well, we don't want to stay indoors, do we, eh, Blandish? What about a quick flip around the park? Who's game?"

There was no escape. When Emmy pleaded the unsuitability of her shoes, Vere brushed the objection aside. "Of course you can't go out in those civilian shoes," he said, "but we've plenty of boots for you. Come along to the cloakroom, both of you. We'll fix you up in no time."

He led the way to a large walk-in closet in the hall. Inside was a jumble of boots, walking sticks, dog collars, old raincoats, and other characteristic impedimenta.

"Now, what's your size, Blandish? Five? Hope we've got some small enough. You're a number nine, aren't you, Henry old scout? Here. Catch!"

Vere swung around and threw a pair of mud-caked Wellingtons to Henry. It was then that Emmy saw the flying boots. They were ancient and dusty, but they stood just inside the door, like new arrivals.

"Oh, Vere," she said, "you've still got your old R.A.F. boots. Weren't they marvelous? We W.A.A.F.'s always tried to get hold of a pair, even if it did mean dead men's shoes. They were quite a status symbol."

Vere looked puzzled. "Flying boots? Good lord, no. Lost mine years ago. I…" He stopped as he saw the black leather boots, with their short sheepskin linings, standing at his feet. "What on earth…?"

From the hall Barbara's voice said, "I found them, darling. In that old trunk in the attic. I thought they might be useful."

"Oh, did you?" Vere sounded a little put out. Then he said, "Much too hot for a day like this. Might be able to wear them in the winter sometimes." He bent down and patted the boots, as if they had been a couple of faithful dogs. "Long time since I've seen these old jokers. But we went through a lot together." He picked up the boots and dumped them at the back of the pile. "Now, let's see. Boots, size five, W.A.A.F. officer for the use of…"

Emmy was soon fitted up, and the three of them were walking through the damp muddiness of the park under sodden brown leaves which fell silently and heavily, like tears. Emmy noticed, with some envy, that it was taken for granted that Barbara should remain in the house.

On their return Vere went into the kitchen, where Barbara was making tea, leaving Henry and Emmy to change their shoes and wash their hands. They were warming themselves by the drawing-room fire when Vere came in. He looked extremely upset.

"Barbara has just told me the most extraordinary thing, Tibbett," he said. "It seems that you have some idea that Lofty was murdered." He sounded not only shaken but frightened.

"She shouldn't have told you," said Henry, "but I suppose she thought that telling you wouldn't count. For God's sake, keep it to yourself. Yes—it's true. But as I explained to your wife, it's only a private suspicion of my own."

Henry went on to ask Vere about his movements on Saturday night, and received a prompt confirmation of what Barbara had said. Old Boys' Dinner—jolly good show…one of the last to leave...didn't get home till after two—Babs a bit shirty about it...

"And the solicitor's letter written to Parker on your instructions?"

"I suppose you found that," said Vere. "It was just a routine precaution. I intended to make sure Barbara didn't expose herself to the risk of a libel suit. You know what some people are like—ready to bleed the last sixpence out of an innocent amateur like Babs."

"Had you anyone particular in mind?"

"In mind for what?"

"Was there anyone whom you suspected might bring such an action?"

Vere laughed shortly. "Any of them, I should think," he said. "Baggot obviously cares for nothing but money; Price is a shark in business, for all his baby-faced look; Annie Day is as hard as nails and has an impecunious husband and a growing family; and as for Sammy—well—we all know *him*. And then there's Beau's father."

"The Reverend Sidney," said Henry.

"You know him?" Vere was surprised.

"No. I've never met him," said Henry truthfully.

"Nor have I." Vere frowned. "But you never know. I don't know how much he—that is to say..."

"How much he knew?" Henry completed the sentence softly.

There was a silence. Then Vere said heartily, "My dear old sleuth, who knows how much anybody knows about anything? Anyhow, I can assure you that the letter from old Pringle had no sinister significance. Just a routine check to safeguard the old bank balance." He threw another log on to the fire. "This is a nasty business. If Lofty really was done in, I mean. I hope you'll be able to keep Babs out of it."

"That's up to you," said Henry.

"To me?"

"Yes. You must get her to drop this book idea."

Vere looked surprised and displeased. "You don't mean that she intends to go on with it, after this?"

"She seems keener than ever," said Henry.

"God Almighty," said Vere. "Well, I'll do what I can."

After tea Henry and Emmy said their good-byes and went to collect their coats. Barbara saw them to the door. Vere did not. As they passed the open drawing-room door, Henry noticed that Vere was standing beside the small table gazing broodingly at the smiling photograph of Beau Guest.

Henry and Emmy did not talk much on the drive to Upper Charwood. Emmy, Henry thought, was quieter and seemed more distressed than at any time since Lofty's death. At last, with as much tact as he could muster, he asked her why this should be.

Emmy was staring straight ahead through the rainy windshield. "It's those bloody boots," she said.

"You mean Vere's flying boots?"

"They weren't Vere's," said Emmy. "I saw the name written inside them. They were Beau's."

Henry did not take his eyes off the road. Softly he said, "How very interesting."

"I don't know about interesting," said Emmy. "I found it upsetting—that photograph and the boots and—what in heaven's name is Barbara doing, Henry?"

"I thought you had explained that to me."

"How do you mean?"

"You advanced the theory that she is suffering from a guilt complex. I think you are probably right."

"Oh, do you?" said Emmy uneasily.

They drove on in silence.

CHAPTER TWELVE

THE DOOR OF THE WHITEWASHED bungalow opened tentatively in answer to Henry's ring.

"Inspector Tibbett?" Emmy hardly recognized the voice. It was that of a tired old man.

"Yes. You must be Mr. Guest. I think you know my wife."

The door opened wider. The Reverend Sidney was visible now, dressed in ancient gray flannels and a sports coat, which made an incongruous frame for his white dog-collar. "Your...? You never told me she was your wife. When you telephoned..."

"I told you I was coming here in my official capacity, and I'm afraid that's true," said Henry. A gleam of hope had appeared in the old man's eyes, but now it died. "But since my wife has already made your acquaintance..."

"You'd better come in," said Sidney Guest despondently.

As he led the way to the cheerless drawing room, he paused to add, over his shoulder, "I'm surprised, all the same, Inspector. Very irregular, I should have thought, bringing your wife on an official visit." Before Henry could reply, they had reached the drawing room. Guest motioned them to sit down and did the same himself. Then he said, "Well, out with it. What is it this time? How much?"

"I beg your pardon?"

"Don't beat about the bush, young man." The fire was coming back into the Reverend Sidney's voice. "I shall allege inadequate supervision, of course. You understand that."

"Mr. Guest," said Henry, "I think you're making a mistake. I believe that my wife wrote you a letter..."

Guest looked completely bewildered. "What has that got to do with it? You can't have come about *that*..."

"I have, in an indirect way," said Henry. "You remember that my wife came to see you last week in connection with a proposed biography of your son..."

"That's right. And then wrote to say that the whole thing was off, which I consider a very sensible decision." The Reverend Sidney was looking a lot chirpier now, sitting back and filling his pipe. He added, addressing Emmy, "I presume that means that you and your colleague will not be visiting me. You may.congratulate him from me on having found something better to do with his time than..."

Henry said, "There is no question of congratulating Mr. Parker, I am afraid. Apparently my wife did not explain the circumstances fully to you. The book is off because Mr. Parker, who should have written it, is dead."

For a moment the Reverend Sidney looked too surprised for speech. Then he said, "What an extraordinary thing. Dead? But I gathered that he was a contemporary of Alan's. He must have been very young."

"In his forties," said Henry.

"A motor car accident, I suppose. Passion for speed, like all these young lunatics. I trust he did not maim any innocent bystanders."

"It was not a motor accident," said Henry, and found that he was speaking a little more loudly than he had intended. "Parker was found dead at his home. Apparently he had committed suicide."

This produced an unexpected reaction. The Reverend Sidney snorted in disgust. "Ha! Typical! Typical of the younger generation. No backbone, no moral fiber. Look at Alan. Exactly the same. Suicide. Oh, I know the official announcement said missing, but I know very well what happened. As soon as things got just a little bit difficult he took the easy way out, with absolutely no consideration for other people. And apparently his friend has turned out to be exactly the same."

"For what it is worth," said Henry, hoping he did not sound as irritated as he felt, "I believe that Charles Parker was a courageous, talented, and unfortunate man. However, that is beside the point. I am trying to establish exactly how and why he died, and I hope that you can help me."

"I? My dear sir, what a bizarre idea. I never met the man. Haven't been to London in months."

"You knew his name and address..."

"I did no such thing!"

"The name and address were on that questionnaire that I left with you, Mr. Guest," Emmy put in.

"Ha! A lot of stupid and impertinent questions. I burned it as soon as you left the house."

"So you did look at it?"

"Certainly I didn't. Put it in the fire."

"All the same," said Henry, "you might just tell me what you were doing last Saturday night between seven and eleven."

The Reverend Sidney stood up, majestically. "I was eating my modest supper and going quietly to bed," he said. "I took early Communion service at Snettle on Sunday morning. The rector is an elderly man and is suffering from a cold in the head. There. Does that satisfy you? If so, you will kindly leave my house. And I would like to put it on record that I consider the whole affair most irregular. If I am pestered again, I shall write to your superiors, my Member of Parliament, and the editor of the *Times*. Good day to you!"

As they got into the car, Henry said, "Phew!" and Emmy said, "I did warn you."

"It's very interesting, all the same," Henry remarked, as he started the engine. He revved up, and then added, indicating a rusty wire fence on their right, "I suppose that must be R.A.F. Dymfield."

"Yes, it must be. As the Reverend Sidney said, this is the tail end of one of the runways."

"Do you think you could locate the main entrance for me? I'd like to take a look at it."

"I think I can find it," said Emmy. "But it'll all be bolted and barred. We won't be able to get in."

Twice Henry took a wrong turn down a narrow lane dripping in the autumn rain, but eventually they pulled up beside an ancient double gate, made of metal and topped with rusty barbed wire. A broken-down hut, still bearing traces of camouflage paint, was all that remained of the Guardroom. Henry and Emmy climbed out of the car and peered through the railings. In the deepening dusk they could see a concrete road, weeds sprouting from every interstice, running bleakly to nowhere. A few hangars still stood, with yawning gaps in their corrugated iron walls giving glimpses of stark girders. There were several overgrown Nissen huts whose broken doors were daubed with the scrawls of young trespassers; and a couple of grassy mounds, from which corners of dirty concrete emerged like bones, were identifiable as old air-raid shelters. A few broken and weather-beaten signs gave warning of "No Admittance" or "Air Ministry Property," while others, older still, bore cryptic markings such as "A," "B," or "C," accompanied by faintly distinguishable arrows. In the damp twilight the impression of desolation was overwhelming.

Emmy shivered. It was impossible to believe that it was through this very gate that Beau had driven her, in the camouflaged station wagon, for her first flight.

"You're very quiet, Blandish."

"Am I, sir?"

"This is your first flip, isn't it?"

"Yes, sir."

"Excited?"

"Oh, *yes*, sir."

"Not nervous?"

"Nervous?"

"You'll be okay with old Vere. Safe as a bloody house. Not like some of us. So just relax and do what he tells you, and you'll find it's a piece of cake. What are you laughing at?"

"I'm terribly sorry, sir. It's just that—well—that you should think I was *frightened*. Do you know, I've spent the last year doing nothing except look forward to this moment, when I could actually get into the air..."

"Sorry I insulted you, little Blandish. I didn't know you felt so strongly."

"Well, I do—sir."

"For God's sake, do you have to call me 'sir' all the time? Yes, I suppose you do. Silly, isn't it? Well, here we are. Out you get. Oh, by the way, Blandish..."

"Yes, sir?"

"Did anyone ever tell you that your eyes were blue?"

"But they're not, sir."

"Aren't they? Let me have a look..."

"I'd better go, sir. Squadron Leader Prendergast will be..."

"You funny child. I won't eat you. All right, run along now. And come to my office when you get back. I shall want a full report."

"Oh, yes—sir."

"Good luck, Blandish."

❃ ❃ ❃

"Let's go home," said Emmy to Henry. "Sammy was quite right. He said it would only depress us."

"Hm," said Henry. He was peering through the window of the old Guardroom. "I suppose records were kept of everybody who came and went. And not a hope in hell of finding them now."

"After all these years? Of course not. Let's go home."

They drove back to London in almost unbroken silence.

Once Henry said, "Isn't it a bit strange that Barbara should have Beau's boots?"

And Emmy replied briskly, "Not at all. I had a pair myself."

"Whose?"

"I don't know. Some poor type who'd had it, I suppose."

As they drew up outside the converted Victorian house in Chelsea where they lived, Henry said, "I shall have to go down again and take a proper look at Dymfield. I'll go to the Air Ministry for permission."

Emmy said nothing.

"I hope you'll come with me," Henry added. "It would be a great help. But of course, if you feel…"

Emmy turned to him and smiled. "Of course I'll come, darling," she said.

The following morning Henry went to his office and spent some time studying the documents found in Parker's rooms. The letter from Messrs. Pringle, Pringle, Pringle and Sprout told him no more than he already knew. Annie's letter was rather livelier:

> Lofty, you blithering idiot, what in hell's name do you think you're up to? It's bad enough for you to go muckraking, but it's a really lousy trick to drag poor little Blandish into it. I'm warning you, you nasty low-down tyke. Drop this nonsense now, or else…
> *Annie Meadowes*

Henry read it several times. A threatening letter? Surely not. This was the sort of affectionate abuse current between close friends or members of the same family. All the same, it was fairly clear that Annie knew more than she would say.

James Baggot's letter was also true to form. He was evidently more interested in the manuscript than he wished Lofty to realize. Henry had the impression that while making a bid to get it on the cheap he would have been prepared to go to quite a high price if pressed.

Lastly, Henry took a look at the questionnaire prepared by Lofty Parker and filled in by Sammy Smith, the only person, Henry reflected, who had done so.

The questionnaire was mimeographed inexpertly. It started with no superscription.

> Please answer the following questions in as much detail as possible and return to C. Parker, 86 Nisbet Road, Earl's Court, S.W.5.
>
> 1. When and where did you first meet Beau Guest?
> 2. What was your impression of him?
> 3. What are the dates of your service at Dymfield?
> 4. What was your job there?
> 5. Give as detailed an account as possible of the evening Beau died, including your own movements and those of other people, when you last saw Beau, etc.

Sammy Smith had not attempted to write his answers on the form. A piece of paper was pinned to the questionnaire, hand-written in a small, neat hand in a bright green ballpoint pen.

> I met Beau at R.A.F. Falconfield in 1941. I hated his guts, although on reflection this was probably Barbara's fault. My impression of the Guests was that I'd never met such a conceited, line-shooting, name-dropping, and generally bloodstained couple in my life. Soon after Guest's arrival I was grounded, owing to senility. I was awaiting posting to the Controllers' Training Course when he crashed. It would be quite untrue to say I was heartbroken about his accident. It

made me feel there was justice in the world after all. Sorry about it, Lofty old scout, but that's the truth.

Question 2: See above.

Question 3: November, 1942, till October, 1943. You surely remember that I was posted to Scotland the very day after Beau bought it.

Question 4: Controller, of course.

Question 5: Simple. I went on a 24-hour leave at lunchtime, but being in the vicinity I dropped into the Operations Room about 6 P.M. to see the fun. You were on duty with Blandish and Annie. Heard Blandish calling up Snowdrop three-two—hell, you know all this. You were there. It did strike me that Guest was failing to master the Tiffie. Has it struck you that he might have ditched out of sheer incompetence? The suicide story sounds to me like an attempt at glamorization on the part of Barbara. Or somebody. Can't think of anything else useful. Sammy.

P.S. If you want to know any more details of my 24-hour leave, my lips are sealed. I'm a respectably married man now.

P.P.S. Any chance of touching you for ten quid till next Friday?

Henry decided that it was time he met the Smiths. And today was Thursday. He put on his raincoat, and set off for Finchley.

CHAPTER THIRTEEN

HENRY WAS IN LUCK. The ugly little house was occupied once more. Windows were open, and from them pop music blared mechanically. In the next-door garden, Mrs. Tidmarsh was pinning shirts on a wash line. She nodded affably to Henry.

"They're back," she said, enunciating with difficulty through a mouthful of clothes pins. "*She's* in. *He's* at work. I told her you'd called." She took the pins out of her mouth, secured the last shirt with a vicious jab, and added, "I was right. Paris. Didn't I tell you?" With that, she picked up her empty wash basket and went indoors.

The pressure of Henry's finger on the front doorbell provoked an outburst of chimes which almost drowned the pop music. Almost at once an upstairs window opened and a voice called, "Who is it?"

Henry looked up. Leaning out of the window was a young woman of such eccentric appearance that for a moment Henry was completely taken aback. She was wearing a pink silk kimono, and her young, tough little face was heavily made-up. The extraordinary thing about her was her hair. She seemed to have a great deal of it, and it stood vertically on end, framing her face in a bright yellow sunburst. She looked exactly like the cover illustration of that frightening children's book, *Struwelpeter*. The quills upon the fretful porpentine had nothing on Mrs. Smith's coiffure; and, like the porpentine, she also seemed fretful.

"Who on earth are you and what do you want?" she demanded.

"Mrs. Smith?" Henry asked tentatively.

"Of course I'm Mrs. Smith. What do you want?"

"A word with you, if I may."

"If you're selling anything, we don't want it."

"I'm not selling anything," said Henry. Out of the corner of his eye he saw that Mrs. Tidmarsh had come out into the garden again with a fresh load of washing. He had no desire to broadcast his identity, either from his point of view or from the Smiths'.

"Well then, go away," said Mrs. Smith irritably. "Can't you see I'm doing my hair?"

"I called the other day," Henry went on, "but you were away. In Paris, I believe."

"Persistent, aren't you?" retorted the girl. A thought seemed to strike her. "If my husband owes you money, it's nothing to do with me. And ditto if you've been fool enough to buy one of his damned cars and now it doesn't work." With that she withdrew, slamming the window.

Henry sighed. Then he pressed the bell again. The chimes rang out. The window flew open.

"I told you to go away!"

"Mrs. Smith," said Henry, "I want to talk to you about the book my wife is writing. I believe she telephoned you."

"Oh, that! Why didn't you say so before, you silly man! Half a tick. I'll come down."

The curious fuzzy head disappeared. Mrs. Tidmarsh smiled with knowing satisfaction as she picked up her basket. She nodded to Henry and went indoors, just as Mrs. Smith opened the door to admit her visitor.

The house was furnished with cheerful vulgarity. In the small hallway Henry had to duck to avoid hitting his head on the chime of cowbells. On the table was a plastic tray ornamented with illustrated cocktail recipes and bearing a single letter. Through the cellophane window of the envelope, Henry could see that it was a bill addressed to S. Smith, Esq.

Mrs. Smith led the way into the living room. Here, two large felt dolls with simian faces and bouffant hair-dos reclined on the piano. A six-inch-long nude female torso in painted metal turned out to be a bottle-opener, and a jointed wooden monkey hung by one elongated arm from the picture rail.

Mrs. Smith said, "I do apologize. You've caught me at a bad moment. It'll take me a good twenty minutes to get it done."

"Get what done?"

"My hair, of course. Will you wait, or shall I bring my mirror down and get on with it while we talk?"

"Do, by all means," said Henry.

"I'd ask you up," said Mrs. Smith, "only Sammy's that jealous, I daren't. Specially with that old cat next door watching every move I make. Shan't be long. Sit down and pour yourself something cold."

She was back in a couple of minutes with an array of brushes and combs and a portable stand-up mirror. She sat down in front of it and said, "Right. Fire away," and began doing intricate things with a tail comb to the tousled mass of hair.

"I hear you're just back from Paris, Mrs. Smith."

"Yes." The comb flickered busily. "Call me Marlene, for heaven's sake. Yes, only got back this morning. Hence the hair-do. Lovely, it was!"

"And you left London on Saturday afternoon?"

"That's right. Caught the..." She stopped suddenly. "Here, what is all this anyway? I thought you'd come to talk about that book. The one about Sammy in the Air Force."

"I have," said Henry, "in a way."

"What do you mean? Aren't you that lady's husband—the one that telephoned?"

"I am, indeed," said Henry, "but as a matter of fact I'm here in a rather different capacity."

Marlene Smith sighed. She seemed not angry, but resigned. "I knew it," she said. "Which is it—selling or dunning? Whichever it is, you can get out." She did not look at Henry, but was entirely absorbed in transforming her cloud of hair into a towering edifice of which Madame de Pompadour would not have been ashamed. Henry would not have described himself as a fashion expert, but he did live in Chelsea. Even to his male eyes, this massive beehive was tinged with the tawdriness of a dying fad.

"I'm not selling *or* dunning, Mrs. Smith. I'm a policeman."

This did produce a reaction. A momentary freezing, a tiny pause in the combwork. Marlene's eyes never left the mirror. She said, "A policeman? How extraordinary. Whatever do you want? Has Sammy been parking in the wrong place again?"

"No, no. Nothing like that. Just a few questions—in connection with that book of my wife's, actually."

"Goodness. Some mystery about it, is there?"

"Not exactly a mystery," said Henry. "The man who was doing the actual writing had an accident on Saturday, and we're trying to check up on anybody who might have seen him."

"Well, you've come to the wrong place, haven't you? We were in Paris."

"But you didn't leave England until quite late, I believe?"

The comb flicked deftly. "Depends what you mean by late. Afternoon, it was."

"I believe you left here about noon, with a suitcase."

Marlene combed a lank wisp of hair into position over the wiglike cocoon. "Been talking to Mother Tidmarsh, have you? Yes, that's right. I left before lunch. Parked my case at Victoria and did some shopping."

"And what time did your plane leave?"

This time Marlene did look at him. The hair-do was finished, except for a few spiky strands which stood out behind each ear. "Who said anything about a plane? We went by train and boat."

"Can you remember when the train left, then, and what time you arrived?"

"I'm not sure of the exact time. Sammy said I had to be at Victoria by four. We got in at about—oh, I don't know. Late. We had a meal in a little café somewhere—don't ask me where, I haven't the foggiest. Lovely, it was. Veal, with a sort of sauce and mushrooms. Isn't it marvelous the food you can get in Paris, even in the middle of the night?"

"You can't remember what time it was?"

"What the hell does it matter? Must have been nearly midnight. Then Sammy took me to a little cellar place and we had brandy and danced. We didn't check in at the hotel till the wee, small hours." The last strands of hair were in place now, and Marlene was busy applying fixative from a spray. "Hotel Etoile, Place Colombe, if you're interested." She turned to look at Henry. "Are you?"

Henry grinned. "I'm interested in everything," he said.

Marlene gave him a long, speculative look. Now that her hair was done, she was ready for her part as the femme fatale. "I'm sure you are," she said, in a smoldering voice. And then, "Do you know, I've never met a detective before."

Henry felt that he ought to apologize for not ripping off the pink kimono and breathing hot passion down Marlene's neck while at the same time picking off a brace of concealed gunmen with his .32. Instead, he stood up and said, "Well, I think that's all, Mrs. Smith. Thank you very much. You've been very helpful."

"I could be even more helpful—perhaps..." Marlene, too, had risen and was standing facing him, resting her weight squarely on one foot and pushing the other thigh toward him. Her voice trickled out from between her half-closed lips.

Henry edged toward the door. "No, no. Please don't trouble, Mrs. Smith. I'll let myself out."

"You haven't told me," Marlene said, "what happened to the author guy. Was it a slight case of murder?"

Henry began to have fears about getting out alive. He said, "Nothing so dramatic, I'm afraid. An accident in his kitchen. Accidents in the home, you know, account for a greater number of deaths than…"

"You're taking one hell of an interest," said Marlene, "in a simple kitchen accident, aren't you? You see—I know your name."

"My name is Tibbett."

"Exactly. We shall meet again—Henry Tibbett."

By this time Marlene had swayed across to a small table where a carved wooden cigarette box began tinkling out *"Auprès de ma Blonde"* as she lifted the lid. She lit a cigarette and deliberately blew a cloud of aromatic smoke into Henry's face. He fled through the front door and did not breathe freely again until he was safely in the tube train which bore him toward the Euston Road.

Sammy Smith was not alone in the showroom when Henry reached Supercharged Motors. Through the plate-glass window, he could be seen engaged in earnest but inaudible conversation with a small man, who wore a neat dark suit and a thin but bristly mustache. Henry pushed open the swing door and went in.

"Now, Trimble, old man," Sammy was saying.

"Don't you Trimble me, nor old man me either," replied the small man with spirit. "I've told you before, Mr. Smith. Not another day do we wait. Not another day."

"Now, be reasonable, old sport. I was in Paris…"

"You haven't been in Paris ever since April," said the small man nastily. It was then that Sammy caught sight of Henry.

"Well, Trimble," he said, with obvious relief, "you must forgive me, but I see I have a customer to attend to. As for the other little matter, I hope to have news for you very soon."

"You'd better," said the small man. He slapped a diminutive bowler hat on to his head and marched out into the street.

Sammy watched him go with a rueful smile and a shake of the head. To Henry, he said, "Impatient—impatient like all these youngsters. He knows I can't guarantee delivery of a Panther Special 1928 in a matter of weeks, but..." He shrugged, and changed gears vocally. "And now, sir, what can I do for *you?* I see you're admiring my girls. That's what I call them. Every one a beauty. Believe it or not, sir, I refuse to sell these cars unless I'm satisfied they're going to good homes. Like horses. It's not good business, I suppose, but then, I'm a sentimentalist." He shot a rapid, shrewd glance at Henry. "Were you interested in any particular model, sir?"

"No, not really," said Henry. "You *are* Mr. Smith, I take it."

"I am."

"Good. Then perhaps we can have a quiet talk somewhere. I am Chief Inspector Henry Tibbett."

Henry pulled out his official card.

Sammy looked at it, and then said, "Why, you're Blandish's husband!"

"That's right," said Henry, slightly irritated. "But this isn't a social call."

"How very alarming," said Sammy, but he did not sound alarmed. He adjusted the carnation in his buttonhole. "Shall we go into the office?"

The office was a dingy room at the back, full of motoring magazines, accessory catalogues, and bills. Sammy sat down at the untidy desk, motioned Henry to a seat, lit a cigar, and then said, "Now, what's it all about?"

"I understand," said Henry, "that you've just come back from Paris."

"Correct. This morning. A most successful trip. We do a lot of business on the Continent, you know."

"And you left here on Saturday afternoon by train?"

"Certainly I did. You don't catch me flying unless I have to, old man. Had quite enough of that during the war. Downright dangerous, if you ask me. But where is all this leading, if you don't mind me asking?"

"Since you've been away," said Henry, "you may not know that Lofty Parker is dead."

"Dead?" Smith was bewildered. "But he was working on this book about Guest. Goodness me, I—I wrote to him only last week. He can't be dead. Was it an accident?"

"I don't think so. There was a suggestion of suicide."

"Well, this is a blow." Indeed, Sammy looked shaken. "A great blow. He was always an unstable type, of course. Artistic," he added, as if that fact would account for any eccentricity.

"When did you last see Parker, Mr. Smith?" Henry asked.

"Last see him? Good lord, what a question. No, wait. I can tell you. October 14, 1943, the day I was posted away from Dymfield. I hadn't given the fellow a thought in years until your charming wife turned up the other day and told me about this book. She left a questionnaire thing with me. That's why I wrote to him, to return it."

"I know," said Henry. "We found it in his room."

"When did all this happen?" Smith asked. "I mean, Blandish seemed bright-eyed and bushy-tailed when she was here last week..."

"It happened on Saturday night," said Henry, "sometime after nine o'clock. That's why I'm just checking up on who might have seen him..."

"I see. Bit of luck for me, then. What you might call the perfect alibi. At nine o'clock, I was on a train hurtling across northern France."

"Just for the record," said Henry, "when did you get to Paris and where did you stay?"

"We got there for a late dinner. Then we went to a night club. It must have been pretty late when we got to the hotel, the Etoile in the Place Colombe—nearer three than two, I'd have thought. The night porter might remember more accurately."

"Well, that seems to be that," said Henry. "By the way, what did you think of the idea of writing a book about Beau Guest?"

Sammy shrugged. "None of my business, old man. What'll happen to it now?"

"Nothing. The project is off. Emmy's letter explained that, surely."

"Letter? What letter?"

"I'm surprised you haven't received it."

"I couldn't have, old man. Haven't been home. Came straight here from the train this morning. So it's all off, is it? A wise move I'd say. Start digging into the dead past—and what happens?"

"Sometimes," said Henry, "one finds where the body is buried."

Sammy looked startled. "What on earth do you mean by that?"

"Oh, nothing. Purely metaphorical."

At this Sammy laughed. "Hm. Yes. I'd take a small bet that the metaphorical body in this case belongs to Barbara Guest. Not that she was ever my type. I like 'em a bit more curvaceous."

"Which reminds me," said Henry, "I met your charming wife this morning."

"My wife? You mean, you went out to Finchley?"

"Yes. I hope you don't mind."

"Bit of a liberty, wasn't it, old man? You might have asked my permission first. How do I know what you and Marlene got up to?" He sounded worried, and—remembering Marlene—Henry was not surprised.

"I assure you," he said, "it was perfectly blameless. Mrs. Smith was entirely absorbed in creating a really remarkable hair-do."

"God, these women!" said Smith. His good humor seemed to have returned. "Do you know, old man, she spends at least an hour a day working on that edifice. It's all very well when it's done, but in the early stages...!"

Henry laughed. "I know. I'm afraid I arrived at a crucial moment this morning. She looked just like Johnny Head-in-Air."

It was a perfectly genuine slip of the tongue. Thinking of Shockheaded Peter, Henry had inadvertently named another character from that sinister volume. He was therefore considerably taken aback to see the effect that his innocent remark had on Sammy Smith. The older man went as white as a sheet. Then, in a flinty voice, he said, "What do you know about Johnny Head-in-Air?"

Henry was in the dark, but it was too good an opening to miss. He said, "I know a certain amount. And I shall find out more."

"Really? From whom?"

"From Annie," said Henry, backing his hunch that Mrs. Meadowes had been less than frank.

It seemed that his guess had not been right, however, for Smith relaxed visibly. "You can ask her, of course," he said, "but I doubt if you'll get much joy. It's none of my business, of course. None at all. But if you'll take a word of advice from an old pal of Emmy's, let it drop, old man. Just let it drop, eh?"

Outside the showroom Henry slipped into a phone booth and contacted his office with a couple of queries. He then repaired to his favorite pub for a late lunch.

By the time he got back to Scotland Yard the answers were on his desk. The first report assured him that no airline had any record of a Mr. and Mrs. Smith flying to Paris on Saturday afternoon or evening. A Mrs. Smith, alone, had traveled on the 2.15 P.M. plane, a Miss Smith had caught the 4.50, while no less than three separate Mr. Smiths had booked on the 5.30, 7.15, and 11.59 flights. It was, of course, impossible to check on individual rail-and-boat travelers, but the Hotel Etoile had confirmed the Smiths' visit. They had most certainly been in Paris, and had arrived there by train. Henry felt the depression that always accompanied an exploded theory.

The second report, however, cheered him up a little, for at least it gave him a lead. It stated that, in accordance with his request, a check had been made on telephone calls outgoing from the number of Supercharged Motors that day. Most of them were local calls of no significance; but, within five minutes of Henry's leaving the showroom, a call had been put through to Whitchurch.

CHAPTER FOURTEEN

THE AIR MINISTRY had been puzzled, but cooperative. Certainly, said the Squadron Leader who had finally agreed that Henry's request was "his pigeon," certainly the Chief Inspector might visit what was left of Dymfield. But he doubted if there'd be much to see. Just a few broken-down buildings and overgrown runways—most of the airfield had been handed back as agricultural land. The Officers' Mess had disappeared altogether, of course. As for the Operations Block—yes, it was still there, on Care and Maintenance. It was used for occasional training courses. The Squadron Leader agreed to provide Henry with a junior officer, armed with the necessary authority and keys, to act as a guide; he was also happy that Emmy and Detective-Sergeant Reynolds should complete the party.

So it was that the four of them set out from London on Friday morning, a bright, shiny day. The countryside was looking new-washed after the rain, and the pale blue sky was scudding with small white clouds. Henry drove the police car himself, with the Sergeant sitting stiffly beside him. In the back Emmy tried to make conversation with the young officer, who had introduced himself as Pilot Officer Simmonds.

He looked, Emmy thought, far too young to be in uniform at all, let alone to hold a commission. He couldn't be more than nineteen. Then she remembered that at the same age she had held an equivalent rank and rather more responsibility. Suddenly she laughed aloud. Pilot Officer Simmonds looked startled.

"I'm so sorry," said Emmy. "I was thinking."

"Oh, yes?" said Simmonds politely.

"I was thinking that one doesn't really grow older; it's just that other people grow younger."

"Oh, really?" Simmonds was definitely alarmed now.

"You haven't an idea what I'm talking about," said Emmy. "But just you wait for twenty years or so."

"Er—yes, Mrs. Tibbett. I'll do that."

The conversation languished. Emmy had gathered that Simmonds had recently completed his flying training course and was temporarily at Air Ministry waiting for a posting, which he hoped would be overseas. He showed a most correct reluctance to talk about the new aircraft on which he had trained, and an amused tolerance when Emmy mentioned the antiquated models of her own epoch. It was like chatting to a jet pilot about one's experiences in a Tiger Moth. She gave up.

The Dymfield operational site looked extraordinarily unchanged. The buildings were shabbier, of course, and to Emmy's eyes had suffered the inevitable shrinkage of places revisited; but the Guardroom was still there, and the grass and concrete mounds with their heavy metal doors looked the same as ever—to an outsider, bleak and forbidding, leading to underground caverns of concrete; but to Emmy, warmly welcoming and secure, her own remembered domain.

Simmonds produced a key and unlocked the main gate into the compound. Emmy ran ahead and arrived at the door of the Operations Room. There she paused, with her hand on the big iron handle, and listened to the footsteps coming up the concrete path behind her—and the years fell away.

"Hey, Blandish!"

"What...? Oh, yes sir."

"Less of the 'sir' from you. There's nobody listening, idiot."

"It's not that; it's a question of discipline, Beau. All the other junior officers have to…"

"To hell with the other junior officers. Going on duty, are you?"

"Yes."

"You're early. It's only ten to two."

"I know. But I didn't want to be late. After all, it's a very special afternoon, isn't it?"

"I'm glad you're going to be on duty, Emmy. I'll be in safe hands."

"Don't be silly. You won't need any help."

"You really believe that, don't you?"

"Of course I do."

"I was—I was hoping to catch you. To say 'good-bye.'"

"Good-bye? Whatever do you mean?"

"I'm going to—that is, I've put in for leave. Starting tomorrow. Barbara is—oh—you know how she is. So I've arranged a surprise for her. Three weeks in Scotland."

"But Beau, there's the tennis match next week and—why didn't you tell us you were going away?"

"Didn't know myself. Spur of the moment, half an hour ago. As a matter of fact—can you keep a secret, Blandish?"

"You know I can."

"Well, then, try this one for size. I'm not coming back to Dymfield. I've applied for a posting."

"A—posting…?"

"I think you know why, don't you?"

"No, I don't. I don't."

"Well, think it out…"

"Beau."

"What is it?"

"You've never given me my photograph, the tennis team one."

"I haven't got it. Lofty gave it to Annie to sign and she's to pass it on to me, but she hasn't yet."

"So I'll never get it now."

"Of course you will, idiot."

"But not with your signature…"

"Well, don't look so tragic. You can send it to me at my new station and I'll sign it for you. Okay?"

"I suppose so."

"Well, don't just stand there, woman. Go on in. It's five to two."

"Beau, are you sure you're all right?"

"Of course I'm all right. Steady as a rock."

"Be careful this evening. Please be careful."

"I'll be careful, all right. D'you think I want to break my neck?"

"I must go now. Good-bye, Beau."

"Good-bye, Blandish."

"Here we are then, Mrs. Tibbett. This is the Operations Room entrance, isn't it? Let's see, Operations Room—this is the key…" There was a click as the key turned, and then Pilot Officer Simmonds pushed open the black door. "Better let me go first."

"No, I'll go," said Emmy. "I know where to find the light switches."

"Be careful, Mrs. Tibbett! There's a steep flight of steps…"

"I know."

Slowly, Emmy went down the familiar concrete steps in the darkness. Automatically, her hand reached out to the panel of light switches. As the lights came on, the three men came clattering down behind her. The young Pilot Officer was whistling the latest pop hit, and the Detective Sergeant remarked that it smelt a bit musty down here. Emmy turned to her left, and walked down a short corridor, through a heavy soundproof door, and into the Operations Room.

It was like coming into an empty theater. The central area of the large underground room was flooded with light. Here, more than six feet below the glassed-in gallery where Emmy stood, the big map-topped table filled the semicircular space. A section of the eastern coastline of England was boldly drawn and the whole surface squared like graph paper for grid reference. Red and blue arrows—relics of the last training operation—showed the tracks of nonexistent aircraft approaching the coast. Around the table lay the paraphernalia of the plotters—the telephone headsets, the boxes of colored arrows, the sticks, like billiard cues, for pushing the arrows into position out of arm's reach.

Henry came into the gallery and stood beside Emmy in the dimness, looking down on the floodlit table. It took very little imagination to people the room with young figures in pale blue battle dress, and to visualize the red arrows as the actual paths of Heinkels or Dorniers and the outgoing blue tracks as the courses of defending Typhoons.

Henry put his arm around Emmy. He could feel that she was shivering.

"That's the plotting table," she said, unnecessarily. "We worked up here. It was always dark up here on the gallery, so that we could see the table more clearly."

"Dismal old holes, these, aren't they?" said Simmonds. "And what with steam radar, and horse-drawn aircraft—it's a wonder to me they did as well as they did."

Emmy was nettled. "A certain amount of skill entered into it, you know," she said. She was pleased to find that the spurt of irritation improved her morale.

"Oh, yes, Mrs. Tibbett. Of course."

Young Simmonds had gone very pink, and Emmy realized that she must have spoken more sharply than she had intended. She also realized, with a pang, how old and awe-inspiring she must appear to this boy.

Henry made a painstakingly thorough investigation of the Operations Room. He questioned Simmonds about old records and was not surprised to hear that they had long since been destroyed. He also learned that there was no permanent staff at Dymfield.

"Well," he said at last, "I don't know what it was that Lofty hoped to find here, except atmosphere." He turned to Emmy. "Just one thing. Could you show me, on the table here, the approximate course of Guest's aircraft?"

Emmy picked up a plotter's rod. "Radar picked him up here." She indicated a spot about ten miles to the northwest of Dymfield. "He was circling, gaining height. At about angels fifteen, fifteen thousand feet, he stopped stooging about and set a course on zero-nine-zero which is due east—heading for the coast." The rod moved over the enormous map. "That's when I called him up and got his answer. He came out over the sea in a wide loop, something like this..." The rod traced a circle, which crossed the coast, then turned northward, and finally came inland again. "I couldn't make out what he was doing. And he wouldn't answer my radio calls. Then he turned east again, about here..." The rod hovered just inland, some fifteen miles north of Dymfield. "That was when we got the 'Tally-ho' call. Then, due east, losing height all the way. We lost him about here..." She marked a point about twenty-five miles out to sea. "The radar stations couldn't get him any longer, because he'd gotten too low by then. He must have gone into the water about here." The rod touched a spot a few miles farther on. "Not so far off the Dutch coast."

"And nothing was ever found?"

"Not that I know of. Some bits of wreckage were washed up, I believe, but nothing identifiable. There were quite a few wrecked aircraft strewn around in the sea in those days."

"Supposing the aircraft had come right down, almost to sea level, and then carried on toward Holland? Would it have looked any different on your table?"

"Well—no. But it would never have survived over the other side. The German guns would have gotten it." Emmy paused and then said, "You've been talking to Annie, haven't you?"

"I'm only trying to consider all the possibilities," said Henry.

"But we all know what happened…"

Henry looked across to the other side of the gallery where Pilot Officer Simmonds was giving an elementary lecture on radar to a fascinated Sergeant Reynolds. Then he said, "I'm afraid, darling, that you'll have to face the fact that the official explanation is pretty unsatisfactory. And don't forget that Lofty was murdered."

Emmy nodded. "I'm not really frightened," she said, "but I do wish I understood."

"So do I," said Henry.

When they were out in the pale sunshine again, Emmy said to Henry, "Sammy was perfectly right. I can't wait to get to the local pub and have a stiff drink."

"Right," said Henry. "We'll have lunch now and come back to look at the rest of Dymfield afterward. Where's the best place to go?"

Emmy considered. "We always used the Duke's Head in Dymfield village. Heaven knows what it's like now. It used to be excellent."

The pub turned out to be as good as Emmy had remembered, even though the landlord she had known had left some years before. The thatched and half-timbered exterior had not changed for three hundred years, nor had the oak-beamed bar parlor. The parking lot had recently been enlarged and a splendid rotary grill installed in the dining room, but the bitter beer tasted the same as ever.

After lunch Henry looked at his watch and said, "We'd better be off soon." He gave Emmy a meaning look, which she interpreted correctly as a hint to go and powder her nose.

When she came back the three men were standing near the door, chatting and laughing. There was a moment of silence as they saw Emmy.

Then Henry said, "I was just thinking, darling. You don't really want to spend the afternoon hanging around a drafty airfield, do you? Why don't you stay here and have another cup of coffee. We won't be very long."

"Hey, what is this?" Emmy demanded, laughing. "Did I disgrace myself this morning? Or are you three up to something?"

"Of course not," said Henry. "It's just that I don't think it will interest you..."

Emmy was about to insist on going with them, when she checked herself. She knew Henry so well, and was so accustomed to cooperating with him, that in normal circumstances she would have appreciated instantly that he wanted her to stay at the Duke's Head for some good reason which he could not at the moment explain. With a jerk she realized that this was not a sentimental journey for Emmy Blandish, but a murder investigation for Henry Tibbett. She said, "No, you're quite right. And I think it's clouding over. I'll stay here."

Sitting on the chintzy window seat and watching the car drive off toward Dymfield, Emmy felt desolate. At first she put it down to a rather childish sense of being unwanted, but after a minute or so she pinned down the unpleasant sensation and identified it for what it was. It was fear.

She shook herself. This was ridiculous. Soon Henry and the others would be back. She tried not to think about the hints Henry had dropped concerning her own safety; but little stabbing tremors kept rising in her mind, like water snakes breaking the surface of a dark pool. She was quite alone. The hotel seemed deserted.

Then she heard the whisper of tires on the gravel of the parking lot. The car itself was out of her range of vision, but she heard the engine being switched off, the bang of a slammed door, and footsteps. In her state of nervousness these simple sounds took on a sinister significance; and as the heavy footsteps crunched nearer and nearer, she felt herself going rigid with fright. And then she laughed aloud with relief, for around the corner of the house came the familiar beanpole figure of Hildegard St. Vere Prendergast. She threw open the window and called, "Hey! Vere!"

"Good lord. What on earth are you doing here, Emmy?"

"Having lunch. At least, I was. Come and cheer me up. I've been abandoned by my husband and I'm horribly bored."

Vere came in, stooping low to avoid cracking his head on the beam over the doorway. He greeted Emmy, rang the service bell, and said, "So Henry's not with you?"

A sour-faced waitress appeared, obviously far from pleased at being summoned. Her expression lightened, however, when she saw Vere.

"Oh, good afternoon, Mr. Prendergast. I didn't realize it was you." She gave Emmy a speculative look. "How's Mrs. Prendergast, then?" she went on pointedly.

"Fine thanks, Dora. She's in London today. Now, be a sport and get us a drink."

Dora glanced at the clock. "Fred's just shutting up the bar, but I dare say I could get something for *you*, Mr. Prendergast."

"Good show," said Vere. "What's it to be, Emmy?"

"Oh, just coffee for me, thanks."

"Coffee's off," said Dora with satisfaction.

"Then a cup of tea..."

"Tea's not started yet."

Vere laughed. "You see? Alcohol or nothing. Have a brandy."

"Oh, all right."

"Two large brandies, Dora my love." He watched the waitress as she disappeared into the bar, and then said, "Po-faced old biddy. Have to butter her up a bit or we'd never get a drink in this place."

"It's funny to think this is still one of your locals."

"I'd hardly call it that. We come here quite a lot in the summer... So Henry's not with you, eh? Where is he?"

For a moment Emmy hesitated. Then she said, "As a matter of fact, he's at Dymfield. The airfield, I mean."

Vere did not appear surprised. He nodded and said, "Pity. I must just have missed him. On his own, is he?"

"Two brandies, eight and sixpence if you please, Mr. Prendergast." Dora had reappeared with a small tray, which she put down on the table noisily.

Vere put some coins on the tray, raised his glass, and said, "Down the hatch!" And then, "What's he doing at Dymfield? Nothing left of it now. I think you said he was on his own."

"No, he's got a Sergeant with him—and a rather touching little Pilot Officer from Air Ministry."

"Touching?"

"Well—he's a bit like you were twenty-five years ago, Vere," said Emmy smiling.

For a few minutes they chatted in a desultory way. Then Vere drained his glass and said, "This is a pretty dim sort of hostelry, if you ask me. Why don't we go back to the old ancestral heap?"

"To Whitchurch Manor?"

"Where else? Barbara is in town for the day. Will you come into my parlor, Blandish?" Vere leered at her and twirled his mustache.

Emmy laughed. "I wish I could," she said, "but Henry will be calling for me here at any moment."

"Don't worry," said Vere. "I will leave a message with the dreaded Dora, or her deputy. I presume Henry has transport."

"Oh, yes. A police car."

"Then he can instruct it to drop him off at Whitchurch for a snort and then proceed to London with the odd bods."

"And how do Henry and I get home?"

"Simple. I drive you. Barbara is attending some grisly committee meeting, and will be overjoyed to see us all when it's over. We might have a spot of dinner somewhere, all four of us. Well? Any questions?"

"No, sir."

"Right. Go and get your coat while I brief Dora."

Emmy stood up. "Gosh, Vere," she said, "I *am* glad you turned up."

"Yes," said Vere. "Yes, it was a bit of luck, wasn't it?"

❀ ❀ ❀

The wind cut an icy swath through the sunshine of the deserted airfield, and Henry shivered.

"I don't know what you want to see here, sir," said Simmonds. "Nothing left, except a few old hangars."

Henry rubbed the back of his neck with his left hand. Diffidently, he said, "It's just a hunch of mine. I wanted to look at..."

"Hey! You over there!"

Henry and the others turned. The main gate of the airfield was swinging open, its rusty padlock having yielded reluctantly to Simmonds's key, and through it now came a strange, scarecrow figure gesticulating with a ragged umbrella.

"You! Yes—you in the uniform! Come here, boy!" The umbrella waved menacingly as the harsh voice came ringing down the wind.

Simmonds sighed. "Some local maniac, I'm afraid," he said to Henry. "I'd better go and send him packing."

"You may find that difficult," said Henry.

"You know him, sir?"

"I'm afraid so. He's Squadron Leader Guest's father."

"Squadron Leader who?"

"Beau Guest."

"I thought that was a book or something."

"It is," said Henry, "but that's beside the point. You'd better leave this to me."

By now the Reverend Sidney had reached them, and he stood for a moment panting for breath but indicating clearly with his umbrella that he wished to be the first to speak. The umbrella traced a wavering, circular movement embracing the whole group, but finally came to rest, its ferrule pointed fair and square at Henry's stomach.

"You! Tibbett! What are you doing here?"

"Taking a look around," said Henry blandly. "May I introduce Mr. Guest—Pilot Officer Simmonds, Sergeant Reynolds."

"Humph," said the Reverend Sidney. "You're in the Air Force, young man," he added belligerently to Simmonds.

"That's right, sir."

"Then you've no right to encourage this tomfoolery. This airfield has been closed for years. No admittance to the public. Says so." The umbrella waved in the direction of the battered notice at the gate.

"We are not the public, Mr. Guest," said Henry.

"You're not in the Air Force, so don't try to pretend you are," replied the old man triumphantly, as though making an unbeatable point.

Simmonds said, "There's only one person here who is unauthorized and that is you, Mr. Guest." He spoke firmly, and suddenly looked very much older than nineteen. "This is Air Ministry property, and for the time being I am responsible for it. You will kindly leave at once."

Beneath the shabby wind-whipped raincoat, the old shoulders sagged. The voice quavered. "Of course, I'm only an old man. That means nothing to the young—why should it? Throw them on the scrapheap; they've outlived their usefulness. Shout at them; they're too feeble to answer back..."

Simmonds was a well-brought-up young man. He reacted at once, as planned. "Please don't misunderstand me, sir." He had gone very pink and now looked not a day over fifteen. "I didn't mean to imply..."

"If my son had been here..." added the Reverend Sidney, driving home his advantage.

Henry felt thankful that he was in his forties and therefore too old to be subject to this sort of intimidation. "Yes, Mr. Guest," he said, "go on. What about your son?"

"Well, what about him?"

"How much do you know?"

"Know? What about? I don't know anything."

"About Johnny Head-in-Air," said Henry. "And Johnny Under Ground."

Embarrassingly, the old man began to weep; but whether from grief or rage, it was impossible to say. "As if things weren't bad enough, what with the stories, and the hospital—and the money—and people coming to the door—asking questions. Telephoning. Writing. No peace…"

Suddenly things became clearer in Henry's mind. "You've only just found out, haven't you?"

"Writing—telephoning…"

"Where is he?"

"All I ever asked for was a little peace…"

"Where is he?"

The Reverend Sidney did not reply. He turned and ran away from them toward the gate, his raincoat flapping like the wings of a bedraggled crow. But as he ran, his black umbrella seemed to wave despairingly in the direction of the disused air-raid shelters.

Henry watched him go. Then he said, "Right, Sergeant. Get the shovels from the car, will you?" He turned to Simmonds, who was looking completely bewildered. "Sorry about that. This is an unusual business, to say the least of it. Tell me, how does one get into those air-raid shelters? Are they locked?"

Simmonds seemed to pull himself together with an effort. "Air-raid shelters?" he repeated. "I've no keys for them. I imagine you just walk in, unless the entrances are bunged up with rubble."

"I expect they are," said Henry. "That's why I brought the shovels. Let's go and look."

As they walked, leaning into the wind, Simmonds said, "What a weird old boy. Is he mad, do you think?"

"Yes, slightly."

"You said he was the father of a squadron leader."

"That's right."

"Well, the old boy must be eighty if he's a day, so his son must be pretty senior by now. Where is he, do you know?"

"I think," said Henry, "that we shall find him in one of those air-raid shelters."

What they found was a skeleton. It was dressed in the uniform of a squadron leader, and the rotted remnants of medal ribbons still clung to the cloth. The jaw was sufficiently well-preserved to make dental identification possible, but it seemed hardly necessary. Beside the right hand, a rusted service revolver lay on the concrete floor, and the skull had been shattered by a bullet which had passed through it to lodge in the wall behind. There was nothing else in the shelter except an empty whisky bottle.

CHAPTER FIFTEEN

O F COURSE, THE FORMALITIES took time. Leaving Sergeant Reynolds guarding the air-raid shelter and Pilot Officer Simmonds, looking rather green, pacing the road outside, Henry drove to Dymfield Police Station. From there, he contacted the local Police Headquarters, and after some lengthy confabulations between the Chief Constable and his senior officers, it was agreed that the local force should send their experts to Dymfield, but that Henry should remain in charge of the investigation. It was after half-past three before all was arranged and Henry was free to go back to the Duke's Head to look for Emmy.

He pulled up in the forecourt, still undecided what or how much he should say to her. He would only be able to stay a few minutes, for he was on his way back to the airfield to meet the team of experts. At least he was thankful that he had managed to dissuade her from coming with them.

The doors of the public and saloon bars were firmly locked, and neither knocking nor ringing produced any sign of life. The place seemed deserted. Then he went around to the back of the pub. Here, things were more hopeful. The kitchen door was open and a youth in a dirty apron was walking across the yard with a bucketful of potato peelings.

"Excuse me," said Henry. "I'm looking for my wife."

The youth gazed at him expressionlessly.

"My wife. The lady who lunched here. She's waiting for me inside."

"Ar," said the youth. After a long pause, he added, "I ain't seen no lady."

"Well, perhaps you could inquire..."

Moving slowly, the youth took the lid off a dustbin and dumped the peelings into it. Then he wiped his hands on his apron, turned his back on Henry, and went into the kitchen.

Annoyed, Henry followed him, only to find that he had misjudged him. Here was a strong, silent young man, who did not believe in wasting words. In fact he said only one.

"Daw—ra!" he bellowed, directing the volume of sound through the serving hatch which communicated with the rest of the building.

From far away came an answering shriek. The youth jerked his head in the direction of the sound, as though to indicate that help was at hand, and went out into the yard again. A few moments later Dora appeared.

"What is it now?" she demanded. And then, seeing Henry, "Who are you? Where's Perce?"

"I'm sorry to bother you," said Henry, "but I'm looking for my wife."

"Well, you can see for yourself that she's not here."

"She was supposed to be waiting for me. We lunched here, and then..."

"Oh, *her*. She's gone."

"Gone?"

"With Mr. Prendergast. In his car. Best part of an hour ago."

"Didn't she leave a message for me?"

"Not that I know of. She might have left one with Fred in the bar."

"Well, could you...?"

"Only he's off duty now. Gone to Ipswich."

"Perhaps Fred might have written it down?" Henry suggested.

"I'll look if you like," said Dora, in the tone of one who is put upon. She disappeared into the house again, and a minute later was back with a piece of paper in her hand.

"Who'd have thought it?" she said. "Here it is. Are you Mr. Rabbit?"

"Tibbett."

"Rabbit, it says here."

"It comes to the same thing," said Henry.

"Well," Dora said doubtfully, "it says to tell Mr. Rabbit that Mr. P. and the lady has gone, and he's to send a sergeant and take the car up to London."

"To do what?"

"That's what it says. Look for yourself, if you don't believe me."

"Is that all it says?"

"Wait a minute. There's something else. Mr. P. will drive lady to London."

"That's not much help," said Henry.

"Well, it's not my fault, is it?" said Dora aggressively. She thrust the paper into his hand. "Here's your message. You'd best take it and go. Can't you see we're busy?"

"I wonder if I might use your telephone?"

"No, you can't," said Dora flatly. "Mrs. Bramble has the public one—at the post office. Three doors down on your left."

Mrs. Bramble was a delightful old lady in a beige knitted cardigan, and she made up in kindliness what she lacked in efficiency. The post office was but one department of her tiny shop, and Henry had to wait while a small girl was served with bulls' eyes and admonished for being out in this weather without woolen stockings. Mrs. Bramble then gave her attention to Henry, and took little more than five minutes to find the local telephone directory. She refused to surrender it to Henry, but insisted on looking up Vere's number for him.

"No trouble at all, sir—it's what we're paid for, after all, isn't it? Now, where did I put my glasses...? I know I had them. Ah—here they are. Now, let's see. Whitehaven, you said?"

"Whitchurch."

"Ah, yes. A lovely village, Whitchurch. My married daughter lives not five miles from there, at Snettle... Whitchurch—Whitchurch," added Mrs. Bramble, flipping slowly through the volume marked A to M.

"It'll be under W," said Henry. He was getting a little desperate. "If you'd just let me—"

"No, no, sir. No trouble at all. We're here to give the public service, that's what I always say. Whitchurch—Whitchurch—well, bless my soul, I do believe this is the wrong book. A to M. Yes, just as I told you. Wrong book... This'll be the one. Whitchurch—Postlethwaite, the name was, wasn't it?"

Between them, they found the number in the end, and Mrs. Bramble dialed it. There was no reply. It was a much easier and shorter process to make contact with Henry's Chelsea home, but there was no reply from there either. Henry glanced at his watch. It was now half-past four. The doctors and photographers would be arriving. He simply had to get back to the airfield. There was only one thing for it.

"Can you get me Whitehall 1212?" he asked Mrs. Bramble.

She raised her eyebrows so high that her spectacles fell off. "One-two-one-two? But that's Scotland Yard. As they always say on the radio. Will anybody who saw the accident ring Scotland Yard, Whitehall one..."

"I know it's Scotland Yard," said Henry. "I want to ring it."

"Have you seen an accident, then? I wouldn't be surprised. Terrible it is, the speed these cars go nowadays. But we haven't had an accident here, not in a long time. Nice and quiet it is, now, ever since the Air Force left. Fine, brave boys," she added, a little hastily, "but I won't say we were sorry to see them go, because we weren't. Do you know, there was one that used to go into the Duke's Head and when he'd had a bit too much, he'd begin eating electric light bulbs! Just sit there, crunching them. Well, we don't want that sort of thing back again, do we?"

"Please," said Henry, "will you get me Whitehall 1212?"

"Well," said Mrs. Bramble, doubtfully, "I suppose you know what you're doing..." She began to dial.

Henry gave the extension number of his office and was delighted that it was answered by a friend and colleague. "Oh, Bert," he said, "this is Henry. Look, if Emmy rings, will you tell her I've been delayed but that I'll see her at home this evening... No, no... Everything's fine... Thanks a lot, Bert. 'Bye."

He rang off, and said to Mrs. Bramble, "How much do I owe you?"

"You weren't reporting no accident."

"How much...?"

"Nor burglary neither."

"If I could just..."

"Are you sure it wasn't a wrong number?"

"Look, I'm in a great hurry, Mrs. Bramble..."

"Two and a penny."

Henry put half-a-crown down on the counter and fled.

The airfield was the scene of considerable activity by the time that Henry returned. Several police cars and an ambulance were grouped around the air-raid shelter, and men in dark uniforms moved quietly but importantly between them. Henry was just turning his car into the gate when he noticed a gaunt figure, some way down the road, standing peering through the wire fencing of the airfield.

Taking a quick decision, Henry reversed the car out of the gateway and drove on down the road. He pulled up just behind the Reverend Sidney, but the latter was so intent on watching the airfield that he did not notice. Henry got out and walked over the grass to him.

"Good afternoon again, sir," he said.

Guest jumped. "Oh, it's you. Gave me a fright."

"I'm sorry."

"What's going on in there?"

"Don't you know?"

The Reverend Sidney sighed. "Nobody will tell me anything," he said. "But I presume that they have found Alan."

"Yes," said Henry, and waited.

The old man's next words surprised him. "The disgrace!" said the Reverend Sidney angrily. He turned to Henry. "It was bad enough before, but there was supposed to have been something noble about the ridiculous gesture. I never considered it so, of course. I knew Alan, *and* his mother. However, it was hardly for me to say. Don't you agree?"

"Of course," said Henry cautiously.

"Well now," the Reverend Sidney went on, "you're in some sort of position of authority, I gather—as far as I can gather anything. I have never known such deliberate obstruction. That young whippersnapper of a constable on the gate refused to let me in. Me, the boy's own father! There's my unfortunate son, lying in there with a bullet through his head, and..."

"We don't know for certain that it is your son."

"Of course you do. *I* know."

"How long have you known?"

The umbrella waved vaguely. "Oh, some time. Some time."

"I don't think," said Henry, "that you knew until very recently. Yesterday, or even perhaps today. After all, you are a conscientious citizen, and I am sure that you would have reported..."

The Reverend Sidney drew himself up with tattered dignity. "Anonymous letters and telephone calls," he said, "are beneath contempt. I would not accord their perpetrator the satisfaction of knowing that I had bothered to report them to the authorities."

"What you mean is," said Henry, "that you didn't really believe what you were told, but you came along this afternoon just in case—and there we were..."

"And very late, too," remarked Guest snappishly. "I'd have you know, sir, that I was hanging around this Godforsaken place all the morning. I might easily have caught a chill. In fact, I am not sure that I am not running a temperature at this moment."

"I hope you have preserved the anonymous letters."

"Letter. There was only one. I burned it at once."

"That's unfortunate. Can you remember what it said?"

"The usual thing. Words clipped out of newspapers and pasted on paper. It started with a piece of doggerel about Johnny Head-in-Air, whom I always imagined to be a character from a children's rhyme. It then went on to tell me that my son had not died a hero's death but had taken the coward's way out by shooting himself in an air-raid shelter at Dymfield while intoxicated. That the police—which I presume means you—suspected this and were coming today to look for him; and that, if he were found, a most unpleasant scandal would result." The umbrella made an ineffectual movement. "I dared not ignore it. I came here—risking a nasty go of bronchitis—and when you came, I did my best to stop you. I was not successful. I suppose it is now too late to appeal to your better nature? That is to say, does this matter have to be made public? Country people are very uncharitable, you know. There are—certain things, which I prefer to keep to myself. The spotlight of publicity at this stage would be intolerable—intolerable…"

"And the telephone call?" said Henry. He was determined not to be moved to pity by the sagging shoulders and quaver in the voice.

"That came this morning, just after the letter arrived. In case it had missed the mail, I suppose. Urging me to be sure to come along and stop you. Though how she thought I…"

"She?"

"Oh, yes. It was a woman, all right."

"Did you recognize the voice?"

"Of course not. 'I just rang to remind you,' she said, or words to that effect. 'Go to Dymfield and get rid of the police or you'll regret it.' I said, 'Speak up, can't you?' And she repeated it, louder. Then I said, 'Who's speaking?' But she'd hung up by then."

"Was it an educated voice?" Henry asked.

"She didn't drop her aitches, if that's what you mean," replied the Reverend Sidney tartly. "As to the extent or efficacy of her education, I am hardly qualified to judge. I wish you young men would use the English language with some semblance of accuracy."

"I'm sorry," said Henry. "I was really inquiring about the aitches. I agree that 'educated' isn't the right word, but..."

"Mealy-mouthed," said the Reverend Sidney. "Why didn't you ask me if she was a lady? Because that's a dirty word nowadays, isn't it? We're all ly-dees and gents, ain't we?" he added, with a ghastly parody of what he probably imagined to be Cockney.

"What time was this call?"

"Must have been soon after eight. I was listening to the news."

"Mr. Guest," said Henry, "I have to go now. I'll be in touch with you again soon. Meanwhile, please don't mention the letter or the phone call to anybody."

Guest gave a bark of sarcastic laughter. "Do you think I am likely to? I venture to suggest, sir, that it is you and your organization who are about to let loose the hounds of publicity."

"I promise I'll do my best for you," said Henry.

"Ha!" said the Reverend Sidney loudly. He looked across the bright, windy wasteland of the airfield to the little knot of men and vehicles. Then he rammed a shabby trilby hat on his head and set off down the road at a sort of loping run. Henry got into the car and drove back to the airfield.

They were waiting for him with some impatience. The experts had done their work; the pathetic remains had been assembled in a temporary coffin; and there was nothing except Henry's absence to detain the group of officials in this drafty and depressing spot. Henry gave permission for everyone to leave, and promised to join them shortly at Police Headquarters.

Left alone, Henry went back into the shelter. Chalk marks on the floor showed the exact position of the body and of the revolver. It seemed that Beau Guest had been standing with his back against the far wall, facing the entrance. The bullet had passed through his brain, and he had slumped to the ground, the revolver falling to the floor from his limp right hand. So it seemed. Who, then, had taken up the Typhoon on that patrol? Who had crashed with it into the sea? Who had answered Emmy's radio call, and who had shouted "Tally-ho!" into the microphone with no enemy in sight?

For a short moment Henry felt almost inclined to believe in ghosts. Then reason returned, and he remembered that somebody knew about Beau's body in the shelter, somebody sufficiently alive to murder Lofty Parker before he had a chance to investigate Dymfield. Henry began to worry about what had happened to Emmy.

Back at Police Headquarters he made another attempt to telephone to his home and to Whitchurch Manor. Once again there was no reply from either number. Scotland Yard informed him that Mrs. Tibbett had not rung. There seemed nothing to be done. Henry returned to his colleagues.

Things were progressing as far as the formal aspects of the affair were concerned. Simmonds had reported by telephone to the Air Ministry and departed thankfully for London. A preliminary check with Air Ministry Records indicated that the insignia and medal ribbons on the rotting uniform tallied with those which Squadron Leader Guest had been entitled to wear. Information on the revolver and dental details were still awaited, as was the pathologist's report. One bullet only had been fired from the revolver, and it had been recovered from the wall behind the body and sent off to the ballistics experts. A short and noncommittal statement had been issued to the press, stating that the skeleton of an unidentified man had been found in a disused air-raid shelter on the former airfield of Dymfield. No more.

It was nearly eight o'clock before Henry and Sergeant Reynolds left for London. They drove straight to Scotland Yard, where Henry found an interesting item of information awaiting him. At ten o'clock that morning, it seemed, a Mr. Smith of

Finchley had reported to the local police that he had received an anonymous letter in the morning mail. This letter now lay on Henry's desk.

The envelope was of the cheapest and least distinguished variety and bore a Central London postmark. Inside, words and phrases had been cut from newspapers and pasted roughly on a sheet of plain paper. The text ran:

> Johnny Head in air will be found to-day by Scotland Yard if you can't stop Henry T from digging stop him talking or you will regret it you know what I mean

The accompanying report stated that Mr. Smith had specifically requested that Chief Inspector Tibbett should be informed, and said he wished to discuss the matter with him personally. Henry studied the document carefully, and then put it aside while he wrote his reports. At nine he went to a pub around the corner and dined on beer, cheese sandwiches, and sausages. At half-past ten he went home.

The Chelsea house, in which Henry and Emmy lived in the ground-floor flat, was in darkness. Henry opened the front door with his key, turned on the hall light, and then unlocked his own front door. He had no time even to switch on a light before the telephone started to ring. Henry picked up the receiver.

"Tibbett here," he said.

"This is Vere Prendergast."

"Thank God for that. I've been trying to ring you. I've only just this moment gotten home."

"I know."

"What do you mean, you know?"

"I'm speaking from the phone over the road. I've been waiting for you."

A small tremor of alarm ran down Henry's spine. "Where's Emmy?"

"We'll talk about that in a minute," said Vere. "We have a number of things to discuss, you and I, my old clue-catcher."

"Where is Emmy?"

"All in good time, old man. Don't worry, she's fine. But I thought it would be pleasanter for everyone if she was kept out of our discussions for the time being. Now, I want to talk to you. I'll come over to your house, shall I, since I'm so close?"

"I think you'd better," said Henry grimly.

"Good show. I'll be right over."

Henry had no time to reply before the receiver was replaced. And he barely had time to make another quick call before the front doorbell rang.

CHAPTER SIXTEEN

VERE LOOKED GROTESQUELY TALL, standing on Henry's doorstep, outlined by the light from the street lamp on the pavement. On each side of his thin face the bristling ends of his mustache stood out, catching the light, giving him the look of a rangy, bewhiskered tomcat.

"Come in," said Henry

"Thanks, old man," said Vere. He stepped into the hall. "I hope you don't think I'm…"

"I think nothing about you," said Henry. "I want to know where my wife is."

"She's with Barbara." Vere looked at Henry, apparently with dawning understanding. "Good lord, old scout, you didn't think…?"

"I was simply wondering," said Henry, "why she wasn't home." He opened the sitting-room door and motioned Vere to go in.

"My dear old sleuth," said Vere. "I've known Blandish since pre-history. I assure you I never had any designs on her then and I haven't now."

"That's hardly the point," said Henry.

"Isn't it? It sprang to mind, if you know what I mean. No, I left Blandish and Barbara together. I thought it would be better if you and I had a quiet talk alone."

"Where did you leave them?"

"Oh, for heaven's sake. What does it matter? In a club, actually." There was a little pause. Then Vere went on, "I understand you went to Dymfield today."

"Correct."

"And you found—something."

"What makes you think that? Do sit down. A drink?"

"No thanks, old boy." Vere lowered himself into an armchair, and gave a sudden, loud laugh in which there was no trace of amusement. "No sense in beating about the bush. You want me to be the first to say it, so I'll oblige. You found Beau, the poor old sod."

"We found a body," said Henry. "It hasn't yet been identified."

Vere looked at him with owlish shrewdness. "I get it," he said. "Unidentified. Full marks."

"I said," Henry pointed out, "that it hadn't been identified *yet*. It certainly will be. The dental evidence will be conclusive." He paused. "So Johnny Head-in-Air was Johnny Under Ground after all."

"Funny you should say that," said Vere. "It's just what I said."

"I'd like to get this straight," said Henry. "You knew that the body was there. You and who else?"

"Oh—some of us…"

"All right. Tell me what happened."

Vere said, "I think I'll change my mind about that drink, old chap."

"Whisky?"

"Please."

Henry poured two drinks, handed one to Vere, and waited. At last he said, "Well, if you won't tell me, I'll tell you. Beau Guest died soon after five o'clock on the evening of October 13, 1943. He wasn't even in flying clothes—which suggests something else, but we'll come to that later. You took that Typhoon up and deliberately faked a suicide. You only risked one short remark to Emmy over the radio telephone, in case she recognized your voice in spite of the distortion in the mike."

Without a great deal of conviction Vere said, "What nonsense, old man. Duff gen. If I'd been in that kite I'd be good and dead now—full fathoms five in the drink."

"Oh, no. Your plan was quite ingenious, and the story stood up so long as it wasn't investigated too closely. And it wasn't likely to be. After all, Beau had disappeared, and you were demonstrably alive. What you did, in fact, was to make a big circle out to sea in order to jettison nearly all your fuel. You then flew in overland again, set the aircraft on an easterly course pointing downhill, and—please don't tell me that's not the right expression, because I'm sure of it, but I don't know the jargon—and then you bailed out. No wonder there was a scare about German parachutists that evening. But the weather was bad and so was the visibility. It wasn't unusual even for pilots bailing out over enemy territory to land unseen, so it's not surprising that you got away with it. You ditched the parachute somewhere in the countryside and prudently kept away from Dymfield until the next day.

"I dare say that, as Beau's greatest friend, you had the job of going through his clothes and other possessions. It must have been a nasty moment when you found his flying boots. You'd forgotten all about them. Still, by good luck nobody else had seen them. You couldn't very well dispose of them—they're too bulky not to invite comment—so you quickly gave them to Barbara. That got them safely out of the Mess, and you knew she'd be leaving Dymfield almost at once."

"You've got no proof of all this."

"I don't need any. The pilot in that aircraft was not Beau Guest, so it had to be somebody else. The list of possibilities is very short."

"Sammy Smith was an ex-pilot."

"Agreed. But he's shortish and thick-set. It's bothered me from the beginning—how Guest was able to fool the ground staff into thinking that he was you. In his case it would just have been possible. Sammy Smith certainly couldn't have done it. In fact, of course, there was no question of having to fool anybody. The ground staff accepted the pilot as you for the very good reason that the pilot *was* you. Any comments?"

"Not at this stage." Vere leant back and sipped his drink. He seemed more at ease. "Do go on, old sleuth. It's fascinating."

"So far," said Henry, "I've given you the facts as I see them. From now on, I'm guessing. The question is—why did you do it?"

"Let's have your theory," said Vere.

Henry sighed. "I wish I didn't distrust obvious explanations."

"Meaning?"

"The obvious explanation is almost too neat," said Henry. "You arrange to meet Guest at the airfield well ahead of the time for the take-off. You shoot him with his own revolver and take his place in the aircraft. Nobody questions the story of an heroic suicide."

"And my motive for this extraordinary action?"

"I don't think that you'll deny that you were in love with Barbara even before she married Beau."

Vere smiled. "No, I don't deny that."

"Well—there it is. You dispose of the husband and marry the widow. For many years all goes well. Even when the plan of writing a history of Dymfield is mooted, you have no objections, until the point at which the nature of the project changes. Lofty is too clever by half. He has smelled out a mystery connected with Beau's death. He is planning to visit Dymfield. He is talking too much, to too many people. So he is silenced. After all, you've killed one man already. I'm told that the second time is always easier. I dare say that it seemed monstrously unfair that after so long the dead past should threaten your orderly life."

Vere nodded, ponderously. "Yes," he said. "Yes, you're nearly right. I do realize that I'm in a serious position. That's why I want to point out to you that your own is little better. There's always a way around these tricky situations, you know."

"Is there?" said Henry grimly. "What do you mean by 'nearly right'?"

"Well, old man, you're assuming that Beau was murdered."

"And wasn't he?"

Vere looked shocked. "Good God, no. He committed suicide." There was a pause, and then he added, "The great hero, the golden boy. It's pathetic, isn't it?"

"What is?"

"How he went to pieces. I knew him during the Battle of Britain, when he really was a hero. The rot must have started at Falconfield. I understand he was as tight as an owl when he crashed that kite."

Henry looked at Prendergast, and wondered. From his recent inquiries at the Air Ministry, he was now satisfied, beyond any shadow of doubt, that the crash at Falconfield had been caused by engine failure in the aircraft. In fact, he had been assured it was thanks to Guest's supreme expertise as a pilot and his total disregard for personal safety that the plane had come down in the sea rather than in the main street of a coastal village. It seemed that somebody had been going out of their way to blacken Beau Guest's memory.

"Did your wife tell you all this, about Beau?"

"Well…" Vere hesitated. "People talked, you know. These things get around. And I myself saw him staggering about more than once at Dymfield. I think even Blandish noticed it, but of course she'd never hear a word against him."

"Please go on with your story."

"What else is there to tell? Beau found himself in a cleft stick. He'd made a public song and dance about taking up the Tiffie, and couldn't get out of it without tremendous loss of face. On the other hand, he was dead scared even to take the thing off the ground. So what did he do? He simply went to pieces. He got drunk and then he sloped off to that disused air-raid shelter and shot himself. Not a pretty state of affairs. Some of us—his friends—decided to take matters into our own hands. That's why I took the kite up."

"Your motives are still not clear," said Henry.

"My dear fellow, I was thinking of Barbara. Barbara and little Blandish—not to mention Beau's old father and the honor of the old squadron, the one we'd served in together. A noble suicide is much easier to stomach than a squalid, drunken one, don't you agree?"

Henry said nothing.

Vere went on, shaking a bony finger in the direction of Henry's face. "Now get this straight, Tibbett. Blandish I don't care about, but Barbara still believes in Beau and in his memory. I don't intend that she shall be disillusioned. What you found today was a body too far gone for identification. A relic of an air raid in 1940 or thereabouts. Understand?"

"Are you out of your mind?" Henry asked, genuinely amazed. "Do you realize what you are asking me to do?"

"Oh, I dare say it sounds a bit unusual to you," said Vere, "but I'm sure you'll agree with me once you've appreciated the alternative."

"What alternative?"

"I'll have another whisky, if you don't mind."

Without speaking, Henry refilled Vere's glass and handed it to him. Prendergast's hands were trembling as he took it, so that some of the golden liquid spilled on his tweed suit. He said, "Yes. The alternative. You see, if it comes out that it is Beau's body, then there's bound to be an inquiry, isn't there? People will want to know why he arrived at the airfield so early, and what he was doing in the air-raid shelter, and who saw him last, and all that sort of thing."

"If you are right, and he killed himself, that would provide answers to all your questions," said Henry.

"Ah, but you see," said Vere, "it's perfectly easy to prove beyond all doubt that Beau had a date with somebody that evening. And it was after speaking to—that person—that he committed suicide. If he did. It might be easier to say—that he died."

"If you're implying that he had a date with Emmy," said Henry, "it's nonsense. She was on duty."

"Oh, yes," agreed Vere, "certainly she was. She arrived rather early for her two till seven stint. Annie will tell you that. She was on duty as well, and found Blandish already installed when she arrived on the dot of two."

"And Sammy Smith found her hard at work when he got to the Operations Room at six," Henry pointed out.

"I know that," said Vere, "but no matter what people tell you, it's the bits they leave out that are really interesting. You should know that, my dear old bloodhound. I don't suppose Blandish has mentioned to you that, having done a two-hour stretch of work from two to four, she was entitled to an hour or so off. In fact, she left Dymfield Operations Room at five past four, and came back at twenty past five. I may as well tell you that there are witnesses who saw her cycling away from the Operations Room soon after four and coming back at five."

"What witnesses?" Henry asked. His throat felt dry.

"I won't worry you with their names for the time being, old sleuth," said Vere. "Naturally, they'd much rather not remember anything about it. On the other hand, if there should be a full inquiry, you can hardly ask them not to tell the truth, the whole truth, and nothing but the truth—can you?" He drained his glass and stood up. "Well, I'll be off now. Thanks for the whisky. Just mull over what I've been saying. I want to protect Barbara, and I'm sure you feel the same way about Blandish."

"You haven't yet told me," said Henry, "when I may expect to see her again."

Vere laughed. "Dear old soul," he said, "you don't think I've abducted her, do you? In fact, with your permission, I'll ring the joint where I left our two ladies together and suggest to Barbara that she shoves Blandish into a taxi and sends her home. I dare say you'll have a lot to talk over with her."

"The telephone is there," said Henry.

Vere picked up the receiver and dialed. "Hello—is that the Blue Parrot? Ah, Mabel, light of my life, this is Vere Prendergast. If my old woman is still sober enough to stand, would you propel her toward the telephone, there's a love... what? Oh, has she? And her girl friend? With whom—? Oh, I see... Well, not to worry, old top. She'll be home before me, in that case. Toodle-oo." He rang off and turned to Henry. "Missed them," he said. "Mabel tells me they got sick of waiting and pushed off about ten minutes ago. Barbara was planning to drive home in her own car—hope to God she's sober. Blandish left with a gentleman friend. Don't look so po-faced, old sleuth. Mabel describes him as a stout, elderly gentleman with gray hair and glasses. So there's no need to get in a flap. She'll be home in a few minutes."

"Where is this Blue Parrot place?" Henry asked.

"Don't you know it? Quite a bright little spot. Meadow Street, off Park Lane. A bit sordid, of course, but Mabel's a good sort. Well, so long, old bluebottle. You know where to find me. Keep me abreast of events, won't you? Regards to Blandish—and don't worry. Nil carborundum, as they say..." And with a wolfish smile, Vere strode out the front door.

Henry waited at the window only long enough to satisfy himself that his telephoned instructions had been carried out. He saw Vere's Bentley come nosing out into the main road and turn toward the south. Seconds later, a nondescript car followed it. Henry went back to the telephone and spoke to his office again. Then he waited. Vere had left a few minutes after eleven. The hands of Henry's watch crept with agonizing slowness to half-past eleven, and then to midnight. But the telephone did not ring, and Emmy did not come home.

Henry dialed Arthur Price's Edgware number. For a long time the phone rang, unanswered. Then a gruff voice—just identifiable as Albert Bates, despite the absence of dentures—asked Henry who he was and what he wanted. Sibilantly, and with irritation, he told Henry that Mr. Price was not in. No, he had no idea when to expect him. He had dined at home, and then, about half-past eight, had received a phone call. Bates had no idea from whom; the master had answered it himself. He had then rung for Bates, told him that he would be taking the car and going out, and given permission for the household to retire to bed.

A call to Sammy Smith's number produced no reply.

Henry had to get James Baggot's number through Scotland Yard, as it was not listed. Here, again, the phone rang unanswered for a time. Then the receiver was lifted and a confused medley of music and voices surged down the wire. James Baggot was evidently giving a party.

"'Lo—whoosat? Whadderwant?" inquired a slurred masculine voice with an American accent. Henry asked to speak to Mr. Baggot. "Jimmy? For Chrissakes, ol' boy—there's about a thousand guys here... No, make it two thousand—three... Hang on, ol' boy—don't goway—see if I can find him..." The voice ceased, and there was a clatter as the handpiece of the telephone fell off the table. The music and babble was now augmented by a rhythmic bumping as the receiver swung on its cord against the table leg. After several minutes there was another clatter as it was picked up. A shrill feminine voice said, "Some nit's left the bloody phone off the hook." There was a click, and then the dial tone once more.

The next thing that happened was a call from the Yard. A report had been received from the car which was shadowing Vere. He had driven straight home to Whitchurch Manor, had put the car away, and gone in. His wife had evidently arrived home before him and was sitting in the drawing room drinking a whisky and soda. Her car, too, was in the garage. What were Henry's instructions now?

Henry gave orders that the watch on Whitchurch Manor should be maintained, and arranged for a plainclothes detective to gate crash the Baggot party in search of the host. Another detective was already watching for Arthur Price's return home.

Once again Henry sat down to wait. At a quarter to one the telephone rang again. This time it was the C.I.D. inspector from East Anglia.

"I rang the Yard, Tibbett," he said, "and they seemed to think you'd like a report direct. Sorry to trouble you so late at night."

"I wasn't in bed," said Henry. "What's the news?"

"It's about that poor fellow you found today. Doc says he's been dead at least twenty years. Far too late now to establish any details, but from the state of the skull it's clear that the bullet entered the left temple and passed through the brain. The bullet you found is the one from the gun and obviously the one that did the damage. But here's the interesting part. Quite apart from the fact that the gun was near the man's right hand, while it was the left temple that was shattered, the medical and ballistics chaps all agree that the wound couldn't possibly have been self-inflicted."

Henry said nothing.

The detective said, "Are you there, Tibbett?"

"Yes."

"Well, did you get what I said? This Squadron Leader Guest—oh, the identification's been confirmed, by the way—this Squadron Leader Guest of yours didn't commit suicide. It may have been an accident or it may not, but somebody else shot him."

At half-past one more reports began to come in. Arthur Price had just arrived home, driving himself in his Austin limousine. A constable in Hampstead had stopped a Mercedes of ancient vintage which was weaving an uneven course up Avenue Road, and the driver had proved to be Sammy Smith, with his wife Marlene as passenger. They told the police they were returning from an evening with friends in the West End. Sammy had gone through all the usual sobriety tests with a calm fluency and equilibrium which suggested long practice. He had also demanded to see his own doctor, who was now awaited. The local Sergeant saw no hope of making a charge stick, but wanted to give Sammy a severe fright. The woman, added the Sergeant's report, seemed quite sober and very angry.

The gate-crasher described James Baggot's party as still in process but not going strong. The host had departed with "some popsy." The more responsible element had long since gone home, and the guests who remained were all more or less intoxicated. A few were dancing to a phonograph, some were necking in the bedrooms, and others had passed out quietly. While Henry was still on the line, a further report came in. Mr. Baggot had returned home, alone, and was now kicking the last of the revelers out of his house. Meanwhile, all was quiet at Whitchurch Manor. Vere and Barbara had finished their nightcap, locked up the house, put the cat out, and gone to bed. What were Henry's instructions?

It would be hard to say which emotion was uppermost in Henry's mind—anxiety, anger, or bafflement. It seemed ludicrous to imagine that a television celebrity, a candy manufacturer, a country squire, and a tippling second-hand car salesman had entered into a conspiracy to kidnap Emmy—and all because of an incident that had occurred more than twenty years ago. And yet, that incident had almost certainly been murder, and a twenty-year-old killing was as serious in the eyes of the law as—yes—as the killing of Lofty Parker last week. Better, Henry decided, to risk appearing ridiculous in the eyes of his colleagues than to take any chances with Emmy's safety.

Briskly he outlined what he wanted. The strictest check on the movements of the entire Dymfield group, including a report from Scotland on Annie Meadowes; then, a full description of Emmy to be circulated to all stations and patrol cars, with the highest priority. The Sergeant at the Yard kept his voice carefully free from expression as he read back Henry's orders, but Henry was well aware of what was passing through his mind. Chief's fussing like an old hen because his wife's gone out on the tiles for once—like to know what he'd say if it was one of *our* wives and we mobilized the entire country to get her home—pretty silly he's going to look when she comes tripping in at half-past two, saying, "Oh, darling, am I late?"

The Sergeant was a good prophet. It was, in fact, two thirty-seven when Henry, who had dozed off in his armchair, was wakened by the sound of a key in the latch.

Before he had aroused himself enough to stand up, the sitting-room door opened and Emmy came in. She looked exhausted, and what she said was, "Henry! What on earth are you doing here?"

CHAPTER SEVENTEEN

"**W**HERE HAVE YOU BEEN?**" said Henry.

Emmy did not seem to notice the exasperation in his voice. She was entirely concentrated on pulling herself together, on behaving naturally. When she spoke, her voice was light and unconcerned.

"I've been having a marvelous evening out, darling. Gossiping with old friends and living it up in the fleshpots of the West End. But when did you get back? I understood from Vere that you were spending the night in Dymfield." She slipped off her coat and threw it on the sofa. "I am sorry I'm so late, darling. Of course, I'd never have stayed out until the small hours if I'd had any idea you were home. I hope you weren't worrying about me."

"I have been worrying," said Henry. "And I'm not the only one."

"What on earth do you mean?"

"Your description," said Henry, "was circulated a quarter of an hour ago to every police station in Britain. Excuse me while I go and call off the hunt. I'll be enough of a laughing stock as it is, without prolonging the farce." He picked up the telephone and began to dial. Emmy stood quite still, watching him. Henry said, "Chief Inspector Tibbett here. My wife has just come home, Sergeant. Yes, she's perfectly all right—it was a misunderstanding… I'm extremely sorry to have given you so much trouble… No, it is *not* all over. The other instructions stand."

"I suppose," said Emmy, as he rang off, "that you're furious."

Henry went over and kissed her tenderly. "Actually," he said, "I'm so bloody relieved I could sing. For God's sake, never do that to me again."

Clinging to him, Emmy said, "But you don't know—you don't know anything. Oh, Henry, I didn't want to tell you, but I'm in such a mess, and…"

"I know you are. I also know that what we both need is a long, refreshing sleep, but there's no time for that. So I'm going to pour you a long, refreshing drink, and then we are going to talk."

He handed her a tall glass and sat down in the other armchair. Then he said, "Let's start by you telling me exactly what you've been up to since I left you in the Duke's Head after lunch."

"Well—first of all, Vere turned up out of the blue. We had a drink and chatted, and then he suggested going back to Whitchurch. We left a message for you. Didn't you get it?"

"I got an extremely garbled," Henry began, but she cut him short.

"Silly of me. Of course you got it or you wouldn't have telephoned."

"I got no reply."

"Oh, but you did. You spoke to Vere."

"Look," said Henry, "suppose you stop telling me what I did and didn't do. Just tell me what you did."

"All right. Vere left a message for you saying that we'd gone to Whitchurch. He suggested you drive over there when you'd finished your work, and then let the car go back to London with the Sergeant and that nice boy Simmonds. Barbara was in town, and Vere said he'd drive us up and we could go out and dine as a foursome. I thought it sounded like fun. When we got back to Whitchurch…"

"Just a minute. Did Vere know where I was?"

"He asked me and so I told him. I didn't think it was a secret."

"Okay. Go on."

"Well, we drove to Whitchurch and had a cup of tea, and then Vere was called away to the telephone. He was gone quite a long time, about half an hour. When he came back, he said that you'd phoned. That you'd gotten our message, and that it all fitted in rather well, because something had cropped up about your work and you had to stay the night in Dymfield. Vere said that you'd agreed that he should drive me up to London, give me dinner, and bring me home. It never occurred to me to question it. D'you mean that you didn't ring at all?"

"I told you. I tried, but got no reply. What time was all this?"

"About half-past four, I suppose. Vere suggested we drive to London straight away. Barbara's meeting, or whatever it was, ended at five, and she'd be waiting for us. So off we went. One odd thing was that Vere didn't take the direct route to London. He drove around by Dymfield, past the airfield. I saw several police cars there and the ambulance, but I couldn't see the car we'd driven down in. I was dying with curiosity, but Vere wouldn't stop, and I couldn't see you anywhere."

"I was looking for you," said Henry. "Well, go on."

"Vere asked me point blank if those were your men and cars, and I said they must be. Then he—he told me what it was that you'd found."

"So you know..."

"Yes. It was kind of you to tell Vere so that he could break it to me..." Emmy suddenly stopped. "But you never spoke to him! He must have known all along!"

"Yes, he knew," said Henry. "Never mind about that for the moment."

"Well—he said I'd have to face the fact that Beau wasn't— all that I'd thought he was. I said I couldn't see that it mattered much, how Beau died or where. We'd accepted the fact that he'd killed himself and the details weren't very important. In fact, I told Vere he must have been stark, staring crazy to take that plane up and bail out—oh, of course, you don't know about that..."

"Yes, I do. Don't worry how. Just take it as read that I know."

"Well, don't you agree that it was crazy? It just shows how a man can behave when he's besotted by a—by someone like Barbara. He did it for her, you see. Thought it would be less painful for her to accept Beau's death if she thought it was heroic. I suppose I can understand that he might have done it twenty years ago, but when he said he intended to go on with the play-acting now, it was really too much. Anyway, I said that if Beau's body had been found, it couldn't possibly be kept a secret. And he said, 'I'm relying on you for that, Blandish.' That was when I began to get really worried."

"I'm not surprised. All this conversation took place in the car, did it?"

"Yes. I told him I'd no idea what he meant, and he said that obviously I had a great deal of influence over you. You can imagine my reply to that! By this time we'd arrived in London and Vere made me promise to say nothing to Barbara for the time being. We met her at a drinking club called the Blue Parrot, and then we went out to dinner at some Italian restaurant, and then back to the Blue Parrot again. Then, quite suddenly, around ten o'clock, Vere said he had to go. No explanation—at least, just some feeble story about meeting a chap at his club. He said that there was no need for us to wait for him—he and Barbara had a car each—so if we got bored, Barbara could drive me home and go on to Whitchurch herself. It was all a bit odd, I thought. Anyway, the miserable man pushed off and left me alone with Barbara.

"It was awful, Henry. She wouldn't stop talking about Beau. The book has become an obsession with her. Vere's presence seemed to put some sort of brake on her, but as soon as he'd gone, she let rip. The world had never appreciated Beau.

She'd never appreciated him as she should have. The world must be told the truth—all that sort of rot. I was just about to slide out quietly into a taxi when the most extraordinary thing happened. You'll never guess who turned up."

"Arthur Price," said Henry.

Emmy's tired eyes opened wide. "How on earth did you know that?"

"It wasn't very surprising."

"Not to you, perhaps, but it was to me. He was the last person I expected to see in a place like the Blue Parrot. He wasn't exactly in his element, as you can imagine. I got a curious feeling that he was—I don't know—as if he was on duty."

Henry said, "Is Price a member of the Blue Parrot?"

"Now, that's funny, isn't it?" said Emmy. She sipped her drink thoughtfully. "It didn't strike me at the time. I mean, Barbara and I naturally welcomed old Pricey, and Barbara was just buying drinks and insisted on including him. And then the barman asked her if she'd sign him in, so he can't have been a member. And yet how could he possibly have known we were there?"

"That's one of the things I intend to find out very shortly," said Henry. "Well, go on. What happened then?"

"Well, we had a drink and talked a bit. Then I said I ought to get home, and Barbara said she was damned if she was going to wait any longer for Vere. She offered me a lift home, but Pricey said he'd take me, as it was on his way."

"From Mayfair to Edgware?"

"I never thought of that. Anyhow, I got into Pricey's car, and off we went, heading west. Almost at once he began to explain that he was, in fact, on his way to a party in Jimmy Baggot's house in Chiswick. He said that he hadn't mentioned it earlier because he wasn't keen on Barbara coming along, but he said he knew Jimmy rather especially wanted to see me, and—well—to cut it short, I said I'd go with him. I was feeling pretty battered after all that had happened, and I *did* think you were spending the night in the country."

"I suppose it never occurred to you that you might be in danger."

"No, it didn't."

"Even after all my warnings?"

"Well, it was just a series of odd coincidences. First meeting Vere in the pub, and then Pricey turning up..."

"Very odd," said Henry grimly. Then he smiled. "I begin to understand why you had such a reputation for innocence in the Air Force. I hadn't noticed it before. I suppose on the whole it's better than sharp-nosed suspicion, which is what I suffer from."

"Don't talk to me about being innocent," said Emmy. She got up and lit a cigarette. "I'm getting to the difficult part now."

"I know you are. Let's have it."

"Jimmy's party was ghastly. Really horrible. Braying Oxford accents and smooth men on the make and screeching women calling each other darling and everybody half-tight—you know what I mean. The only person who seemed stone-cold sober was Jimmy himself. It was almost as though he'd been expecting to see me, waiting for me. He brought me a drink, and then said that he had a surprise for me, an old friend had turned up unexpectedly. He took me into a sort of study at the back of the house away from the din, and who should be there but Annie!"

"That is a surprise," said Henry. "That completes the gathering of the vultures."

"What on earth do you mean?"

"Never mind. What did Annie say?"

"Well, you know her. She didn't waste any time on polite preliminaries. She told me she'd been in touch with Vere and that she knew that you'd been to Dymfield and found Beau. She also told me that she'd known all along that—that he was there, and that was why she'd tried to dissuade me from doing the book, even to the point of trying to frighten me by that silly suggestion that Beau might be alive. I said to her what I'd said to Vere—that I couldn't see it made much difference whether

Beau shot himself in an air-raid shelter or deliberately crashed a Typhoon. And then it started."

Emmy paused, and took a deep breath. "You see, Henry, I left the Operations Room that afternoon. I wasn't deliberately concealing it—I'd have told Lofty—but, well, I didn't feel like mentioning it. Annie was also on duty at Dymfield, and it appears she knew I'd been out of the Operations Room for more than an hour. Apparently she'd been looking for me, on some technical thing, and when she couldn't find me, she rang the Guardroom. The guard told her I'd gone past on my bicycle, heading for dispersal. And as if that wasn't bad enough, it seems that Pricey saw me cycling back to the Operations Room when he was on his own way back for dinner. Annie went off and fished poor little Pricey out of the party and made him confirm it. He was wretched and desperately apologetic, but he kept saying that he'd have to tell the truth if he were asked, and so he would, of course."

"Even if you were out on the airfield," said Henry, "it doesn't prove that you saw Beau."

"But I did. I wouldn't deny it. In any case, Annie pointed out to me that there was solid proof of it."

Henry sat up. "Proof? What proof?"

Instead of answering, Emmy got up and went over to the desk drawer. Again, she pulled out the photograph of the tennis team, and threw it over to Henry.

"There," she said. "That's the proof. I told Annie last week that I had this photograph with Beau's signature on it. Tonight she pointed out to me that it had been passed for autographing from Lofty to her to Beau. She had signed it on the afternoon of October 13th, and it was in her pocket when she set out for duty that evening. She met Beau leaving the Operations Block—he'd just been saying good-bye to me at the Operations Room door, actually—and she gave him the photograph to sign and pass on to me. So you see, since I now have it..."

Henry looked down at the rectangle of paper, and at the young faces smiling out from it. All of them were now familiar to him. Annie, tall and gawky in those days; Lofty, smooth-faced and handsome; Emmy, as he remembered her from their first meeting; and Beau, black-haired Beau, with his burn-scarred face and lopsided grin. No, Beau was not familiar.

"I should have thrown it away years ago," said Emmy. "But I didn't—out of sheer sentimentality, I suppose. And now I'm stuck with it."

"Don't waste time on regretting what you might have done and didn't," said Henry. "Get on with the story. What happened next?"

"A Dymfield reunion," said Emmy. She smiled, a little bitterly. "In Jimmy's study. Annie and Pricey and Jimmy—and Sammy Smith was there, too, with his wife. I gather he hangs around Jimmy whenever he can these days. Anyhow, he was tight so he doesn't really count. The general idea was that I was in an awkward spot, and that my old pals were rallying around to help me. What they really meant was that for various reasons none of them wanted the old scandal revivified, and they knew enough to make things pretty hot for me if I didn't cooperate."

"In what?"

"In getting you to suppress the fact that the body you found was Beau's. I'm supposed to persuade you to pronounce that identification has not been possible and that the man must have been an air-raid victim." Emmy passed a hand over her brow. "I don't know what to do, Henry. I know that my being involved is going to make everything frightful for you. I wish to God I'd never gone to that awful reunion."

"I told you to stop regretting things," said Henry. "It doesn't help. For a start, I may as well tell you that the identification is now official, and the matter is out of my hands."

Emmy slumped into a chair. "That's a relief," she said. "I told them, of course, that I couldn't do anything to hold up the ordinary legal procedures, and that was that. The party broke up after that. Annie and Pricey and the Smiths went home. Jimmy came out with me, and eventually we found a taxi—and here I am." She ran a hand through her short, dark hair. "Goodness, I'm tired. Well, we shall just have to face the music of an old scandal; but, honestly, Henry, don't you think they're all making a ridiculous fuss? Who cares now about what happened to Beau Guest?"

Henry went over to Emmy and sat down on the floor at her feet. "Emmy, darling," he said, "I'm afraid things are rather more serious than you think. Your dear friends—or one of them—is very dangerous. Have you forgotten what happened to Lofty?"

"Nothing's been proved about Lofty yet," said Emmy. "In any case Lofty led twenty colorful years of life after he left Dymfield. If he really was murdered, surely it was because of some much more recent trouble. You keep on about my being in danger, but just take this evening. Any of them could have murdered me if they'd wanted to, and all they did was to wine and dine me, and send me home in a cab. So..."

"Emmy," said Henry, "I'm afraid you've got to face an unpleasant fact. You are being threatened with something much more subtle than physical violence." He took her hand. "Now listen to me, darling. You know that I trust you and believe in you absolutely. Now, you've got to tell me the exact truth about everything that happened that night at Dymfield. How and where you saw him, and got the photograph. Because, you see, Beau didn't commit suicide."

Instinctively Emmy cried, "I always knew he didn't!"

"What do you mean?"

"He was in such good spirits. He was looking forward to the flip... But if he didn't, then..."

"Yes," said Henry, "he was killed, either deliberately or by accident. You were presumably the last person to see him alive—except the killer. And your dear friends have made good and sure of the evidence against you. If I'm not very much mistaken, there was a tape recorder in James Baggot's study. You walked right into the parlor, love. I shall now make you a cup of good strong coffee, and you will tell me the end of your story."

"Move over, Blandish."

"Oh, Annie! Is it four o'clock already?"

"Almost. I'll take over."

"I can stay on a bit longer. There's nothing doing."

"Orders, Section Officer Blandish. We can't have you off duty at six, can we? I imagine you *will* want to be controlling Snowdrop Three-two? So you'd better have an hour or so off, and some tea."

"Okay. Thanks, Annie. It's all yours. Nothing exciting. A couple of patrols, but not ours. I'm just listening out."

"There was a swarm of bombers on the table just now heading southeast."

"Yes. They're all away now. Wonder who's getting it today? The Pas de Calais, I suppose. Poor devils."

"Well, we won't be here to see the bomber boys back. Sammy can have that pleasure."

"Excuse me, ma'am—Miss Blandish…"

"Yes, Corporal? What is it?"

"Someone on the phone for you, ma'am."

"Oh, thanks. Who is it, do you know?"

"He didn't say, ma'am. It sounded like the Chief Controller, ma'am."

"Beau. You shouldn't ring me when I'm on duty."

"Are you alone?"

"Yes. But Corporal Dale recognized your voice."

"Hell, if I can't ring my own Operations Room and speak to one of my own officers…"

"Oh, don't be silly. You know what people are saying…"

"As far as I'm concerned, they can all go and…"

"Beau!"

"Sorry. But it makes me flaming mad. You're the only friend I've got in this benighted place. If we were having a scorching love affair, it would be different…"

"If we were, we'd be terribly discreet, and nobody would have an inkling. Anyhow, what does it matter, if you've applied for posting…"

"That's why I rang you. I've got that photograph for you. I've even signed it."

"Oh, good. Will you have time to bring it along here?"

"No. You'll have to come and get it."

"But—you know I can't. I'm on duty…"

"Annie's on watch with you. You're surely entitled to an hour off."

"Yes, but you know very well we aren't supposed to leave the…"

"Section Officer Blandish, you are going to get on your bicycle and come over here forthwith. If anyone tries to stop you, say that those are my orders."

"But…"

"Blandish!"

"Oh, all right. Where are you phoning from?"

"The Guardroom. I'll see you in the usual place in ten minutes."

"But…"

"And wear your mac. It's beginning to rain."

"So you met him," said Henry. "Where was 'the usual place'?"

"The disused air-raid shelter, of course."

"It was, was it? That makes everything much easier."

"Does it really?"

"Of course it doesn't. I was being heavily ironic. You often met him there, did you?"

"Yes. Quite often. Oh, I know it sounds terrible," said Emmy. "Sordid and dreadful. It wasn't. Please believe me. We only wanted to talk; he used to tell me all about Barbara, and how difficult she was, and ask my advice. He really did love her, you see. And we used to laugh about things and—that's all. But we couldn't meet openly, him being the Chief Controller and me very junior. It wouldn't have done. In the summer we used to go for long walks together, leaving the station separately and meeting out in the country. It was while we were walking on the airfield one day that we came across the shelters. They hadn't been used since the dive bombing in 1940. So we made that one our rendezvous for the winter. Beau even kept a bottle of whisky there, so that we could have a drink..."

"Innocent little Emmy," said Henry.

"You don't believe me," said Emmy.

"I do," said Henry seriously. "I know you, and I know that you have a wonderfully sure and quite irrational instinct for judging people. I'm beginning to like this man Guest, but I also know that you were both as stupid and vulnerable as innocent people always are. Darling, I believe you. But who else does?"

"All the Dymfield people," Emmy began indignantly. Then she stopped.

"Yes," said Henry. "A fine loyal bunch of pals they've turned out to be. Did any of them know about this secret meeting place?"

"Oh, *no*. At least, I hope not."

"Well," said Henry, "go on. What happened next?"

"Very little. I rode over on my bicycle, and went to the air-raid shelter. It was raining quite hard by then, and I was very cold and regretting that I'd ever come. Beau was there. He gave me the photograph. He seemed quite different from the way he'd been earlier—I mean, he was in high spirits, not a bit nervous or depressed..."

"Ah, Blandish. Good girl. Come in out of the rain. I won't offer you a drink, because you're on duty. Well, here's your picture."

"Thank you, Beau."

"Don't thank me, old thing. A pleasure. Now, you're not to worry about this flip. *It's going to be all right.* Don't be alarmed if I'm not madly communicative over the radio telephone— I'll have quite a bit to cope with up there. Then, tomorrow, Scotland and fishing. And after that, fresh woods and pastures new. Aha. You thought I was going to say 'fresh fields,' didn't you? You can't catch me like that, you horrid little pedant."

"Beau, you're not—you haven't been drinking, have you?"

"Of course I haven't. Don't worry. And now, much as I love you, I'm going to return you to your duties. I have to see a man about a dog... Well, this is it, Blandish. Come and kiss me."

"No..."

"Coward. You little coward, Blandish. What can it matter, just this once? After all, you'll never see me again... There— that's better. I've been wanting to do that for some time. Think of me now and then, won't you? Oh, God, you're not going to cry, are you?"

"No, of course I'm not."

"Good. Well, off with you. Good-bye, Emmy."

"Good-bye, Beau."

"And that's all," said Emmy. "I swear it. I got on my bicycle and rode back to the Operations Room. I don't remember seeing Pricey, but apparently he saw me. I went back on duty, and the rest you know." Emmy was silent for several moments. Then she said, "I do seem to have made a bloody mess of things. I'm so sorry, darling."

"He didn't say who he was going to meet?"

"No. He just said 'a man about a dog'—which might mean anything."

For a little time Henry was silent. Then he said, "I begin to see a pattern, quite a definite pattern." He looked at his watch. "It's now half-past three," he said, "and time for bed.

Tomorrow, first thing, I intend to forestall the opposition. You see, darling, we've got very little time. With you as the—the star witness, I couldn't possibly stay on the case myself. If I can't clear it up tomorrow or the next day, I'll have to hand it over to someone else."

"So what happens tomorrow?"

"First of all," said Henry, "a second Dymfield reunion party."

CHAPTER EIGHTEEN

HENRY TOOK EMMY with him to Scotland Yard the following morning. As they drove through the Chelsea traffic, he said suddenly, "I hope to God I don't bungle this."

"Of course you won't."

Henry changed gears with a touch of gloom. "It's all very well for you to say that," he said. "As though this were the last chapter of a murder mystery, where the brilliant detective reveals all and unmasks the criminal."

"Well, isn't it?"

"I'm only human," said Henry. "I don't know if I can pull it off. There may be something I've overlooked..."

"I wish you'd tell me what's going to happen."

"Even if I knew, I'd rather that you didn't. It'll be much easier for you to play it that way."

At the entrance to the Yard, Henry and Emmy parted company. Henry went to his office, while Emmy was shown into a large, bleak room furnished only with chairs and a big, plain table. There was a murmur of conversation coming from inside the room, but it ceased abruptly as the uniformed Sergeant opened the door and ushered Emmy in.

At the far end of the room, three chairs had been drawn together into a conspiratorial cluster, and on them sat Vere Prendergast, Sammy Smith, and James Baggot. Their three heads were close together, and there was a distinct element of guilt in the way they drew apart as they saw Emmy.

"Good morning," said Emmy.

Baggot was the first to pull himself together. He came over to Emmy, hands outstretched. "My dear Emmy," he said, "what joy to see you. You can tell us what all this is about."

"Don't you know?" Emmy asked.

"My dear girl," said Jimmy, "I know nothing. I'd barely opened half an eye this morning, and was just trying out my hangover for size, when a couple of ruddy great plainclothes men came barging into the house telling me I was wanted at Scotland Yard. I have the greatest respect and admiration for your husband, but this is really taking things a bit far. Besides, I have a recording session at twelve."

Sammy, who had been sitting with his head in his hands, came to the surface with a sort of bubbling moan. "You haven't got another Alka-Seltzer, old boy, have you?" he said. "'Morning, Blandish. I'd shake you by the hand if I wasn't reasonably certain that my head would come off if I did."

There was a carafe of water and a glass on the table. Jimmy produced a tube of Alka-Seltzers from his pocket, dropped one into a glass of water, and handed it to Sammy. To Emmy, he said, "Poor old Sammy is in a bad way. He got pinched for drunken driving on the way home last night."

Sammy took a long pull at the sizzling drink and made a face. "God almighty, I feel awful," he said. "Now, get this straight, Baggot. I did *not* get pinched. Passed all tests with flying colors and was allowed to go home without a stain on my character. That's why I don't consider that the cops have any right to drag me along here at the crack of…" He groaned. "It's no good. Can't talk. Too painful. Wake me up when the fun starts." With that, he pulled his Teddy Bear greatcoat more closely around his plump form and calmly lay down on the floor, with his face to the wall.

"Poor old Sammy," said Emmy. "Anyhow, I'm sure this gathering has nothing to do with his being pulled in last night."

"It's about Beau, isn't it?" said Vere. He was standing looking out of the window at the dingy area below.

"I think so," said Emmy.

"I gather, then, that our well-meant efforts last night came to nothing," remarked Jimmy. "I'm sorry, Emmy."

"It was too late," said Emmy. "The body had been identified."

"There's something damned irregular about all this," said Vere suddenly. "Surely Henry hasn't any right to be in charge of a case in which his wife is involved. Isn't that right?" he demanded aggressively, addressing nobody in particular.

"Quite right," said Emmy. "I think that's why we're here this morning."

"Eh?" said Vere. "Come again."

"What I mean is, I think Henry's hoping he may be able to clear everything up this morning without it going any further. If he can't, he'll have to hand it over to somebody else..."

"Which will be much more unpleasant for everybody," said Jimmy. "Well, I appreciate Henry's zeal for our welfare. But I don't understand why he's picked on us four."

Emmy opened her mouth to reply, but speech proved unnecessary, for at that moment the Sergeant reappeared heralding Arthur Price and Annie Meadowes. Annie came over to Emmy at once.

"Blandish, I *am* sorry about all this. I did my best..."

"I know you did, Annie. Never mind."

Arthur Price came bustling up. "Mrs. Tibbett—oh, dear, oh, dear... This is all most unfortunate, most unfortunate... Do you think it will be possible to see your husband...?"

"Very soon, I imagine," said Emmy.

"I meant—em—that is, *privately*." Pricey's pink cheeks were even rosier than usual, and his eyes looked almost tearful behind their spectacles. "It's all so *distressing*." He lowered his voice. "I blame myself. Oh, dear me, yes. I should have taken action sooner, but—well—I'm sure your husband will understand—such a charming man, so human... One has to be very careful, with the law as it stands, and a man in my position..."

Quite suddenly, and for the first time, a simple truth dawned on Emmy. She looked at Price with real compassion. She saw his neat, plump hands and feet, his gestures, his tendency to fuss—"a bit of an old woman," they had called him in the Mess. "Why didn't I see it then?" Emmy wondered. "I suppose I was too innocent. Poor Pricey. And now somebody's blackmailing him."

"Don't worry, Pricey," she said, reassuringly. "As far as I know, this is just an informal sort of inquiry into Beau's death. But don't quote me. I'm as much in the dark as anyone." She felt glad that she could say this honestly.

Price smiled, but without much hope. "You're very encouraging, Mrs. Tibbett. One can only hope, I suppose. I thought perhaps that if I could just see your husband alone..." At that moment he noticed the supine form of Sammy Smith, and gave a little jump. "Who—what—what's that? Is he—is he ill, poor fellow?"

"It's only Sammy with a hangover," said Emmy.

"Oh, dear. *That* won't create a good impression. Perhaps we should try to revive him..." Pricey pottered off.

Emmy became aware that Annie was still beside her. She looked very strong and sure of herself, rather like a robust headmistress supervising a rowdy school outing.

"The main thing is not to brood, Blandish," she said. "This is bound to be unpleasant, but it won't last long. We seem to have been spared Barbara's company, which is a mercy." She blew a smoke ring and looked around. "I should have said we were a quorum. Ah, here comes your husband."

But it was not Henry. It was a highly belligerent Sidney Guest. The room was a large one, but it seemed too small to contain him. The other occupants gave the impression of being flattened into two-dimensional shapes against the whitewashed walls.

"I demand to see Tibbett," he was shouting. "It's an encroachment of the liberty of the citizen, and I shall complain with the utmost vigor to the highest authority. It's no use his whining that he sent a car for me. What if he did? That has nothing to do with it. Are we living in a police state, that an innocent man can be dragged from his bed and virtually frog-marched to police headquarters? Well?" He fired the last word like a salvo at the Sergeant, who had been doing his best to beat an unobtrusive retreat.

"Couldn't say, sir," said the Sergeant, smiling rather nervously.

"Then you should be able to say! Or are you just an unthinking cog in a brutal machine? Answer me!"

"It was Chief Inspector's orders," said the Sergeant, backing toward the door.

"What did we fight the last war for?" demanded the Reverend Sidney. "What did my son and his brave comrades sacrifice their lives for? Answer me that!"

"Isn't he marvelous?" said Jimmy Baggot quietly to Emmy. "Who is he?"

"He's Beau's father," said Emmy.

"That's why his face is vaguely familiar, I suppose. Well, we'll certainly keep him in."

"Keep him in what?"

"The series. I've got a first-class writer working on it now. Lucky I got a foot in the door before this story breaks—about finding Beau. Everyone will be after it. Lofty would have made a packet if he'd lived."

By now, the Sergeant had made his escape, and the Reverend Sidney turned back into the room. His eye fell on Emmy and he made straight for her.

"Mrs. Tibbett! What are you doing here? Don't tell me that you, too, have been subjected to this intolerable persecution? Where is your husband? Who are all these people?"

Emmy answered the last question first. "We are all colleagues of Beau's, that is, of Alan's."

The Reverend Sidney looked taken aback. "What an extraordinary thing," he said. He raked the room with his powerful spectacles. "You mean that all these—these nondescript people are colleagues of my son Alan? I understood from the popular press that he and his companions were the epitome of British *jeunesse dorée*."

"That was a long time ago," said Emmy.

"Nonsense," replied Guest. "No time at all. Matter of a few years. And look at them, a collection of middle-aged deadbeats, with—bless my soul, whatever is that?"

Emmy turned, following the Reverend Sidney's pointing finger, and realized that he had just seen Sammy, who was sleeping peacefully on the floor.

"He's asleep," said Emmy.

"Another colleague of Alan's?"

"Whazzat?" said Sammy. He rolled over on his back and opened one eye. When it encountered that of the Reverend Sidney, gazing down on it from a great height, it immediately closed again. "God almighty," said Sammy, and rolled over on his face again.

Emmy was beginning to think that it was high time Henry put in an appearance, and it was with great relief that she saw the door opening once again. This time it *was* Henry. All conversation stopped. He smiled, said, "Good morning," walked up to the table, and sat down.

"It's very kind of you ladies and gentlemen to give me your valuable time," Henry went on.

"Kind?" The Reverend Sidney was on the point of explosion. "Kind, do you call it? We were dragooned here. I intend to make a complaint."

Sammy opened his eyes again. "What's going on?" he demanded. "Izzat Tibbett?"

"It is, Mr. Smith," said Henry. "I hope you're suffering no ill effects from your excessive sobriety last night."

This raised a small laugh and Henry felt guilty, like a nervous schoolmaster who picks on the obvious butt of the class in order to ease his own position.

Sammy sat up and blinked. "I feel fine," he announced. Rather unsteadily, he got to his feet. "Now, let's get this over and we can all go home, what?"

"Very well put," said Henry. "If you'd all like to find chairs and make yourselves as comfortable as this rather austere room permits, I'll explain why I asked you to come here."

There was a good deal of scraping and rustling and eventually everyone was seated. Henry began.

"I expect you have a pretty good idea of what this is all about. Yesterday, in a disused air-raid shelter at Dymfield R.A.F. Station, we found the body of Squadron Leader Guest. The doctors say that he died more than twenty years ago. He was shot in the head."

No sensation was produced by this remark. Henry's audience merely looked at him expectantly, waiting for more.

Henry grinned. "I can see that this does not come as news to anybody here. I think that some of you heard about it yesterday, whereas some of you have known for years. For the moment, however, that aspect does not interest me. A death by shooting twenty years ago is hardly a matter of pressing importance. I am more interested in a modern blackmailer."

The silence in the room was absolute now. Emmy could almost feel the currents of emotion, like electric impulses. A surge of relief, simultaneously with a quickening of apprehension.

Henry seemed unaware of any tension. He went on. "I believe that several people present have received letters or telephone calls, or both, in connection with our discovery yesterday. Only one person, Mr. Smith, took the correct step of informing us at once." He smiled at Sammy, who gave a little mock-bow of acknowledgment. "Now, I want to say at once that nobody has anything to fear from making a full statement. Matters which have no direct bearing on the case will be treated in strict confidence." He paused and looked around the table. "I seem to be talking like a legal machine. Please, will the people concerned tell me about it?"

There was an awkward, shuffling pause. Then the Reverend Sidney said, "I have already told you. I received a letter and a phone call pointing out to me the desirability of keeping you and your men away from Dymfield. I destroyed the letter, and did not recognize the woman's voice."

At this, Annie looked up sharply. "If that was all you wanted of me, Tibbett, it was monstrous to drag me all the way to London."

"Thank you, Mr. Guest," said Henry. He looked around hopefully. "Anybody else?"

Arthur Price had gone the color of an apoplectic beetroot. After a moment's struggle, he said, "I received an—em—a communication. "

"Will you tell me about it?"

"I—surely I am entitled to divulge such a thing to you privately, Inspector? All these people..."

"I take it that the letter was of a threatening nature?"

"Most definitely so. Threatening to make public certain—certain things, if I did not—em..."

"Mr. Price," said Henry. "Did you know that Squadron Leader Guest's body was at Dymfield?"

"Certainly I didn't," said Price indignantly. "Biggest shock of my life when Annie told me."

"Annie told you?"

"Well—yes." Price looked appealingly at Annie. "No harm in telling, is there, Annie?"

"It's a little late to ask that now," said Annie.

"Can we go back a bit?" said Henry. "What did this letter tell you to do?"

"Frankly," said Price, "I couldn't make it out. Wanted to refresh my memory, it said, that I'd seen Emmy Blandish leaving the Operations Room on her bicycle at a quarter past four on the day when the Chief Controller died." Price stopped and looked around, almost apologetically. "I always called him the Chief Controller," he said to Henry, who saw no need for an explanation.

"Call him what you like," said Henry. "Go on."

"Well—imagine!" Now that Price realized that his private life was not going to be made public, he seemed to be enjoying

himself. "I couldn't make head nor tail of it. I've a dim recollection, it's true, of seeing Emmy cycling away from the
Operations Room that evening, but as for saying definitely
what time it was—well..." He shrugged. "The letter went on to
say that Annie had also seen Blandish leaving the Operations
Block, and that I'd better contact her to make sure our stories
tallied. Well, I had Annie's address, of course, because of the
reunion. So I telephoned her."

"This would have been yesterday morning—Friday?"
Henry was making a note.

"That's right. I telephoned Annie around nine in the
morning. That was when she told me about the Chief Controller.
It gave me a nasty turn."

Henry glanced up from his notebook. Emmy was looking
at Annie as though she had never seen her before. Annie,
serene as ever, was lighting a cigarette. Henry noticed how
large and strong her hands were, and how steady.

"She said," Price went on, "that we should meet. Didn't
you, Annie dear? She said she'd catch a plane to London,
which she did. She arrived at midday, and we had a talk at
my house."

"What was said?" Henry asked.

Price looked appealingly at Annie. "I don't want to speak
out of turn," he said unhappily. "Can't Annie tell you herself?"

"Perhaps she can," said Henry. "Well, Mrs. Meadowes?"

Annie seemed quite composed. "I did my best to get him
to keep his mouth shut about seeing Blandish," she said. "He
yapped a bit about committing perjury, but I soon got the truth
out of him. He'd had this letter and he dared not disobey it.
Poor Pricey, he was in a hell of a flap," she added, with more
contempt than pity. "Anyhow, I decided something should be
done. I decided to find out just what was going on."

"Had you any theory about who might have sent the anonymous letter?"

"Yes," said Annie promptly. "Obviously Vere."

"Here, I say!" protested Vere.

Annie did not even look at him. Sammy Smith, who was nursing his aching head again, winked at Vere. "Very enterprising, old cock," he said. "Did it take long—pasting all those words on the paper?"

"Wrap up, Sammy," said Vere. "It's not funny."

"Go on, Mrs. Meadowes," said Henry.

"Well, I telephoned Vere. Talk about flaps! First Pricey and then Vere!"

"You never said a word about anonymous letters! Not a word," said Vere.

"I didn't get a chance."

"If you'd just explained quietly..."

"Quietly!" Annie appealed to Henry. "Ever tried having a quiet conversation with a jumping bean? From the incoherent babble, I gathered that Barbara was in London, that you were due to visit Dymfield with a shovel, that the whole sordid story was about to be revealed, including Vere's part in it, that Barbara would never get over it, and so forth. I asked him what he proposed to do, and he said he'd done all he could, which I took to mean the issue of Price's anonymous epistle."

"Meant nothing of the sort," mumbled Vere. He had gone very red in the face. "I'd persuaded Barbara to go to London. Thought that was a sound move. Get her out of the way."

"Vere, you're hopeless," said Annie. Turning to Henry, she went on. "It was my idea that he should go over to the Duke's Head. I felt sure you'd be lunching there, and I thought he might be in time to head you away from Dymfield. I gave him my phone number—I was at my London club—and told him to keep in touch. The next I heard from him was that he'd missed you, but had collared Blandish and brought her back to Whitchurch. I then told him what to do next—bring Blandish to London and dump her somewhere with Barbara, and then go to Chelsea and tackle you. He said he'd leave Emmy with Barbara at the Blue Parrot, which seemed satisfactory. Did he run you to earth in Chelsea?"

"Yes," said Henry. "He obeyed your orders faithfully. I wonder why?"

"I'm a forceful woman," said Annie simply. "I suppose he cut no ice with you?"

"None, I'm afraid."

"I might have known it. He was the wrong person to send."

"I wish," said Vere, "that you wouldn't talk as though I weren't here."

Annie ignored him. "Shall I go on?" she asked Henry.

"Just a minute, Mrs. Meadowes," said Henry. He turned to Vere. "Mr. Prendergast," he said, "apart from packing your wife off to London, did you take any other steps before Mrs. Meadowes rang you?"

"He rang me," said Sammy. He laughed and then winced. "Annie's right. A jumping bean sums it up nicely. Wanted to know what I thought he ought to do. 'Let Nature take its course, old scout,' I said. 'I suppose it was you who sent me that cloak-and-dagger letter this morning? Well, you'll live to regret it, old top, because it's now in the hands of the coppers.' That put the wind up you, didn't it, old man? 'Take my advice, old man,' I said, 'make a clean breast of it. It's ancient history now, and nobody cares a rap one way or the other about Beau Guest.' But old Vere wouldn't listen to reason. Suggested talking to you, Tibbett, and trying to persuade you to hush the whole matter up. I told him what I thought of *that* little scheme."

"You wished me the best of luck," said Vere.

Sammy winked at Emmy. "The best of British luck, dear old soul," he said. "Those were my words. You may quote me."

Henry had to suppress a smile. "Would you like to go on, Mrs. Meadowes?" he said to Annie.

Sammy held up a shaky but decisive hand. "No," he said. "My part in the saga is not yet over. May I continue?" Henry bowed assent. "The next thing I did," said Sammy, "was to telephone Jimmy. I'm so sorry—*Mister* Baggot. Or would it be premature to say 'Sir James'?"

"Don't be more of an idiot than you can help, Sammy," said Baggot. He did not, however, sound displeased.

"I rang him," Sammy went on delicately, "for certain personal and financial reasons, which I need not go into now. Suffice it..."

"Probably trying to borrow money," said Vere to Henry in a stage whisper. Annie gave a great laugh, and Henry found it difficult not to join in.

However, he kept his face straight as he said, "Very well, Mr. Smith. No need to go into them."

"He flatly refused to lend me ten quid till next Thursday," said Sammy with dignity, "but he was most interested in what I had to tell him about—well, we all know what about. Most strangely interested."

Baggot did not appear to be at all embarrassed. "Certainly I was interested," he said to Henry. "I'm planning a series along the lines of 'Unsolved Mysteries of the Second World War.' That's just the working title, of course. Each episode to be a short serial, in three or four installments. Beau was to have been my first subject."

"Your script to be based on my wife's research?" asked Henry.

Baggot reddened angrily. "I explained to you," he said. "The whole thing is in the hands of the copyright department."

Henry grinned. "Okay," he said, "go on,"

"Well, it seemed to me, from what Sammy said, that we might be on to something quite sensational. In most series of this sort, I mean, the best we can do is to present all the old evidence, plus perhaps a few inconclusive bits dug up recently—hitherto unpublished letters and so forth—and then finish the program with an appeal to the viewers to decide for themselves. But supposing, for once, we could produce new and absolutely convincing evidence, revealed for the very first time on the television screen..." He stopped and smiled. "Sorry. I'm talking like a story conference. But you see what

I mean. I was prepared—I still am—to go to considerable lengths to insure exclusivity."

Henry looked at him unbelievingly. "You want police evidence suppressed until you can produce it on your T.V. program?"

"I wouldn't exactly say 'suppressed,' Call it soft-pedaled. Anyhow, Sammy pointed out to me that Blandish was rather more involved in the matter than you might be aware of, and it struck me that it would be a sound move to get her on my side, as it were."

"By blackmail?" said Henry.

"*Blackmail?*" Jimmy was shocked. He appealed to Emmy. "Did anybody blackmail you, Blandish?"

"No," said Emmy. "I thought you were trying to help me."

"I was trying to help you," Annie cried. "Jimmy, you're a low-down underhanded..."

"Please," said Henry. "Let's cut out the abuse and get on with the story. Mr. Baggot?"

"Well," said Jimmy, "I arranged a party. I thought we should all get together, and it seemed a natural and unobtrusive cover for our little reunion. I invited Sammy, and then I rang Price, who told me that Annie was in town, which was great news. And Annie actually knew that Blandish was going to be at the Blue Parrot with Barbara. Naturally, I didn't want Barbara hanging around, so we sent Price off to ease Emmy away from the bar and bring her along. You know the rest."

"Yes," said Henry, "I know the rest."

Annie shrugged. "Well," she said, "the plan didn't work, and since I've heard Jimmy's sordid motives, I'm not altogether sorry. So, the dirty linen is hanging out on the line; you'll be handing the case over to a disinterested party; Barbara will have her nervous breakdown—or whatever it is that Vere's afraid of—Jimmy will go ahead regardless with his horrible series; and Blandish will have some very swift explaining to do. Can we all go home now?"

"No," said Henry. "I want to know how many of you knew about Beau's body being in the air-raid shelter." There was dead silence. Henry went on. "Vere Prendergast knew. So did Sammy Smith and Annie Day. I am pretty sure that Arthur Price, James Baggot, and Mr. Guest, senior, only heard the news yesterday. Is anyone going to question that?"

Once again an almost tangible silence.

Henry went on. "Between the three of you—Prendergast, Smith, and Day—this grisly bit of information was known by the code name of Johnny Head-in-Air. A reference, of course, to the famous wartime poem contrasting Johnny Head-in-Air with Johnny Under Ground." Henry was looking stern now. "Come along," he said briskly, like a games master inviting a reluctant class to jump into the swimming pool. "You first, Mr. Prendergast. Go back to the night of October 13, 1943. Who told you that Beau Guest had shot himself in the air-raid shelter?"

Vere said nothing.

"Oh, I dare say you had some sort of pact of honor not to tell," said Henry impatiently, "but I really can't tolerate this childishness. This is a police inquiry."

Slowly Vere said, "I can't see that it matters telling you, since you know so much already. Sammy told me. Telephoned me. I was in the Mess. I went down and met him at the Duke's Head. He told me, and I took the kite up myself. You know that."

"Thank you," said Henry. "Well, Mr. Smith. Who told you about Guest?"

"Annie did. Rang me at the pub."

"How did she know where to find you? I thought you were on leave?"

"Not leave, old boy. Just an S.O.P., as it were."

"What's an S.O.P.?"

"Sleeping Out Pass. Permission to spend the night other than in official quarters. Everyone knew where I was. My girl-friend was visiting me, you see."

"I see. Well?" Henry looked inquiringly at Annie.

She was looking angry and puzzled. "Vere told me," she said. "I was on duty at Dymfield, as you know. He telephoned me and told me. Blandish was still away from the Operations Room."

"That's a lie," said Vere. "I never telephoned you."

"You did. You suggested I should ring Sammy. You were in a flap, as usual."

"That's not true."

"It is, and you know it."

"Just a moment," said Henry. "Let me get this straight. Smith told Prendergast. Prendergast told Day. Day told Smith. We're back to the old daisy chain. A tells B who tells C who tells A who..." Angrily, he thumped the table with his bulky file of papers. "It's exactly the same as your account of what happened yesterday. Everybody's actions were apparently triggered off by somebody else's. But, Goddamn it, the thing started somewhere. *Someone* set the mechanism going, and then slipped into the ring to join the dance. And someone," Henry added, "killed Lofty Parker, and for a very good reason."

There was a shocked silence. Henry went on. "Yes, Lofty Parker did not commit suicide. He was murdered. He was murdered, because he was on the point of making a discovery, the discovery that all those years ago Beau Guest did not commit suicide either. He was shot by somebody else. By the person who started the ring-of-roses games. And I intend to find out who that person was."

It was at that moment that Henry realized that the five pairs of eyes were no longer fixed on him. They were looking at Emmy.

Henry stood up. "That's all for the moment," he said. "I must ask you all to remain available for further talks as our inquiries progress. Can you stay in London for a few days more, Mrs. Meadowes?"

"Certainly," said Annie. "I shall be at the Ladies' Cavendish Club."

Henry made a note. "Good," he said. "The rest of you, please inform my office if you intend to go away from home. We'll be in touch soon."

There was a bewildered silence.

Then Sammy, who had been nursing his head again, looked up and said, "You mean—we can go?"

"Yes," said Henry.

"Bit of an anticlimax, isn't it?" Sammy sounded positively disappointed. "No spectacular arrest? No master criminal unmasked?"

Henry smiled. "Not today, I'm afraid." He looked around the room. "I'll be frank with you," he said. "You are all intelligent people and I can't believe that any of you would shield a murderer, even if he—or she—were an old friend. I'm depending on all of you to help me. I've narrowed the field," his glance traveled around the room, "but what I lack is motive. If I can find *why* Guest was killed, I shall know who did it. I'm convinced that positive proof of such motive exists. Tomorrow my men will be taking the Dymfield Operations Room apart, looking for it. But I doubt if they'll find anything. I think that my proof will come from one of you—when you decide to come and tell me about it."

"You're pretty cryptic, aren't you, old sleuth?" said Vere. "I didn't understand a word of that."

"Then you are very fortunate," said Henry. "I am quite sure that somebody did. Well—that's that. I'd like a word with Mr. Guest and Mr. Price. If you'd come with me to my office, Mr. Guest…? Emmy, will you wait here with Mr. Price for a few minutes? The rest of you may go."

There was a scraping of wood on wood as everyone stood up. Then the little group straggled out into the corridor. It was noticeable that nobody was talking to anybody else. They walked out into the watery sunshine and went their various ways.

Henry wondered how many of them would be aware of the fact that they were being shadowed.

CHAPTER NINETEEN

IN HIS OFFICE Henry faced the Reverend Sidney, and felt glad that there was a stout oaken desk between them. The old man had been strangely subdued during the inquiry, but he had now recovered all his old fire.

"The whole matter is a disgrace!" he shouted, banging the desk with his fist. "Why was it not discovered years ago? What do we pay our taxes for? What is being done about it now? Nothing. Dragging me up from the country to witness the spineless performance we saw this morning..."

Henry managed to get a word in. "I wanted to speak to you," he said, "about your wife."

The effect was instantaneous. It was like watching the air go out of a balloon.

"Oh, dear me," said the Reverend Sidney, "I should have known. More trouble, I suppose. What is it this time?"

"She is a patient at Sandfields Hospital, is she not?"

"You know very well that she is."

"Being treated for alcoholism?"

"Treated? Ha. That's one way of describing it. She's long past curing, Inspector. Has been for years. The trouble starts when she gets out, as she does, far too frequently. Inadequate supervision. I've complained time after time. And what happens?"

"I was hoping that you would tell me that," said Henry.

"The trouble is," went on the Reverend Sidney, "that she is so plausible. Or so they tell me. I have not seen her for many years, of course. I could hardly be expected to visit her, under the circumstances. I merely pay the bills."

"Under what circumstances? Why don't you visit her?"

The old man looked anxiously around. "This will go no further, I trust."

"Not unless it has a direct bearing on the case."

"Well—since it is every citizen's duty to assist the police—I will tell you the whole story. In confidence. When my son Alan was less than two years old, my wife deserted me. Ran away with a jazz-band player. They lived together for some years, and she had a child by him. They were extremely anxious to marry, but naturally I refused to divorce her."

"Wasn't that rather harsh?" asked Henry.

"I am a Christian," snapped the Reverend Sidney. "Hard cases make bad law, as you should know. One cannot consider the individual when the sanctity of family life is at stake."

Henry did not trust himself to say anything. Instead, he lit a cigarette.

Guest went on. "My wife apparently became hysterical over the situation. She was always an unbalanced personality. Eventually she took to alcohol. Her condition deteriorated to the point where her paramour could stand it no longer. He had the impertinence to write to *me*, if you please. Some story about the child having been very ill, and of feeling compelled to take him away from June, my wife, for the boy's sake; and asking me if I would do something to help the wretched woman. Simply evading his responsibilities, of course. However, I was still June's husband—I still am—and just as my convictions prevented me from divorcing her, so they compelled me to remain responsible for her. I found her living in a slum in Soho in a lamentable state. Lamentable. I arranged for her to go to Sandfields, a most expensive proceeding considering the size of my stipend. I do not think that anyone can accuse me of being ungenerous. Why do you smile?"

"I wasn't smiling," said Henry. "Please go on."

"Well, there she remained, on my orders. Once or twice, in the early days, the hospital attempted to convince me that she was cured and discharged her. She was always brought back, hopelessly intoxicated, within a short time. They now agree that she is incurable. It was the matter of her son which utterly deranged the poor creature."

"Alan?"

"No, no. The illegitimate boy. She was always looking for him. Still is, even now. She gets out of the hospital, you see, and battens on unsuspecting strangers. Apparently, she can appear completely normal, and she was always an attractive woman. She borrows money from these people and disappears, ostensibly to look for her son. She is invariably picked up by the police, dead drunk and penniless. And I have to pay out large sums to recompense the people she has swindled and to hush things up. You can imagine the effect that it would have on my life if the story got about."

"So that was the threat contained in the anonymous letter?"

"Precisely. It was not specified just how the discovery of Alan's body would lead to exposure of the other matter, but I was not prepared to take any chances."

Henry suddenly felt very tired and longed to be rid of the Reverend Sidney. He said, "I suppose your wife's second son took his father's name?"

"I suppose so."

"And that name was…?"

"I have no idea."

Henry looked up sharply. "Of course you have. You had a letter from the man."

The Reverend Sidney moved unsteadily in his chair. "I can't see that it is of the slightest importance…"

"It's extremely important," said Henry, "if the name is what I think it is."

"And what is that?"

"Parker. Jeremy Parker."

The Reverend Sidney sat quite still. His breathing grew harsher and more audible as he did his best to hide any sign of emotion.

"I'm not guessing," said Henry, "I know."

"How can you know?"

"The other day," said Henry, "I saw a photograph of your son, Alan, taken before his crash. It was not the one used by the plastic surgeons when they rebuilt his face. The photograph immediately struck me as being familiar, although I couldn't quite think why. And then I realized. It was astonishingly like Lofty Parker. Apart from the fact that one was dark and the other fair, the half-brothers were extraordinarily alike." Guest said nothing. "It was foolish of you to make a mystery out of the name. After all, there are plenty of Parkers in England. As it is, it's obvious that you knew who Charles Parker was. The question is—did *he* know?"

"I am not in a position to answer that," said the Reverend Sidney. He seemed to find speech difficult.

"Did Alan know that he had a half-brother?"

"I imagine so. Alan used to insist on visiting his mother, against my wishes. Since she was obsessed with the other boy, she must surely have talked about him. Naturally, Alan and I never mentioned the matter."

"Naturally," said Henry, with an irony that was lost on Guest. "Did the boys ever meet, that is, before coincidence threw them together in the R.A.F.?"

"Not to my knowledge."

"How did you know Charles Parker's identity?"

"I would prefer not to tell you."

"I'm sure you would," said Henry. "Nevertheless, you will do so. This isn't a friendly chat, Mr. Guest; it's a murder investigation."

The Reverend Sidney had gone very red in the face. "I have a sense of responsibility," he said. "This boy is—was—after all, my wife's son. Shortly before the last war, Parker, the father, got in touch with me again. He was, it seemed, quite without funds, but had been offered a job in America. He wished to leave England, but had no means of supporting his son, who was then in his last year of school. I paid for the boy to finish his schooling, and since then I have made him a small allowance. Fortunately, I have certain private means, not great, but enough to… I arranged carefully that the boy should be under the impression that the money came from his natural father. When Jeremy Parker died in America, the solicitors were instructed to tell Charles that the money came from his father's estate."

The old man was by now beetroot-colored. The confession of a genuine philanthropy seemed to upset him greatly.

"You told us," said Henry, "that you had thrown away that questionnaire without looking at it. That's not true, is it? You looked at it and you saw Parker's name and address. You knew he was writing this book."

"I don't deny it. But I want to emphasize that I never met Charles Parker. Never. I knew his address, and I helped him financially, from a sense of duty. That is all there was to it."

Henry stood up. "All right," he said. "That'll be all for the moment. I'll be in touch with you again."

"And you won't divulge…?"

"Not unless it's absolutely necessary."

At the door the Reverend Sidney paused, turned back, and said, "I repeat that I never met him. A scamp and a wastrel, by all accounts. Only got what he deserved."

He rammed on his hat and stalked out.

Henry sent for Arthur Price.

Left alone by themselves in the bare interview room, Emmy and Arthur Price regarded each other with mutual embarrassment. After a long silence and a couple of false starts, Price said at last, "I'm extremely sorry about all this, Mrs. Tibbett. Extremely sorry."

"So am I," said Emmy. "For you, I mean."

Price went pinker than ever. "Oh, pray," he said, "don't concern yourself with my affairs. Believe me. I would gladly have—em—forgotten the events of that terrible night. But you understand my predicament. I *did* see you—on your bicycle... I don't suppose you saw me..."

"Where were you?" Emmy asked.

Price mopped his brow. "I, that is, there was a young corporal at Dymfield, a mechanic, one of the ground staff... I had taken an interest in his welfare... He had financial problems—a most talented lad..."

"I understand," said Emmy gently.

"We met that evening, briefly—just for a chat... Naturally, it had to be well away from the Mess—wouldn't have done, you see, mixing with other ranks... We were near his billet, as a matter of fact. Gave me quite a fright when you came by. But you didn't see us."

"No," said Emmy. "I didn't. I wonder who did?"

Price gave a nervous little jump. "Whatever do you mean?"

"You know what I mean, Pricey," said Emmy. "Somebody has been blackmailing you very efficiently."

"I assure you," said Price, "that the letter I received made no mention of *that* incident. No, no. The reference was to a more recent..."

"I'm sure it was," said Emmy. "But somebody who knew you in the old days knew enough about your private affairs to—to know what direction to look in. Don't you agree?"

Price had no time to reply before the door opened and the Sergeant informed him that Chief Inspector Tibbett would like to see him. When Price had gone, the Sergeant returned and said to Emmy, "The Chief Inspector says he won't be long now, Mrs. Tibbett. He thought you might like to have a cup of coffee in the canteen while you're waiting for him."

"Thanks a lot," said Emmy. "Actually, I think I'll treat myself to a cappuccino. Will you tell my husband I'll be in the espresso shop around the corner? He'll know where I mean; we often meet there."

"Very good, Mrs. Tibbett," said the Sergeant woodenly. Secretly, he was eying Emmy with some interest. He had not met her before, but he was well aware of the rumpus caused by her escapade of the previous night. Funny, he thought. Doesn't look the flirty type. Just shows you never can tell. It's the quietest ones that spring the biggest surprises. Poor old Chief. Pretty silly she made him look last night.

Unaware of this scrutiny, Emmy gave the Sergeant a friendly smile, and left the building. In the street outside she met a woman whom she knew slightly, and gladly agreed it would be pleasant to take a cup of coffee in company. They walked off down the road together.

Henry had very little trouble with Arthur Price. He started straight off, without preamble. "Now, Mr. Price, I want the truth of where you were last Saturday evening."

"I told you, Inspector…"

"You told me a pack of lies."

"You can check with my club…"

"Oh, yes," said Henry, "that part was true. Certainly you played bridge in most respectable company until half-past six. After that you told me a flimsy falsehood, which you hoped could not be checked. You were wrong."

Price looked up, startled. "Was I?" he asked ingenuously.

Henry found it hard not to smile. "I suppose you saw *Boadicea* earlier in the week?"

"Well—I…"

"You should have taken the trouble to find out," said Henry, "that it closed on Friday. It was not playing on Saturday night."

"Oh, dear me. That was foolish of me, wasn't it? I thought these things always ran for months. You must think me very stupid, Inspector."

"I shall think you a lot stupider," said Henry, "if you don't now tell me the exact truth."

It was a sordid but predictable little story. Price had spent the evening at the flat of "a friend." This friend was particularly anxious that his name should not be mentioned, and it was to respect his friend's wishes that Price had, as he put it, "exercised a little innocent deception." Of course, there was nothing *wrong* in the friendship, if Henry understood what Price meant. It was simply that the young man in question was sensitive about publicity, and...

Henry said dryly that he understood perfectly, but that it was necessary for the friend's name to be divulged. After much humming and hawing and polishing of spectacles, Price agreed and told Henry the name. It was not unknown to Henry, and had no further relevance to the investigation, but Henry was well able to understand that a man in Price's position would not wish such a connection to be bruited abroad.

"I presume," said Henry, "that the anonymous letter threatened to expose this friendship of yours."

"Well—yes, I fear so. It's so *unfair*," added Price with pathetic vehemence. "It isn't as if there was anything *wrong*; I have been trying to help the boy. He has so much *good* in him..."

Henry said, "I am sure that your motives are purely philanthropic, Mr. Price, but I really wouldn't waste your good will on that young man."

Price looked sharply at Henry, unable to make up his mind whether or not he was being mocked; then decided to take Henry's remark at its face value. He thanked Henry for his kindness, and took his leave hastily, only partially reassured by Henry's promise not to make use of his friend's name unless it proved strictly necessary.

When Price had gone, Henry went in search of Emmy. Briefed by the Sergeant, he made for the coffee shop. It was crowded, and Henry wasted several minutes ascertaining that Emmy was not among those present. He supposed she must have grown tired of waiting and gone to do some shopping. He went back to Scotland Yard, and organized the use of a police car and the services of Detective Sergeant Reynolds. He also spoke to his colleague in East Anglia. Then he tried to telephone his home. There was no reply.

By now Henry was distinctly cross. Emmy should surely have realized that he was worried about her, but after the debacle of last night, he was not going to risk raising another false alarm. She could not be in any danger since all her old chums had left Scotland Yard accompanied by discreet police shadows; nevertheless, Henry was unhappy about leaving London without knowing where Emmy was. And he could not tell her of his plans, except by leaving a message in his office in case she called. It was all extremely annoying, and it was all Emmy's fault.

Shortly before he left the Yard, Henry received the first reports telephoned in from the detectives detailed to follow his group of suspects. Prendergast had taken a taxi to the Blue Parrot club, where, as the only customer, he had been drinking whisky ever since. The detective had observed him in conversation with Mabel, the proprietress, who had left with a shopping basket shortly after their conversation. To get away from Prendergast, the detective surmised. Vere had had a distinct air of the Ancient Mariner, and Mabel must have been relieved to hand over the role of Wedding Guest to the barman.

Annie Meadowes had traveled by bus to Knightsbridge, then walked across the park to the Ladies' Cavendish Club. She was now in the lounge writing letters.

Sammy Smith had made straight for the nearest bar, where a young woman with a beehive hair-do was waiting for him, clearly in a state of some anxiety. They had had a drink together, and then parted—the young woman heading for the West End, while Sammy himself entered the Turkish Baths in Northumberland Avenue. He was still there—"and likely to remain so," thought Henry.

James Baggot had been met by a chauffeur-driven car containing, besides the chauffeur, a very smart, dark-haired young lady. The car had driven them to a recording studio in Oxford Street.

The Reverend Sidney Guest had walked to Liverpool Street Station and taken a train for home. No report had yet been received on Arthur Price, who had but recently left Scotland Yard.

All very ordinary, characteristic behavior, Henry reflected. Nothing in the least suspicious. He called Reynolds and together they drove off, heading northeast.

❖ ❖ ❖

It was a cold, blustery day. Some brave chrysanthemums still stood in the country gardens, but they looked like bedraggled survivors of a battle, barely able to hold their tattered banners upright. October was at the gates and autumn was in full retreat.

Henry dropped Reynolds off in Whitchurch village, and felt a pang of envy as he watched the Sergeant's broad back disappearing into the snuggery of the inn, where he was to await Henry's return. Whitchurch Manor looked uninviting. It seemed to be huddling and hugging itself against the dismal chill of the outside world, and Henry had a strong feeling that visitors would not be welcome.

Barbara answered the doorbell so quickly that she must have been waiting and watching ever since the car turned into the drive. She was not so much hostile as desperately nervous.

"Where's Vere?" were her first words.

"Still in London, I presume," said Henry. "May I come in, Mrs. Prendergast?"

Barbara stood aside to let him enter and closed the door behind him, saying, "Is he in prison?"

"Of course not," said Henry. "Surely you weren't worried...?"

"Worried?" Barbara laughed harshly. "I suppose you never stop to think of the effect it's going to have on people's families when you send policemen to drag them out of their beds at all hours…"

"I'm sorry," said Henry. "I had to see your husband."

"And now that you've seen him?"

"I want a word with you."

They were in the drawing room by this time. Logs crackled and smoldered in the big fireplace, giving out an aromatic, wintry smell. From the table, the photograph of Beau Guest grinned at Henry.

"Let's have a drink," said Barbara. She sounded a little more at ease. "Please forgive me. I'm not a nervous person as a rule, but… Now, what will you have? Whisky? Sherry? Gin? You will stay to lunch, won't you? Just cold meat and salad, but there's plenty of it. Now, please tell me where Vere is and what he's doing. Why isn't he with you?"

As she paused for breath, Henry said, "I suppose I ought to reply—'sherry, yes, no, I don't know, possibly.' Or something of the sort. To tell you the truth, you went too fast for me. Anyhow, for a start, I'd love a sherry—dry, if possible."

"Of course," said Barbara. It sounded as though a thaw had set in.

"Second," said Henry, "it's very kind of you to ask me to lunch, and I accept with pleasure. Third—what was the third? Oh, yes. Where's Vere? I really don't know. He came to a little conference at my office this morning, but he was away from Scotland Yard by eleven o'clock. I dare say he went off for a quiet drink and a bite of lunch."

Barbara was smiling a little shamefacedly as she handed him a small glass of pale golden sherry. "Isn't it idiotic how hysterical one gets?" she said. "Vere has been—well—rather strange lately, and what with Lofty's death and everything, I suppose I'm inclined to be jumpy." She looked at the photograph and then away again.

At that moment a plump countrywoman in a white apron came in and said, "What will it be for lunch, then, madam?"

"Just a cold lunch, Mrs. Rudd. For two."

"In that case, it's ready," said Mrs. Rudd. She turned and walked out.

Henry did not see her again.

After lunch Barbara settled Henry into a large armchair by the fire and went off to make coffee. "My marvelous Mrs. Rudd only comes in the mornings," she explained. "Eight till one. Still, I suppose I'm very lucky. She will come and cook dinner sometimes, if I'm having a party."

Outside it was raining again, and the slender, bare arms of the wisteria were beating against the leaded windowpanes. Barbara came back with the coffee, sat down, and said, "So you wanted to speak to me?"

"Yes," said Henry. He glanced at the table. "That's an old photograph of your first husband, isn't it? Taken before his crash, I mean."

"Yes—the day he got his wings. Before I met him. He must have been—let me see—just twenty..."

"And Lofty Parker must have been seventeen or eighteen."

Barbara sat up very straight. "What has that got to do with it?"

"When did you first meet Lofty?"

"Why—at Dymfield..."

"No, no, no." Henry shook his head impatiently. "You knew Lofty long before that. I realized it when I saw you here together. You met him in 1940, when he was assistant stage manager to *Summer Song*."

It was, strictly speaking, a guess, but Henry knew at once that he had been right. Barbara froze, her cigarette halfway to her mouth. Before she could say anything, Henry went on. "You had a small part in the show. You were eighteen, or thereabouts. You were a gay young thing, and Charlie Parker was your steady boyfriend. But there were others, weren't there? Soldiers, sailors, and airmen, passing through London on leave. Especially airmen. Then Charlie did you a good turn. He introduced you to his half-brother, the famous Beau Guest, the fighter ace. Beau and Vere became rivals for your favors.

You were on the upward path, all right. I don't suppose you gave another thought to Charlie until you arrived at Dymfield in 1943 and found him there, as one of your husband's junior officers. Did either of them explain to you why they weren't acknowledging their relationship to each other?"

Barbara had evidently decided that things had gone too far for denial. She said, "What, and have the whole sordid story made public?"

"I must say you have nerve," said Henry. "You tried to get Lofty to write all those lies about Beau's parents..."

"What possible harm could it have done?"

"I don't think," said Henry, "that he was planning to play along with you. Did you know that he had sent Emmy to interview Beau's father?"

"The rotten little tick," said Barbara. She did not sound unduly worried.

"Let's go back a bit," said Henry. "Beau was killed. You married Vere. You lost touch completely with Lofty. When you met at the reunion, you saw at once that he was down on his luck, and you decided to make use of him for a plan you were hatching."

Barbara blew a smoke ring. "Clever little detective," she said. "And what was this plan supposed to be?"

"You wanted a biography of Beau."

"Well, why shouldn't I want it?"

"The question is rather, why should you?" said Henry. "My wife thinks you may have a guilt complex. I would doubt that, myself. I think the reason was much simpler. You wanted to establish, once and for all, that you were really married to Vere—and, of course, to his money."

This did not amuse Barbara at all. "Just what are you getting at?"

"Beau Guest was reported missing, presumed killed. Before you and Vere married, you should have made sure that Beau was declared legally dead by a court of law. You didn't bother with this formality. I imagine Vere was against it."

"That's quite right," said Barbara. "He wouldn't let me do it. I never knew why."

"He had good reasons," said Henry, "for not wanting to stir up any legal inquiries. However, cases have occurred—as I'm sure you know—of people turning up years after their supposed deaths and claiming their rights. If they've been declared legally dead, there's not much they can do; their marriages have been dissolved and their ex-spouses set free to remarry. But your husband was never declared legally dead. A memorial book would have—what shall I say—would have strengthened your case. The surprising thing is that you waited twenty years."

Henry waited hopefully for Barbara to say something. She had gone very pale and was twisting her hands nervously together.

"Supposing," said Henry at last, "that I tell you that Beau Guest is without doubt and demonstrably dead and has been for at least twenty years?"

She turned and clutched Henry's hand. "Is that true? Do you swear it? Are you sure?"

"I'm absolutely sure," said Henry.

Barbara began to cry, tears of sheer relief. "Thank God! Thank God!"

"I suppose you've been getting letters alleging that he was alive."

"Yes. For the last six months—about once a week..."

"Purporting to come from him?"

"Yes..."

"Signed?"

"No—typewritten... Of course, I couldn't be sure they were from him, but I didn't dare take the chance. He was threatening to come back... I had to send money..." She dabbed her eyes. "Who sent them, then? How did he manage to know so much about us—Beau and me? That's what made me think they were genuine..."

"I think I know who sent them," said Henry, "but I can't tell you for the moment. The next time you are blackmailed, for heaven's sake go straight to the police. If you'd done that, Lofty would probably have been alive now. In any case, you can set your mind at rest. You won't be troubled in that way anymore. Your first husband did die in 1943, but not quite in the way that you imagined at the time. In fact, I have seen his body."

"You've—*what?*"

"We found him yesterday, in an old air-raid shelter at Dymfield. Vere knew about it, and that was one of the reasons I wanted to talk to him this morning."

"Vere knew yesterday? Then why didn't he tell me?"

Henry smiled, a little wryly. "He was afraid of upsetting you," he said.

Back in Whitchurch village Henry called at the post office and tried to phone Emmy. There was no reply. He then contacted his office and got the latest reports on his suspects. Sammy was still in his Turkish Bath. Baggot was still in his recording studio. Vere was en route for Whitchurch in his car. Annie was closeted in her bedroom at her club. Arthur Price was in his City office. The Reverend Sidney had arrived home, and had set out almost at once for a country walk. Henry found these reports a little puzzling. People were not reacting in the way he had expected. He was very thoughtful as he walked over to the inn to pick up Sergeant Reynolds.

(HAPTER TWENTY

IT WAS FOUR O'CLOCK in the afternoon before they were all ready—Henry and Reynolds and a strong-arm squad from the local force. The Scotland Yard car, with Henry at the wheel and Reynolds beside him, led the procession; after it came two radio cars bulging with purposeful-looking officers. It was a conspicuous cavalcade, and for this reason Henry halted it in a country lane some distance from the entrance to R.A.F. Dymfield. He and Reynolds were to go ahead on foot, followed after a discreet interval by the rest of the party.

Taking no chances—for he could not be sure that nobody had arrived at Dymfield before them—Henry motioned to Reynolds to keep well in toward the hedge as they proceeded in Indian file up the lane. These precautions proved futile. As Henry edged his way toward the gate, he was greeted by a loud, cheerful young voice.

"Ah, there you are, sir!"

Feeling exceptionally foolish, Henry emerged from the hedge, followed by a sheepish Reynolds. At the open gate of the Dymfield compound stood Pilot Officer Simmonds, all smiles.

"Thought you might turn up, sir," he announced blithely. "Lucky you got here in time. He must be almost through down there by now. Another half-hour and you'd have missed him."

"Missed who?" asked Henry.

"Why—the flight lieutenant—didn't get his name—who came along to the Air Ministry. And Mrs. Tibbett, of course. As soon as I saw her, I knew it would be in order. About opening up the station, I mean."

"My wife turned up at the Air Ministry? When?"

"About one o'clock. Lunchtime. I was alone in the office."

"And she was with a flight lieutenant?"

"That's right. He'd served on this station during the war, he said, and he was helping you in your inquiries here. He wanted to take another look at the Operations Room."

"And you gave him the key?"

Simmonds looked reproachful. "Oh, no, sir. That would have been against regulations. That's why I came down here with them. I opened up the Operations Block for them, but the key's here." Simmonds patted his pocket smugly.

"Did you speak to my wife?"

"Not actually. The flight lieutenant had his own car, you see, and he drove her down. He said she was very tired; I saw her dozing in the back. I came down with my own transport. The flight lieutenant explained that he was going straight on to Hull after he'd finished this job. He said that Mrs. Tibbett would stay on a bit in the Operations Room after he'd gone—so many memories. Quite understandable, of course. He said you might come to collect her, but if you didn't, I was to drive her back to town about six." Simmonds glanced at his watch. "The flight lieutenant said he'd be about half an hour, and he's been down there over ten minutes, so..."

Henry could hear his own breath coming fast and jerkily, like that of a man who has been running long and hard.

"Listen, Simmonds," he said, "I've no time to explain, but this is deadly serious. Get in your car and drive down the lane toward Whitchurch until you meet a couple of parked police cars. Bring them back here as fast as you can, and tell them to come to the Operations Room entrance. Tell them I said so. And also tell them not to come any farther than the entrance without orders from Sergeant Reynolds or myself in person. Is that clear?"

"But, sir, I..."

"Do as you're told," snapped Henry. "Come along, Reynolds."

He set off at a run down the concrete path. Simmonds stood watching him, open-mouthed. Reynolds, forgetting the deference due to a commissioned officer, shouted at him, "Get a move on, you stupid bastard!" as he ran to join Henry.

Shocked, Simmonds scuttled toward the gate.

The black iron door which led to the Operations Block was closed, and there was no sound except for the wind howling in the trees outside. Henry was uncomfortably aware that a pitched battle could be taking place in that underground fastness without so much as a murmur reaching the outside world. He took hold of the heavy bar-shaped handle and moved it down. Thank heavens for Simmonds's strict security training, which made him retain the key, he thought. The door was closed, but it was not locked. Silently, he pushed it open.

Inside, all was quiet. The concrete steps led down into that secret little world and, at the foot of the steps, a faint light was shining from the passage that led away to the left. Somebody was in the Operations Room.

Still in the fresh air of the world above, Henry whispered to Reynolds. "You stay up here. I'm going down alone."

"Sir..."

"Don't argue. He's certainly armed, and he can pick off anybody going through that door against the light. We must split up. You know your way around this place. Wait there for the others, and then bring them down."

He did not wait to hear Reynolds' reaction. A moment later, he was moving down the dark staircase.

On the bottom step Henry stood still. To his left the short passage that led to the Operations Room was dimly lit. He knew that the gallery would be in comparative darkness, as always, and the passage light itself would be much brighter. So that faint glow must come from the strip lights placed above the plotting table, which stood in the center of the Operations Room at a lower level than the gallery. It was not as bad as he had feared. It seemed that the intruder must be occupied at the lower level near the plotting table. With any luck, it should be possible to observe him from the dark gallery, unseen. Not daring to breathe, Henry eased himself around the corner and into the corridor.

The swinging door at the end of the passage had been propped open and Henry could look through into the darkness of the gallery. Beyond, through the sloping glass observation panel, the lights burned over the plotting table. Slowly, quietly as a cat, Henry edged his way along the passage. For the murderer—the man who was desperately trying to save himself by destroying evidence under these neon lights—Henry had little time or worry to spare. The place was surrounded; the poor devil hadn't a chance. What mattered was that Emmy was down there—"dozing in the back of the car." That almost certainly meant drugged.

Henry had no illusions about why she had been brought here. The murderer, all evidence safely destroyed, would leave the station. The innocent Simmonds would eventually become alarmed about Emmy and would investigate. He would find—a suicide. Beau Guest's body had been found. He had been shot, deliberately or accidentally, by somebody else. Henry Tibbett, of all people, had made the discovery. Emmy's dear friends had established beyond all doubt that she had been infatuated with the dead man, and that she had been the last person to see him alive—having left her duty station to meet him in what would undoubtedly appear as the most sordid of love-nests. It would be only too natural if, faced with that situation, Emmy should have taken a sentimental journey to Dymfield with an old colleague, made an excuse to stay behind—and ended her own life.

As for Lofty's murder, hadn't Emmy plenty of motive for that, once one assumed her guilty of Beau's death? And how could even Henry be certain that she had stayed at home all that evening? He had watched television for two hours while she was supposed to be working in the bedroom, and she had had remarkably little to show for it. It might be crazy to suppose that she had sneaked out to Earl's Court and killed Lofty, but it *was* possible. A jury might well think so. If he had been ten minutes later arriving at Dymfield this afternoon— Henry's blood ran cold and he forgot to be frightened.

He had reached the door leading to the gallery, when the silence was shattered by a horrifyingly strident noise—a harsh, insistent buzzing somewhere on the gallery to the left of the door. Of course. A telephone. In a place like this, buzzers rather than bells would be used because they were less distracting. This one only sounded so shockingly loud because of the utter silence in that dead place. Henry braced himself. Discovery was inevitable now. It would be a question of fighting it out. He waited in the shadows for his enemy.

Nobody came. The telephone buzzed again. And then the truth dawned on Henry. It would be immaterial if twenty telephones buzzed or twenty clog-dancers performed on that gallery. So perfect was the soundproofing that anybody on the floor below would hear absolutely nothing. All Henry's elaborate precautions to remain silent were a waste of time. So long as he could not be *seen* from below… He ran forward, careless of noise, and snatched up the phone, which was buzzing again.

"Oh, good," said a voice. "That is the plotting table, isn't it? Thought I might have the wrong extension. Simmonds here, sir. I thought you'd like to know that Inspector Tibbett has arrived. I do hope his wife is better; she looked very groggy as we came in, I thought. Anyhow, he's asked me to take my car and go down to meet some police cars that are on their way, but I thought I'd better…"

"Christ Almighty!" said Henry.

"Eh? What? Who are you?"

"By the grace of God," said Henry, "I am a wrong number. Now get going, Simmonds."

"Oh, I say. Inspector Tibbett. Yes, sir. Thank you, sir."

The phone went dead. From the shadow of the gallery, Henry looked down on the floor below.

At first he thought that there was nobody there. The big table stood under lights, the blue and red arrows still marking the courses of long-departed aircraft. Outside the perimeter of light, the darkness was intense, far blacker than the dimness of the gallery above. Henry pictured the Operations Room as it must have been when in action, and decided that anybody wishing to dispose of a small object unobtrusively would certainly have done so downstairs, somewhere outside of the bright circle of light on the plotting table. And sure enough, something was moving down there in the shadows.

Henry stepped forward. Below him, in the far corner of the lower room, under the jutting gallery, he could just make out the figure of a man in uniform. His back was toward Henry, and he seemed to be working with a screwdriver on something in the wall about a foot up from the floor. Then Henry saw Emmy. She had evidently been given another dose of tranquilizer, for she lay sprawled in a chair in the shadows, for all the world as though in a deep and peaceful sleep. Henry had a moment of panic, and then reassured himself. From where he stood, he could see that she was breathing deeply and regularly.

He looked quickly around him and saw the stairs that led from the gallery down to the plotting area. The murderer had taken the elementary precaution of placing Emmy between himself and the only entrance to his rabbit burrow. She was within arm's reach of him, and he had only to grab her to use her as a shield, and to...

Henry ran back along the passage and up the stairs into the fresh air. Reynolds stepped forward anxiously.

"Everything all right, sir?" he whispered.

"No," said Henry. "And no need to whisper. He can't hear."

"You mean—he's...?"

"He's in a soundproof trap," said Henry. "My wife is in there too, sleeping peacefully. Drugged."

"There's no sign of Simmonds or the other cars, sir."

"No, thank God. At all costs, you've got to stop them coming down. Keep them up here, and *whatever happens*, take no action without my orders. The only way we can save my wife is to…"

"To let him get away?" Reynolds asked with badly masked disappointment.

"Of course not. He'd kill her before he went. No, my only hope is to go down and make him think I'm on my own."

"I don't see what good that'll do, sir," said Reynolds. "He'll kill you both, like as not." Reynolds' square face was puckered with anxiety.

Surprisingly, Henry said, "Oh, I don't think so. He's a nice fellow, you know. Very nice indeed."

And before Reynolds could reply, Henry had disappeared down the stairs again into the gloom.

The swing door that led into the lower section of the Operations Room was heavy, padded, and silent. Henry pushed it open and went in, keeping in the shadows outside the ring of light. Then the door closed behind him with a small sound, like a sigh, and the man in the corner straightened and turned in one rapid, frightened movement. Henry saw that he had a gun in his hand. He stepped forward into the light.

"It's only me, Mr. Smith," said Henry. "Sorry. Flight Lieutenant Smith. I've come to take Emmy home."

Sammy Smith stood there, the gun trembling in his hand—a nice fellow.

Henry said, "Haven't you done enough? You've had a good run for your money, after all. Twenty years." The muffled silence in the soundproof room was almost too oppressive to bear. Henry took a step forward. "You've killed two men," he said, "but each time in hot blood. I agree that there's nothing to prevent you from shooting both Emmy and me—this moment. But I don't believe you'd do it. Not in cold blood. Not while she was sleeping."

Sammy Smith said, in a voice which cracked from strain, "Are you crazy? Where's your bodyguard?"

"I sent them away."

"You expect me to believe that? They'll be here in ten minutes storming the place with tear gas and Tommy guns."

"They won't, you know," said Henry. "They don't possess such things. Oh, they're up in the compound all right. I don't deny it. But they're under orders to do nothing—absolutely nothing—without my permission. You could walk straight out of the gate now and nobody would stop you."

Sammy gave a curious half-smile, an echo of his old, bouncy self. "Where would I walk to, for heaven's sake?"

"I don't know," said Henry. "That's your problem. I can't do everything for you," he added, with a spurt of irritation.

Suddenly Smith laughed, a real laugh. He put the gun down on the plotting table, under the bright white lights. "How long have we got?" he asked.

"As long as you like."

"You said I'd killed in hot blood. It's true. I hope you believe that."

Henry nodded. "I believe it."

"Why don't we sit down, old man?" Sammy sounded quite normal. He pulled forward one of the swivel chairs that the plotters had used and motioned Henry to do the same. They sat down, one at each side of the checkerboard of a table.

Sammy pulled out a pack of cigarettes and lit one. Then he pushed the pack over to Henry with one of the long rakes—like a croupier's in a casino—which the plotters had used to push their arrows into position. He laughed.

"I wonder if your faithful but flat-footed minion is still waiting outside the Turkish Bath," he said. "I should strip him down, if I were you, falling for the oldest trick in the business. In through the front door with a small parcel, strip off, change into uniform, out through the back door as a flight lieutenant. I was as free as air inside of fifteen minutes."

"Yes, I'm afraid we slipped up," said Henry. "But why don't you start at the beginning."

"The beginning? Where was that, I wonder? Falconfield, I suppose. I'm not trying to justify what I did to Beau. It was a dirty trick. But go back to Falconfield, and you must admit that I'd suffered enough from the pair of them—Beau and Barbara. I'm an easy-going type, Tibbett, but I never could stand being mocked, made a monkey of. You know what I mean."

Henry nodded, but said nothing.

"Old Lofty got plastered one night and told me about being Beau's half-brother and about their mutual and alcoholic mother. Perhaps I'd better explain."

"No need," said Henry. "I know."

"Good. Well, I was saving up that little tidbit of information to use when the time seemed ripe. Come to think of it, I didn't actually make use of it for twenty years. Funny, isn't it? No, the moment I realized I had Guest where I wanted him was when I grasped the fact that, for all his bravado, he was seriously worried about taking that Typhoon up. Well, I bided my time. Let him sweat it out—and he was as jumpy as a cat. I knew that he had to decide by five o'clock that evening, one way or the other. Up until five he could withdraw his challenge, and be made a laughing stock, but a live laughing stock. Vere would then go up on patrol in the usual way. At five, if Vere had heard nothing, he'd know the bet was going ahead, and would put Plan A into action; that is, disappear and leave the coast clear for Beau. After five it was too late to back out without getting Vere into serious trouble.

"Well, about half-past two I telephoned Beau from the Duke's Head, where I was staying. I asked whether he was going to take the kite up. He told me frankly that he'd been having trouble with his dizzy spells and that he was going to call Vere and withdraw his challenge. He was very upset about it, and he'd asked for a posting. Well, I begged him not to do that. I told him—it was a lie, of course—that I'd had experience in flying Typhoons and that I wanted to go up in his place, for a bet. He was very dubious, but I told him to be a sport, and at last he agreed.

"I said we'd better meet somewhere quiet to fix details, and he suggested that disused air-raid shelter at five o'clock. As it happened, I got there rather early, and I saw several things which came in useful later on. Like Beau kissing Blandish in the corner when she should have been on duty, and old man Price having a petting party with a handsome young corporal behind a Nissen hut. Charming, you'll agree. Our brave boys in blue."

"Very human," said Henry.

"I don't know why everyone assumes that being human is a virtue," said Sammy. "My behavior that night was extremely human, and look where it's landed me. I was determined to make Guest squirm, and so I did. I met him and let him ramble on about how nobody would ever know, as he was off to Scotland next day. And then I let him have it. I told him I'd no earthly intention of taking the kite up, and that he'd bloody well have to do it because it was too late to back out. I don't suppose anybody has ever had a more complete revenge for humiliation than I had that night."

"You knew he'd be killed if he went up."

"Oh, sure. But he wouldn't have gone up. He'd have had to go into that Mess at Dymfield and confess that he was afraid. And by leaving it so late, he'd probably have got Vere court-martialed. And he couldn't have breathed a word about my part in it without revealing that he'd been prepared to let me go up instead of him, a much older man, mind you, and with less flying experience. Not cricket, old man. Dear me no. *That* would have been the end of Beau Guest, the young chevalier, the golden boy. Do you see how perfect it was? I had him cold."

"So—what happened?"

"Something I hadn't bargained for. He said that he had something to say to me. It seems that—did Blandish ever tell you that I was Messing Officer at Dymfield?"

"Yes, I think she did," said Henry.

"I was Messing Officer at Falconfield, too. A nice, cosy little job that nobody else wanted, involving the handling of quite tidy sums of money. Apparently our sharp-nosed Squadron Leader Guest had smelled a rat, even in the Falconfield days. Not that it was very serious—a few quid here and there 'converted to my personal use,' as the courts say. Very grave offense for an officer and a gentleman, of course. Great mistake to commission types like me—one of nature's bums, that's all I've ever pretended to be. Give Sammy the chance of a fiddle on the side, and... Anyway, Beau was senior to me at Dymfield and he'd commandeered the account books from the Mess Sergeant. Normally I got them nicely fixed up for the quarterly audit. He'd had his suspicions for some time, and he'd intended to confront me with the evidence and give me the chance to make up the money before the audit. But when I threatened to roll him in the dirt, he came right back at me. He had the books there with him, in the air-raid shelter, and he said that if I didn't take the Tiffie up, he'd have me court-martialed. I didn't mean to kill him when I pulled the gun on him. Only to frighten him. But he came straight for me and the bloody thing went off—and there he was, done for.

"For a moment I didn't know what to do. Then I had an inspiration. I hurried back to the Duke's Head and telephoned Vere at Barbara's flat, where I knew he'd be skulking by then. Asked him to come down to the pub. After all, the patrol wasn't due to take off till six. I told Vere a story that wasn't too far off the truth—that Beau had begged me to take his place in the kite, that I'd agreed to meet him at Dymfield to talk it over, but that I'd realized I couldn't do it. That when I had finally refused, he'd gone all to pieces—and had pulled out a gun and shot himself. He was drunk, I said, just as he had been when he crashed at Falconfield. All totally untrue, of course, but Vere believed it. I emptied a whisky bottle all over the shelter, and I told Vere where the body was and that he could go and see it for himself. I don't know whether he did or not, but he certainly had a hand in getting the entrance discreetly blocked up with rubble afterward."

"And what was Prendergast's reaction?" Henry asked.

Smith laughed, not pleasantly. "Just what I'd expected. Thought of nothing except the cow Barbara and how she'd never get over it and how she'd blame it all on him. That was just what I wanted. I pointed out that there was still time for him to take the plane up himself, head her out over the sea, and bail out. That would rate as a number one heroic suicide, and would be simple for the most sensitive widow to bear. And he agreed." Smith leaned forward and banged the flat of his hand on the table. "He actually agreed! I've always said he was certifiable. There's not much more. I said I'd go down to Operations to watch his progress. He was to sing out 'Tally-ho!' just as he bailed out, so that if he didn't turn up, I'd know roughly where to look for him in order to render first aid. Fortunately for him, it wasn't necessary, because there's no need to tell you that I'd have done nothing of the kind.

"After Vere had gone, I rang Annie. Just to confuse the issue, if you follow me, old man. My motto is—if there's a guilty secret, the more people who know about it the better. I've always been a fair mimic, and it's easy to fool people over the phone. Just a super-Mayfair accent and a couple of 'my old Queen-of-the-plotters' thrown in, and Annie believes to this moment that she spoke to Vere. I thought it was rather cunning to suggest to her that she should ring *me* and tell me the horrid news, which she did, bless her cotton socks. It all went off beautifully, though I say it myself."

"But you still had those account books," Henry pointed out.

"Yes, I had, hadn't I? They're here, if you want to see them."

Sammy pushed a couple of very dusty, cardboard-bound ledgers across the table.

"You hid them here, in the Operations Room?"

"My dear chap, what else could I do with them? I couldn't put them into the wastepaper basket at the Duke's Head, not with R.A.F. crests all over them. The landlord would have shot them straight back to the Mess. I couldn't take them quietly back, because Beau had signed for them. I expected they'd be safest here—not up in the gallery, where fellows were working all the time, but down here in the darkest possible corner. Actually, I shoved them into the ventilation shaft. You'll hardly believe it, but I unscrewed the grill, put in the books, and screwed it up again at three in the morning under the noses of three W.A.A.F. plotters. The point being, of course, that a big bomber force was coming home from a raid on Berlin and the girls were far too busy to notice anything. As for noise—this place is completely soundproof, and the plotters were wearing headphones. It's taken me twenty minutes to get that ruddy grill off again today—rusted up."

"It's a pity," said Henry, "that you had to kill Lofty."

"I never meant to."

"Then why did you make all those elaborate preparations—fixing a trip to Paris, sending your wife ahead by train, and taking a late-night plane yourself..."

"I wanted to speak to Lofty, make him see reason. To cover my tracks, Inspector, was an automatic gesture for a man like me. You wouldn't understand. You haven't lived your life on a legal knife edge."

"All right," said Henry. "You fixed your alibi. What did your wife imagine you were up to? She backed up your story gallantly."

Smith smiled, like a wolf. "All I have to say to Marlene," he said, "is that there's money in it. Marlene has a sweet, trusting nature. So long as the cash is solid, she asks no questions. Didn't bat an eyelid about mailing the letters or ringing up old Guest or even waylaying Blandish this morning and slipping the dope in her coffee. She's a useful girl, Marlene."

"Let's go back to Parker. Your pretext for visiting him was to borrow money."

"That's right. I slipped a modest request for funds into that questionnaire thing—thought it would make it seem more natural when I turned up on the doorstep. Yes, Blandish made me very nervous with her talk of mysteries over Beau's death and visiting Dymfield. What on earth gave Barbara this bloody silly idea anyway?"

Henry smiled. "A sort of poetic justice," he said. "You were too greedy. You shouldn't have blackmailed her by making her think Beau might still be alive. This was her way of proving him dead."

Sammy sighed. "Yes," he said, "I've made mistakes all along the line, I can see that. It's funny, isn't it? If I'd made a clean breast about Beau's death at the time, and explained it was an accident, I'd probably have gotten away with it. But I simply couldn't afford to have it discovered after all these years. And I knew neither Vere nor Annie would lift a finger to help me, if they had an inkling of the truth—that it wasn't suicide, I mean. I never thought I'd live to admit that honesty is the best policy, but there may be something in it after all.

"Anyhow, I visited old Lofty and, believe me, I tried in the nicest way to get him to drop the whole idea. But he'd had some sort of an offer from Baggot for television rights and was cock-a-hoop and absolutely adamant. When I didn't get anywhere being nice, I happened to mention his mother—and then he got abusive. And suspicious. And—well, to cut it short, we had a set-to and I hit him. Hard. He went out like a light, and suddenly it seemed so easy to make sure he wouldn't wake up again. So I made him comfortable in the kitchen, sealed the place up, and switched on the gas. Then I caught the plane to Paris and met Marlene for dinner. It was most inconsiderate of you to start asking questions about a perfectly ordinary suicide. Not playing the game, it seemed to me. When it became obvious that nothing was going to stop you from going to Dymfield and digging up poor old Guest—well—I figured I'd give you a run for your money."

"You did that," said Henry. "Tell me, how did you know exactly when I was going to Dymfield?"

"Simple. You told Barbara, who told Vere, who told me. Old Vere has been in a helluva flap these last weeks. Never off the phone to me, reporting developments and asking my advice. I figured there was nothing like stirring up confusion and getting as many people as possible involved. The letters were fun to do, too. Pity I had so little time to spend on the one I sent myself. A bit skimped, I thought it."

"So did I," said Henry. "And you made a bad mistake when you told Emmy that you knew Beau was due to go to Scotland the morning after he died. There was only one way you could have found that out. She put the reference in her notes. So I set this little trap for you. I didn't count on your abducting my wife, of course."

"I thought I had a pretty good weapon in Blandish," said Smith, regretfully. "I knew you wouldn't want to see her rolled in the mud. I wouldn't have harmed her, you know. At least, I hope I wouldn't."

"You hoped you wouldn't harm Lofty."

"That's true. Yes, you were right to take no chances. Pity I bungled it. Poor old Sammy. Never could make a success of anything, not even secondhand cars. Oh, well. Funny, isn't it? The first part, Beau, went like a dream. Second part, Lofty, more difficult. Third part, Blandish, disaster. I'd have been better to lie low and say nothing. Too late now, of course."

There was a long silence. Henry didn't move.

Then Sammy said, "'Do not despair for Johnny Head-in-Air.' That's a poem. Know it? 'He sleeps as sound as Johnny-Under-Ground.' That was Beau, Johnny Under Ground. He slept sound, all right. 'Fetch out no shroud for Johnny-in-the-Cloud, and keep your tears…'"

Henry did not see him take up the gun, so quick was the movement. The shot rang deafeningly around the enclosed cave of a room, echoing and re-echoing between the padded walls. Sammy Smith had not bungled this time. He was lying slumped over the table, and the blood from the wound in his temple ran in a scarlet river across the grid reference squares, like the track of a hostile aircraft making for the coast.

Henry stood up. Emmy was stirring, moaning in her drugged sleep.

For a moment Henry looked down at Sammy—a pathetic, gay, amoral, criminal, kind, cruel, funny human being. A gallant pilot. A cheat. A murderer. An ordinary man. Softly Henry finished the verse which Sammy's death had interrupted—"'And keep your tears for him in after years...'"

Then Henry picked Emmy up in his arms and carried her up the narrow stairway and out into the daylight.